KNIT of the LIVING DEAD

PEGGY EHRHART

KENSINGTON BOOKS
www.kensingtonbooks.com

KENSINGTON BOOKS are published by

Kensington Publishing Corp.
119 West 40th Street
New York, NY 10018

All Kensington titles, imprints, and distributed lines are available at special quantity discounts for bulk purchases for sales promotion, premiums, fund-raising, educational, or institutional use.

Special book excerpts or customized printings can also be created to fit specific needs. For details, write or phone the office of the Kensington Sales Manager: Attn.: Sales Department. Kensington Publishing Corp., 119 West 40th Street, New York, NY 10018. Phone: 1-800-221-2647.

Kensington and the K logo Reg. U.S. Pat. & TM Off.

First Printing: September 2020
ISBN-13: 978-1-4967-2365-9
ISBN-10: 1-4967-2365-1

ISBN-13: 978-1-4967-2368-0 (ebook)
ISBN-10: 1-4967-2368-6 (ebook)

10 9 8 7 6 5 4 3 2 1

Printed in the United States of America

KNIT OF THE LIVING DEAD

The small procession made its way through the trees until the stone building that housed the restrooms came into view. The path, however, was obstructed by the body of a woman.

"What's that?" Gus whispered, as if the circumstances now called for reverence. "Around her neck?" He aimed the flashlight at a spot below the edge of the sunbonnet's brim and above the edge of the organdy collar.

Pamela stepped closer and bent down. Several strands of thick yarn had been wrapped around the woman's neck. "Yarn," she whispered.

"Strangled, looks like," Gus pronounced sagely.

"That's Mary Lyon," said another voice. It was Nell. She had caught up with them and her tone was more wondering than shocked. "My across-the-street neighbor," she added.

"Can't see her face," Gus said. "So how do you know?"

"Bo Peep," Nell said, her voice starting to quaver. "That's her costume—Little Bo Peep."

Pamela had looked up during this exchange, but now she motioned to Gus to redirect the flashlight, and she bent toward the dead woman's neck again. She knew not to touch anything at a crime scene, but she stared—hard. There were no marks on the woman's neck and the ends of the yarn hung loose. It was as if the plan to strangle had been abandoned at the last minute—though the victim had clearly been killed by some other means . . .

Books by Peggy Ehrhart

MURDER, SHE KNIT

DIED IN THE WOOL

KNIT ONE, DIE TWO

SILENT KNIT, DEADLY KNIT

A FATAL YARN

KNIT OF THE LIVING DEAD

Published by Kensington Publishing Corporation

For my Sister in Crime, Ann Ray

Acknowledgments

Abundant thanks, again, to my agent, Evan Marshall, and to my editor at Kensington Books, John Scognamiglio.

Chapter 1

Pamela Paterson was feeling unimaginative. The figures moving in and out of the bright circle created by the bonfire's dancing flames resembled wizards, mermaids, medieval jesters, zombies—and here was her best friend, Bettina Fraser, as a very credible Raggedy Ann, with a red yarn wig replacing Bettina's own equally vivid scarlet hair. Pamela had done her best with her costume, but the outfit she had come up with—black slacks, a black sweater, and a headband featuring cat ears—now struck her as woefully lacking. At least she could have added whiskers and a tail!

The event was Arborville's much-anticipated Halloween celebration, a parade down Arborville Avenue that allowed everyone to show off their costumes, followed by a bonfire in the town park. As Pamela chatted with Bettina, they were joined by Bettina's husband, Wilfred. His post-retirement uniform of blue denim bib overalls formed the

basis of his Raggedy Andy costume, and a plaid
shirt and red yarn wig completed the look. Bettina's costume was more elaborate. She wore a
long-sleeved cotton dress in a colorful old-fashioned print, topped by a ruffled white pinafore.
On her legs were red-and-white-striped stockings
and on her feet black patent leather Mary Janes.

"We've been so lucky with the weather," Bettina
observed as a woman in the flowing draperies of a
Greek goddess strolled by. "It's such a shame to
put a lot of effort into a costume and then have to
hide it by bundling up in a coat."

"Here you are!" said a cheery voice from behind
Pamela. "Hardly anyone looks like themselves
tonight." Pamela turned to greet Nell Bascomb
who, along with Bettina, was a fellow member of
the Arborville knitting club, nicknamed Knit and
Nibble.

"You look like yourself, though, Pamela," Nell
went on. She stepped back to survey Pamela in the
light created by the brightly blazing logs. "What
are you supposed to be?"

Pamela tipped her head forward and pointed to
the cat ears that completed her simple costume.

"Oh, Catrina!" Nell clapped her hands. "Your
sweet kitty."

Nell herself wore a filmy white dress that looked
like it had once been a curtain, topped by a sky-
blue cape and accessorized with a tiara and a
magic wand.

"A fairy godmother?" Bettina suggested and Nell
nodded.

The costume was appropriate. Nell, in her eighties, was Knit and Nibble's oldest member, but her

age gave her a gentle wisdom that was much appreciated by the other Knit and Nibblers.

Wilfred caught sight of one of his historical society friends and excused himself to say hello. Pamela, Bettina, and Nell moved closer to the fire, where they stared at the flames in companionable silence, enjoying the crackling of the logs and the aroma of wood smoke. Despite the fact that the night wasn't cool enough to require bundling up, the air felt restless. Tree branches tossed by wind gusts sighed nearby, and overhead the moon was full and yellow. It wasn't hard, Pamela thought, to share in the awe that had made earlier people see in the transition from summer to winter a time when the line separating this world from the other world blurred.

Despite the festive atmosphere and good cheer, the bonfire awoke feelings more appropriate to a pagan celebration marking nature's mysterious powers. The flames illuminated rapt faces, dramatizing features and rendering the familiar unfamiliar. Pamela felt herself shiver despite the heat, and she was just as glad when, after a time, Bettina said, "I feel like I'm burning up. Let's step back a little and let someone else have a front-row spot."

They eased through the crowd, past the Greek goddess, a jester, a pirate, and several other costumed revelers, and meandered across the grass until they were near the little stand of trees that marked the northeast border of the park. A light on a tall pole illuminated that corner of the park, though—given the bright moonlight—it was hardly needed on this night.

"Harold is here somewhere," Nell said, naming

her husband. "He's probably met up with Wilfred and their historical society pals."

"How about the rest of the Knit and Nibblers?" Bettina asked. "I can't see our straitlaced Roland in a costume, but Holly must be here somewhere. She's one of Arborville's biggest boosters and she'd never miss an event like this."

Bettina took a few steps back toward the bonfire and Pamela followed her, peering toward the crowd. But the contrast between the darkness and the glare of the flames blurred her vision, and the point of the costumes was—after all—to disguise, so it was impossible to recognize any one particular person.

As they stood there staring at the shifting mass of revelers, a sound from behind her distracted Pamela. She grabbed Bettina's arm and whispered, "What was that?"

"Someone screamed," Bettina whispered back.

The sound came again, louder, establishing that it was indeed a scream, and that the person screaming was moving closer.

"It's coming from back in those trees," Pamela said. She turned toward the stand of trees at the edge of the park. Nell had turned too, her filmy dress catching the beams of light from the tall pole.

Pamela took a few hurried steps toward the stand of trees. A dirt path provided a shortcut to the tennis courts and to restrooms in a rustic stone building, and Pamela launched herself onto the path just as the scream came again. It was shadowy back among the trees, but the moonlight offered enough illumination to navigate by.

"Oh my God," wailed a horrified voice. "She's dead!"

The next moment, Pamela found herself hugging a terrified young woman. She backed up the way she'd come, drawing the young woman along with her. After she'd progressed a few feet, two voices competed for her attention.

One voice was Bettina's, calling her name, and the voice was soon complemented by Bettina's presence. Bettina wrapped both Pamela and her young charge—who was by this time weeping—in a hug of her own, and the three of them paused amid the trees.

The other voice was not calling Pamela. It was a young man's voice and it was calling someone named Misty.

A figure darted out from behind a tree, a figure not much larger than the young woman who was still clinging to Pamela, but the full moon provided enough light to reveal the newcomer as a young man—or, really, a teenage boy. And the young woman looked to be a *girl*, really, a girl of about thirteen or fourteen.

"Misty!" he called again, and the young woman pushed away from Pamela. She whirled around, and in a moment the *boy*—Pamela couldn't think of him as anything other—was grasping her as intensely as she had grasped Pamela.

Bettina had by this time let go of Pamela as well. Now she stood beside Pamela and was the first of the two to find her voice.

"What on earth is going on?" she asked.

As the boy stroked the girl's hair and the girl sobbed, Bettina's words were echoed by another voice, Nell's gentle voice. Nell crept up beside them, repeating her query.

"Someone is dead." The boy's arms tightened even more protectively around the girl's back. His voice struck Pamela as an approximation of official voices in the crime dramas on television, as if he was trying to impress his girlfriend with his sangfroid.

"Dead! What do you mean?" Bettina's voice was as frantic as his had been calm.

The girl twisted loose from the boy's embrace and pointed farther along the path that wound back in among the shadowy trees. With a hiccupping sob, she moaned, "There's a body back there. A woman."

Pamela stared into the shadows, surprised to notice a beam of light emanating from behind her, bobbing among the trees. Footsteps approached from the rear and a deep, masculine voice said, "What's the commotion about? Somebody got lost on the way to the restrooms? I keep telling them we need a decent light back here."

Gus Warburton had joined them. He was one of the rec department stalwarts and a key organizer of the Halloween celebration. The beam of light had been cast by his flashlight.

"These . . . these . . . kids say there's a body—" Pamela ventured.

Gus laughed. "People get up to all kinds of things back in these woods. Couples . . . looking for privacy, if you know what I mean." He jabbed an elbow into Pamela's ribs and she winced.

"No, no," the boy stuttered, and it occurred to Pamela that he and Misty *had* perhaps been looking for privacy so they could get up to things undisturbed. "This was a body, just one person, lying there and not moving."

Gus plunged forward along the path, his flashlight beam leading the way. As Pamela started to follow, she felt Bettina grab her arm—not to pull her back, but to assure her own footing on the none-too-smooth dirt path.

Nell's resolute "I'm coming too" floated after them.

The small procession made its way through the trees until the stone building that housed the restrooms came into view. The path, however, was obstructed by the body of a woman. Gus uttered a brief profanity as his dancing flashlight beam picked out details. The woman was wearing a pink-and-white-striped dress in an old-fashioned style, with a scalloped overskirt in solid pink and a wide white organdy collar trimmed in lace. She had apparently once been wearing a blond wig, but that was now lying amid some fallen leaves a few feet from her head. The charming straw sunbonnet that had complemented the outfit had, however, been placed back on her head—though in a way that completely hid her face.

"What's that?" Gus whispered, as if the circumstances now called for reverence. "Around her neck?" He aimed the flashlight at a spot below the edge of the sunbonnet's brim and above the edge of the organdy collar.

Pamela stepped closer and bent down. Several strands of thick yarn had been wrapped around the woman's neck. "Yarn," she whispered.

"Strangled, looks like," Gus pronounced sagely.

"That's Mary Lyon," said another voice. It was Nell. She had caught up with them and her tone was more wondering than shocked. "My across-the-street neighbor," she added.

"Can't see her face," Gus said. "So how do you know?"

"Bo Peep," Nell said, her voice starting to quaver. "That's her costume—Little Bo Peep. Look!" Nell took Gus's hand and guided the flashlight beam to a spot a few feet away from the woman's feet. "There's her shepherd's crook."

A long staff with a curl at the top lay in the dirt. Bettina squealed and reached for Nell's arm.

Pamela had looked up during this exchange, but now she motioned to Gus to redirect the flashlight, and she bent toward the dead woman's neck again. She knew not to touch anything at a crime scene, but she stared—hard. There were no marks on the woman's neck and the ends of the yarn hung loose. It was as if the plan to strangle had been abandoned at the last minute—though the victim had clearly been killed by some other means.

Chapter 2

Stepping into the fluorescent brightness of the library from a night lit only by moonlight and dancing flames had been a shock to the eyes. Now Pamela sat blinking at one of the library's long tables. The festive mood had fled, the costumes, wigs, and makeup that had turned her fellow Arborvillians into fanciful revelers seemed garish under the fluorescent lights, and she was wondering what had become of Nell.

The police station shared a parking lot with the park and the library. Gus had only to run twenty yards to summon an officer to the little stand of woods where the body in the Bo Peep costume lay. Then, within minutes, a police bullhorn had directed everyone in the park to proceed to the library, which had been hastily opened for the occasion. A second officer had joined the first near the body, and Pamela and Bettina had answered enough basic questions to establish they weren't the people who had first come upon the body and had only been drawn into the stand of trees by a panicked scream. Then they had been dismissed and told to join the muttering crowd trooping across the parking lot. But Nell had been instructed to remain behind, along with the quivering young couple who had happened upon the body.

The revelers had been directed into the library's main room upstairs, with the overflow shunted into the large community room downstairs. The children's library, which was also downstairs, had been set aside for police interviews, which were now in the process of being conducted.

"Those poor young kids!" Bettina said from the chair across the table from Pamela in the upstairs room. "They won't forget this Halloween for a long time." She still wore the jaunty red yarn wig and that, plus the circles of rouge she'd added to her usual makeup, made her woeful eyes and downturned mouth seem more playacting than the genuine concern they reflected.

Seated next to her, Wilfred squeezed his wife's arm through the flowery cotton of her puffy sleeve. He had removed his wig to reveal his thick white hair, and his air of genial sympathy made him a familiar and comforting presence.

Harold Bascomb had been talking to Wilfred when the bullhorn's announcement boomed over the park. Now he sat next to Pamela, still wrapped in the long cape that had made him a convincing vampire. He had apparently pocketed his vampire teeth as he and Wilfred climbed the library steps together. Like his wife, Nell, he was in his eighties, but he was rangy and vigorous, with an energy that belied his thatch of white hair.

"Nell's fine, I'm sure," Pamela said. "The police will want to talk more to me and Bettina—and to everyone who was in the park tonight. But Nell recognized the body, or thought she did—though there was a hat over the face. So they'd want to confirm that it's really Mary Lyon before they do anything else."

Bettina nodded. "Clayborn is probably on his way—if he's not already out there—and the crime scene van from the county." Bettina reported on the doings of the Arborville police, as well as nearly everything else that happened in Arborville, for the *Arborville Advocate*. The *Advocate* was the town's weekly newspaper, characterized by both its fans and its detractors as the town's source for "all the news that fits."

"Mary Lyon." Harold shook his head sadly. "She and Nell weren't all that close, but Mary lived right across the street. Mary wrote that blog, *The Lyon and the Lamb: Adventures in Woolgathering*."

Pamela knew the blog, which often touched on knitting-related topics. During a chat on the sidewalk in front of the Co-Op Grocery, she'd once invited Mary to join Knit and Nibble. Mary had protested that she didn't have time, and Pamela—who had regretted the invitation the moment it popped out of her mouth—had been just as glad. Mary could be prickly, and with Roland DeCamp as a member, Knit and Nibble already had its share of prickliness.

Harold, meanwhile, had stood up and was scanning the room. Every seat at every table was full, as well as the comfortable armchairs along the windows and the little stools in front of the computer monitors. People were chatting quietly, or napping with their heads on their folded arms, or staring at their mobile devices—apparently even princess and demon costumes included pockets. Some had shed the most dramatic parts of their costumes. A Big Bad Wolf simply looked like a mild young man with a mop of blond hair wearing a furry set of long underwear, his head, with its long snout and terrifying teeth, resting on the floor next to his armchair.

"Do you see her anywhere?" Bettina asked, tilting her head upward.

"Nell would have found us, I'm sure," Harold said. "We're not far from the door." He swiveled his neck and continued scanning. "I'm looking for Brainard," he explained. "Mary's husband."

Pamela heard herself gasp, a quick intake of breath like a backward sigh. She hadn't thought of that. Mary and her husband would no doubt have come out to the parade and bonfire together. What fun would it be to come alone? So where had he been when her venture into the little stand of trees led to her death? And where was he now? And did he know what had happened to his wife?

"Here you all are," said a voice behind Pamela, a voice that seemed unfamiliar. But Bettina's expression had cheered and she was mustering a version of her usual smile for the newcomer. Pamela twisted in her chair and recognized Holly Perkins. Holly was another member of Knit and Nibble, but not quite her buoyant self under the stress of the current circumstances—thus the fact that her voice had been drained of its habitual enthusiasm.

Holly was one of the youngest members of the knitting club, in her twenties. She and her husband, Desmond, owned a hair salon in Meadowside. For Halloween, she'd used her expertise with hair to create a stunning Bride of Frankenstein coiffure that sprang up from her forehead in rippling waves, accented with white streaks at the temples.

"Have you been here the whole time?" Pamela asked as Holly circled the table to sink into the chair Wilfred had vacated for her.

Holly pointed toward the ranks of shelves that filled a wide alcove near the library's entrance. "Both of us. We ended up back there, in a row of study desks against the wall. Desmond fell asleep with his head on a desk—he can sleep anywhere." She leaned forward. "Somebody said there's a body? And the police are questioning everyone who was at the bonfire?"

Bettina nodded. "Some kids, teenage kids, found it back in those trees along the edge of the park. They were looking for a private spot to make out, I expect, and certainly didn't expect to come upon a dead person. The girl started screaming and Pamela heard her and I followed Pamela, and Nell said it was her neighbor Mary Lyon—"

Displaying a flash of her customary energy—though not the smile that featured perfect teeth and evoked a dimple—Holly exclaimed, "You both saw it too! And Nell!"

"We saw it." Pamela nodded. "But we didn't find it. The kids did. And Nell said it was her neighbor.

So the police made them all stay and sent us in here."

"Poor Nell! What a shock that must have been for her! Is she all right?"

"We don't know," Bettina murmured sadly. "We haven't seen her since . . . then."

They were all silent for a bit. After a while, Holly glanced at the clock above the circulation desk. It was nearly eleven. "When do you think we'll get out of here?" she asked.

Bettina shrugged. "Anybody at the bonfire might have seen something useful, so the police will want to talk to everybody. At least tomorrow's Sunday and we can all sleep late."

At that moment. a police officer appeared at the top of the stairs that led to the library's lower level. Pamela recognized her as Officer Sanchez, the young woman officer who was usually to be found monitoring the grammar school children crossing Arborville Avenue.

Officer Sanchez approached the long table closest to the steps. "Please come with me," she said, and gestured for everyone at that table to get up.

Wilfred helped himself to one of the chairs that had been vacated and pulled it up to the end of the table where the Knit and Nibblers sat. "Might as well be comfortable," he said with a sigh.

Harold stood up again and resumed scanning the room. "He's looking for Mary Lyon's husband," Pamela explained.

"He might be downstairs," Holly said. "The police filled that big room down there with people first. And he might not know what this is all about . . ."

"That's what I'm afraid of," Harold said. "Brainard

might not even have come tonight. I didn't see him at the bonfire . . . of course I might not have recognized him in his costume—whatever it was." He furled his cape around himself and sat back down. "I didn't see Mary either. But with such a crowd, and in the dark . . ." He shrugged.

An authoritative voice drew their attention to the stairs again. A police officer stood there, not Officer Sanchez but the officer Pamela had seen just that morning on Arborville Avenue arranging orange cones around a spot where the asphalt was being repaired.

"Harold Bascomb?" the officer inquired. "Is there a Harold Bascomb here?"

Chapter 3

Pamela would have been happy to remain in bed until ten a.m., or even later. But, though she'd been a widow for the past seven years and her only daughter was away at college, she was not alone in her large house. The two beings with whom she shared it were at that moment crouched on her chest. Catrina, a lustrous black cat with amber eyes, was studying Pamela's face intently, as if for signs of consciousness. Catrina's daughter Ginger, whose name described her color, seemed similarly curious about Pamela's state.

"Yes, yes," Pamela murmured. The cats leaped nimbly to the floor as she pushed herself into a sitting position. "I know it's past your breakfast time."

Down in her cozy kitchen, wrapped in her fleecy robe and with furry slippers on her feet, Pamela scooped a six-ounce can of "fish medley" into a fresh bowl that the cats shared and broke it up into manageable morsels with a spoon. She set the bowl in the corner of the kitchen, where the cats were accustomed to receiving their meals.

Once Catrina and Ginger were crouched over their bowl nibbling at the glistening mixture from opposite sides, Pamela set her kettle boiling for coffee and headed out to retrieve her newspaper. After the distressing events of the previous night, the familiar rituals with which she always started her day promised to soothe.

It had been one a.m. before she was back at home again. When she and Bettina were finally summoned down to the children's library, where the police interviews were being held, she'd had to repeat to Detective Clayborn the story she'd already told to one of the police officers who'd responded to Gus Warburton's summons—how she heard the scream, stepped back among the trees, encountered the frightened teenagers, and followed Gus and the teenagers to the spot where the body lay across the path. Then when she and Bettina and Nell and their spouses left the library, the three women had been set upon by the *County Register*'s ace reporter Marcy Brewer, no less perky for the lateness of the hour.

Back inside, she extracted the *Register* from its flimsy plastic sleeve and laid it, still folded, on the small table that furnished her kitchen. The table, just large enough to accommodate two chairs, was covered with a vintage cloth featuring fruit in unlikely colors—blue oranges!—that she'd found at one of her favorite rummage sales.

At the counter, she measured coffee beans into her coffee grinder, depressed the cover, and waited until the clatter of the beans smoothed into a whir. She slipped a paper filter into the plastic filter cone atop her carafe and transferred the ground beans into the filter. She was just about to reach for the kettle, which had begun to whistle, when the door-bell chimed.

The cats preceded her to the entry, streaking ahead and pausing in the middle of the thrift-store Persian rug that covered the floor's ancient par-quet. They stared at the door, and so did Pamela, but only for a moment. Through the lace that cur-tained the door's large oval window, Pamela could see a woman, none too thin and not very tall, with hair of vivid scarlet. She smiled and opened the door to Bettina.

But Bettina, usually quick to smile, didn't smile back. And the woman who dressed for her life in Arborville with the flair of a dedicated fashionista had crossed the street from her own house and climbed the steps to Pamela's porch wearing a flowered flannel bathrobe and fuzzy slippers. Her face was free of makeup and her bright hair looked untouched by a comb.

"Have you seen this?" she inquired, the rising pitch of her voice reminiscent of a distressed Cat-rina. Bettina held out a section of the *Register*.

"I just brought mine in," Pamela said. "I'm mak-ing coffee." She stepped back and beckoned Bet-tina across the threshold.

Bettina shook her head vigorously. "I have to get dressed. We have to talk to Nell."

Pamela felt a frown take shape on her forehead. She reached for the newspaper. What could the

Register be reporting that was more startling than what they'd experienced firsthand the previous night? And surely Pamela and Bettina wouldn't even appear in that day's issue of the paper. Marcy would have filed her interview with them long after Sunday's *Register* had gone to print.

"It wasn't Nell's neighbor," Bettina said. "That body wasn't Mary Lyon's."

"But the costume—" Pamela stopped. Bettina's lips tightened and she shook her head again.

"The dead woman was Dawn Filbert." Bettina was still shaking her head, and the uncombed tendrils of her hair were bobbing. "She owns—*owned*—Hair Today, the hair salon on Arborville Avenue. We have to talk to Nell."

"But the costume," Pamela repeated.

"That's why we have to talk to Nell," Bettina said, in the tone of someone stating the obvious. "Maybe the killer was trying to kill Mary."

Pamela nodded. "Wandering around in the dark looking for the person in the Bo Peep costume . . ." She paused. "But the killer would need some reason to think the person in the Bo Peep costume was Mary."

"She had the blog," Bettina said. "*The Lyon and the Lamb: Adventures in Woolgathering.* 'Little Bo Peep has lost her sheep' and all that . . ."

"There's a connection . . ." Pamela squinted and pursed her lips. "But would the killer make that connection?"

"That's why we're talking to Nell." Bettina pulled her robe around her. "I can't go like this and neither can you. Get dressed. I'll call Nell and tell her

we're coming and I'll pick you up in ten minutes."
Then Bettina was off, hurrying back across the
street.

The kettle was still on the stove and whistling fu-
riously when Pamela returned to the kitchen. She
turned off the flame, thankful that the kettle hadn't
boiled dry. There was no time for breakfast and the
coffee she'd ground would serve for the next day.
She'd store it in a ziplock bag when she returned
from Nell's, but she paused for a moment to un-
fold the *Register* and scan the front page.

"Arborville Hairdresser Murdered at Town Halloween Celebration" read the bold headline, and
in smaller print below were the words, "Unaware,
Revelers Frolic Around Bonfire." According to the
article's first paragraph, Dawn Filbert had been
killed by a blow to the head shortly before her
body was found by two teenagers whose names
were not being released. Pamela skimmed down a
bit further, but there was no mention of the
strands of yarn. She left the newspaper unfolded
on the table and headed for the stairs.

Unlike Bettina, Pamela was not a fashionista.
Up in her bedroom, she slipped into a cotton
turtleneck and the same pair of jeans she'd been
wearing all week. To the outfit she added a hand-
knit pullover in a soft shade of brown and a pair of
loafers. She was tall and thin, and the casual look
suited her, but Bettina never stopped lamenting
her friend's lack of interest in the clothes Pamela's
figure could have shown off to advantage. In the
bathroom, she ran a comb through her shoulder-
length brown hair and she was ready to go.

* * *

"I started coffee as soon as I hung up the phone," Nell said by way of greeting. She escorted Pamela and Bettina down the long hallway, decorated with souvenir art from the Bascombs' many travels, which led to her kitchen, and invited them to take seats around the table. Holly Perkins, who embraced all things mid-century with the enthusiasm of someone who hadn't actually lived through the era, never tired of expressing her delight in the Bascombs' kitchen. Their house itself predated the 1950s by several decades, but the kitchen had been redone shortly before they bought it in the early days of their marriage and had remained the same ever since, with pink Formica counters and avocado-green appliances.

An ancient aluminum percolator gurgled cheerfully on the stove. "I've had my tea and my breakfast," Nell added, "but there will be coffee soon, and how does homemade granola sound?"

"Or doughnuts?" came a voice from behind the door that led to the mudroom.

That door opened and in stepped Harold Bascomb, dressed for an unseasonably warm fall day in jeans and a flannel shirt faded to a pleasant greenish gray. He carried a white cardboard bakery box secured with a crisscross of white string.

"So that's where you went!" Nell gave Harold a look that a fond but irritated mother might give a mischievous child. Harold responded with a broad grin that creased his cheeks and crinkled the skin around his faded blue eyes.

"I thought we could all use a little treat after last

night," he said. "Especially you." He placed the box on the table, slipped off the string, and folded back the top. Inside were half a dozen plump doughnuts, glistening with a translucent sugary glaze. A look of concern replaced Harold's grin and he gazed at his wife fondly. "You were certainly ready to go home by the time that cop came up and fetched me."

"They had a lot of questions," Nell said. "And I had to wait around while the crime scene people took pictures before they could lift the hat off her face. And then, of course, I could see right away that it *wasn't* Mary. But I had no idea who it was until I saw the *Register* this morning. And sugar is not going to make me feel any better."

But Bettina was eyeing the doughnuts. "I'd love one," she said. The corners of her mouth lifted and she looked a bit more like herself. The aroma of the perking coffee, which had begun to fill the kitchen, might have also contributed to the boost in her spirits.

Nell sighed and her lips stretched into a defeated half smile. She reached into a cupboard, took out four small plates, and transferred them to the table. Like Nell's kitchen, her dinnerware dated from the 1950s, with a coral and gold color scheme, now faded, and a pattern that evoked wildflowers and wheat.

"You're wondering why I was so sure the body of that poor woman was Mary Lyon," Nell said as she set plates in front of her guests, and in front of Harold, who had taken a seat. He put a doughnut on each plate, then jumped to his feet again.

"We certainly are," Pamela said.

"It was her blog," Nell explained. Harold motioned her into a chair and began bustling around the kitchen. As Nell spoke, he busied himself at the counter and then added napkins, spoons, and cream and sugar to the table setting. Nell went on. "Mary had posted photos of the costumes she and her husband planned to wear: Little Bo Peep and a sheep. So anyone who followed her blog . . ."

Pamela nodded. Harold appeared behind Nell and laid a gentle hand on her shoulder. He bent toward Nell's ear and whispered, "More tea, my dear?"

She turned and looked up at him. "Oh, Harold, yes," she said. "That would be so sweet—especially if I'm going to eat one of your doughnuts."

"So how did Dawn Filbert end up wearing the Bo Peep costume?" Bettina asked.

"Mary and Brainard had a fight and he stayed home last night," Harold answered from the counter, where he was spooning tea leaves into a squat brown teapot. "That's why he was nowhere to be seen at the bonfire—or later. Mary recruited her hairdresser—Dawn—to go as Bo Peep. She herself wore the sheep costume."

"Harold talked to Brainard this morning," Nell explained. "They were both outside first thing, collecting the *Register*."

The teakettle began to hoot and Harold stepped toward the stove. He added boiling water to the tea leaves in the squat teapot and began serving the coffee.

"Sad," Nell murmured as she watched her husband focus on these domestic tasks. "So sad when couples can't get along."

Harold slipped steaming cups of coffee in front

of Pamela and Bettina. "That's what comes of marrying after a whirlwind romance," he commented. "Not like Nell and me." He winked at Pamela. "She was elusive," he said, pointing at Nell. "But I was determined. The Lyon-Covingtons, on the other hand—love at first sight, once he got a look at Mary. At least that's how she tells it. Of course, he was already engaged to her sister—" He jumped up. "I'm forgetting the tea!" he said. He reached the counter in two large strides and with two more had delivered Nell's tea.

They were barely settled and taking the first bite of their doughnuts when Bettina, uncharacteristically, reached into her purse and pulled out her smartphone. "I'm just too curious," she said as her fingers danced over the little screen. After a few moments, she exclaimed, "Here it is!" She passed the smartphone to Harold, who glanced and nodded and handed it to Nell.

"That is the blog post," Nell said, handing the phone to Pamela.

Laid out on what looked to be a bed covered with a smooth spread was a pink-and-white-striped dress. A scalloped overskirt in solid pink and a wide white organdy collar trimmed in lace gave it a charming old-fashioned look. Above the dress was perched a straw sunbonnet trimmed with a wide pink ribbon, and a shepherd's crook lay alongside. Next to the dress was a lamb's costume, like a long-sleeved, hooded jumpsuit sewn from a fleecy white fabric, with fleecy mittens attached to the ends of the sleeves. The hood featured ears. A separate mask lay atop the hood, a half mask, actually, with eyeholes and a lamb's snout.

* * *

An hour later, Bettina swung into her driveway and parked her faithful Toyota next to Wilfred's ancient but lovingly maintained Mercedes.

"Well," she said, turning to Pamela. "That was interesting. It certainly sounds like the killer could have been aiming for Mary."

"Could have been," Pamela agreed. "With the blond wig and the sunbonnet—those hats really hide a person's face from any angle except straight on. And it was dark. Anybody stalking Dawn Filbert to kill her would have had a hard time recognizing her. On the other hand, anybody who knew, or thought they knew, exactly what Mary's costume was going to be . . ."

"I'm talking to Clayborn tomorrow, for the *Advocate*," Bettina said. "I'll see if he has any new tidbits. By then, the police will have interviewed people in Dawn's circle. Maybe there was a jealous boyfriend . . . or somebody who hated the way their hair turned out . . ."

"I almost hope so." Pamela reached for the door handle. "That would mean Dawn was the intended target and there won't be any more murders." She stepped out onto the asphalt of Bettina's driveway, but then leaned back into the car. "I'm afraid there will be, though. That yarn around Dawn's neck—I don't think the plan was to leave it hanging loose. But then the killer got a good look at Dawn's face and realized the woman in the Little Bo Peep costume wasn't who he expected."

Bettina's eyes got large and she raised her carefully manicured fingertips to her mouth. "Oh my," she whispered. "And maybe he thought—*hoped* then—that he'd only knocked her out, and so he didn't carry through with the strangling. I'll point that out to Clayborn. And about the costume too."

"What time are you seeing Detective Clayborn?" Pamela asked, still leaning into the car.

"Eleven."

"I'll meet you at Hyler's at twelve," Pamela said.

"You know I never say no to lunch at Hyler's." Bettina smiled and Pamela waved goodbye.

It was a bright fall day, made all the cheerier by the convivial parishioners lingering on the steps and sidewalk of the church next to Pamela's house. They chatted and laughed and called to one another, as if unconcerned about the fact that Arborville's town park had been the scene of a startling murder less than twenty-four hours before.

Arborville was a charming small town, a town untouched by the social problems that afflict urban environments. But, curiously, Arborville had had its share of murders over the years. They weren't committed by frightening people, but rather by ordinary people who one would never think could do such a thing—until they did. And even more curiously, Pamela and Bettina's insights had frequently led them to solve murders that left the police baffled.

Pamela's computer waited at the ready in her upstairs office, its keyboard warmed by the presence of a slumbering ginger cat. She'd checked her email first thing that morning, and now it took only a gentle click of the mouse to awaken the screen. She didn't expect an email bringing work assignments on a Sunday—though her boss at *Fiber Craft* magazine seemed not to observe holidays or recognize weekends. But she suspected there would be an email from her daughter Penny. Penny's college was in Massachusetts, but thanks to friends who emailed and texted, she often knew as much about the goings-on in Arborville as did her mother—or even more.

Pamela transferred Ginger to her lap, clicked to open her email page, and clicked again to open the new message from Penny Paterson.

"Mom," the message read. "I slept late and now I am sending this to tell you I just found out what happened last night because lots of people on campus are from towns not that far from Arborville. I hope you and Bettina are not going to get involved in any way like you do sometimes if there's something to do with knitting."

Pamela thought for a minute as she scratched Ginger between the ears. Then she responded. "You do not need to worry," she wrote. "There's no connection between that poor young woman Dawn Filbert and Knit and Nibble and I'm sure the police will have everything figured out in no time. Love, Mom."

Chapter 4

In contrast to the previous morning, Pamela's routine on Monday proceeded undisturbed. After feeding Catrina and Ginger, she started water boiling on the stove for her coffee. Then she fetched the *Register* from her front walk, slipped it from its plastic sleeve, and set it on the kitchen table. She returned the coffee she'd ground the previous day to her carafe's filter cone and slipped a slice of whole-grain bread into her toaster. While she waited for the water to boil and the bread to toast, she unfolded the *Register* and scanned the front page.

Thankfully, there was no follow-up to the story of the Arborville murder on that page. She set Part 1 aside to reveal the next section. Stories involving events in the county's many small towns often started out as front-page news if they were dramatic enough but then migrated to the Local section. As she had suspected, the *Register*'s Marcy

Brewer had been busy. Her byline appeared on a long article that mentioned Pamela and Bettina by name as "two of the first people to happen upon the gruesome murder scene." But the article didn't add anything to what Pamela already knew of the event or of the police response. Perhaps Bettina would have new information, however, after her meeting that morning with Detective Clayborn.

The kettle's whistle summoned Pamela to the counter, where she poured boiling water through the grounds waiting in the filter cone. Just as she finished, her toast popped up. From the cupboard where she kept her wedding china, she took out a cup, a saucer, and a plate. Pamela didn't see the point in having nice things if one were to leave them behind, barely used, after one was gone. So she always drank her morning coffee and ate her morning toast from delicate porcelain garlanded with roses.

Then, settled back at the table, she paged through the *Register* until nothing was left of the toast but a few crumbs and the carafe had been drained.

Pamela's workday had begun even before she descended the stairs to her kitchen. She'd gone almost directly from bed to her office, where she'd watched as six emails arrived. A few were from friends, one offered coupons from the hobby shop, one informed her that her credit card statement was waiting to be downloaded—and one came bearing five attachments. That one had been from her boss at *Fiber Craft*.

Now, fed and dressed and with her bed made,

she revisited that email. "Please read and evaluate the attached submissions," her boss had written, "and advise me by Thursday at the latest whether you think they are suitable for publication."

Pamela's job as associate editor for *Fiber Craft* allowed her to work from home most days, a feature she'd appreciated when she was raising Penny and then especially after her architect husband was killed in a construction accident and she was left to raise her daughter alone. Her responsibilities included evaluating articles for publication and then copyediting the ones her editor chose, with occasional trips to the city for meetings.

She opened the first of the attachments, each marked with a stylized paper clip, that stretched across the top of her boss's email, and she was soon immersed in "The Feminist Collective Biennale: Subverting the Patriarchy One Stitch at a Time." Two more articles later, it was time to meet Bettina at Hyler's.

With a light jacket added to her uniform of jeans and sweater, Pamela strolled up Orchard Street, past sturdy wood-frame houses that resembled her own. Though fall had been lovely so far, with the afternoon sun still warm despite its autumnal angle, the air had a golden tinge and leaves had begun to turn. Halfway up the block, one particular tree glowed a luminous scarlet.

When Pamela and her husband had been shopping for a house all that long time ago, they'd been attracted by Arborville's smallness and its charm. Most houses were two stories tall, with attics above and basements below and wide porches where people might have sat to drink lemonade in summers a hundred years ago, when the houses were new. The town's commercial district, with the Co-Op Grocery anchoring it at one end, was only five blocks from Pamela's house. There, quaint storefronts dating from the early 1900s, some with awnings and some without, offered most goods and services that any Arborvillian might need—including lunch at Hyler's Luncheonette.

At the upper corner of Orchard Street, Pamela detoured into the parking lot behind the stately brick apartment building that faced Arborville Avenue. A discreet wooden fence hid the building's trash cans, as well as discards that wouldn't fit in the cans. Pamela loved the treasures she discovered at tag sales and thrift stores—her wedding china was nearly her only treasure she'd acquired new. But even more exciting was a treasure that cost no money at all. Recently, a peek behind the wooden fence had yielded a framed sketch of a young woman in an eighteenth-century gown.

Bettina stood up and waved from a booth along the wall as soon as Pamela stepped through Hyler's heavy glass door. The booths, with their high-backed benches upholstered in burgundy Naugahyde, offered the chance for a quieter meal than did the worn wooden tables that crowded the center of the room, especially between noon and one p.m. on a weekday. That was when the restaurant buzzed with conversation as Arborville's bankers and Realtors and insurance agents, as well as the people who staffed Borough Hall, took their lunch breaks.

Bettina had dressed for her meeting with Detective Clayborn in a stylish pantsuit, lightweight wool in a rich shade of amber. The floppy bow of a silk blouse, in a plaid fabric that contrasted amber with deep red and cream, was visible at the neck, and she'd added antique amber and silver earrings to complete her ensemble.

She'd been chatting with a server Pamela had noticed in Hyler's before, a meek-looking young woman with fair, straight hair pulled back into a low ponytail. The young woman greeted Pamela and waited as she slid into the booth across from Bettina. Then she held out the oversize menus that were a Hyler's trademark. As she did so, her left hand, which had been hidden by her right as she cradled the menus, became visible.

As far as Pamela could see, it was a perfectly ordinary left hand, with well-groomed nails painted a pretty shade of coral. But Bettina stared at the hand and gasped. So distracted that she didn't even reach for the menu, she exclaimed, "Your beautiful ring! Where is it?"

"Oh . . . I . . ." The young woman set Bettina's menu on the table before her. She shrugged and twisted her delicate features into a sad smile. "We're not getting married after all."

"You poor dear girl! Whatever happened?" Bettina asked.

From anyone else such prying, except from a close confidante, would have merited a curt "None of your business." But Bettina was such a sympathetic soul, her mobile face so reflective of the genuine concern she felt when she encountered people burdened by sorrow, that the young woman sank onto the edge of the bench occupied by Pamela.

Her head tipped forward and she sighed. "He's down in Princeton and I'm up here . . ." Her voice thinned and then trailed off.

Bettina reached out and grasped the young woman's hands. "Princeton's not so very far away," she said, her expression both concerned and hopeful.

"It's a different world," the young woman said. She blinked a few times. Pamela, observing her in profile, noticed a tear escaping from her eye. "He's a graduate student and I'm working my way through County Community College two courses at a time."

"So he broke it off?" Bettina's concern had given way to indignation. "Then you're well rid of him!"

"It wasn't really him." The tears were flowing now. Bettina released one of the young woman's hands and used her own newly free hand to offer the paper napkin that made up part of her place setting. The young woman dabbed her eyes and the words "It was—" squeezed out of a constricted throat.

"Felicity?" A figure had appeared at the edge of the booth, the middle-aged woman who had worked at Hyler's forever. She was carrying a bundle of menus. "It's the lunch-hour rush," she said. "What are you doing?"

Her tone of voice and the expression on her face suggested a scolding, but her face softened as she looked more closely at the young woman. She shifted the menus to the crook of one arm and laid her other hand on the young woman's shoulder. "You get off to the restroom and wash your face, sweetheart," she said. She watched, shaking her head, as the young woman threaded her way among the tables.

"It's hard to be young," she commented. "Felicity Winkle is as nice as they come and that boyfriend's father is a real—" She paused, as if censoring herself, and raised her eyebrows. "Now then"—she turned back to Pamela and Bettina—"how about ham and Swiss on rye? That's today's special." They both nodded. "And it looks like you need a fresh napkin," the server observed. "I'll hand these menus around and then I'll be back to take your order."

They chatted for a few minutes about the encounter they had just had with the young woman who they now knew as Felicity Winkle. "I earned money for college waiting tables during the summer," Bettina said at last. "It's nothing to look down on—unless somebody's a complete snob."

"I guess the boyfriend's father is." Pamela shrugged.

Then the server returned with her order pad and recorded their request for two ham and cheese on rye and two vanilla milkshakes.

When the server was gone, Pamela leaned across the table. "So—what did Detective Clayborn say?" she asked.

"They've been busy," Bettina reported, "and they plan to be busier. They're interviewing everybody who's been in Dawn's salon for the past six months. When an appointment is booked, the person taking the booking makes a note of the client's phone number, which is handy for the cops."

"They don't really think Dawn was killed by a

customer who thought Dawn had ruined her hair, do they?" A tiny laugh accompanied Pamela's question.

"Not exactly," Bettina said. "But women tell their hairdressers all kinds of things, and vice versa. So talking to Dawn's clients wouldn't be such a far-fetched approach—*if* the killer was really aiming for Dawn."

A vanilla milkshake appeared on the paper mat in front of Pamela and a voice said, "Wasn't that a shame! Such a shocking story!" The voice belonged to the middle-aged server who had taken over from Felicity. She went on, seemingly encouraged by Bettina's nod. "Have you been past the salon? It's closed, of course, but people are leaving flowers on the sidewalk outside. She had a very devoted clientele."

When the server was gone again, Bettina pulled her milkshake closer. She shifted the straw, which protruded from the frothy crest atop the tall glass, to a more convenient tilt. Then she took a long sip. "Delicious!" she pronounced. Her bright lipstick left an imprint on the straw.

"They've already interviewed Dawn's family," Bettina said, returning to the topic at hand. "Sisters and like that—she'd never been married. And friends, and old boyfriends, and—"

Pamela interrupted, "But we're pretty sure the killer wasn't really aiming for Dawn."

"*We're* pretty sure—"

Pamela was typically a model conversationalist, letting others have their say without getting impatient. But this wasn't a typical conversation.

She interrupted again. "Did you tell Detective Clayborn about the Bo Peep costume?"

"Well, *duh*! Of course I told him, and he—"

This third interruption was from the sandwiches. They arrived on cream-colored oval plates, accompanied by slender pickle spears and coleslaw in little pleated paper cups. The sandwiches themselves were oval too, but sliced in half, the rye bread light brown and studded with caraway seeds. The gap between the bottom slice of bread and the top slice revealed the rich pink of ham piled high, topped with a generous layer of Swiss cheese. Frilled toothpicks steadied the impressive constructions. After she settled the plates into place, the server slipped a fresh napkin beside Bettina's.

The revelation of Detective Clayborn's response was postponed as Bettina and Pamela each removed a toothpick from a sandwich half. Bettina took the first bite. Pamela smiled at her friend's look of astonished pleasure and sampled her own sandwich half. It was delicious, the hint of exotic caraway in the rye bread and the buttery nutlike Swiss balancing the sweet smokiness of the unctuous ham. And after a few bites of sandwich, the crisp taste of the pickle offered the perfect contrast.

They ate in silence for a time, punctuated only by appreciative hums. Then, as Bettina was removing the toothpick from her second sandwich half, Pamela returned to the topic they'd been discussing when the sandwiches arrived.

"What did Detective Clayborn say when you told him about the Bo Peep costume?" she asked.

"He didn't see the point." The smile with which Bettina had been regarding the remaining sandwich half vanished. "He said people wear all sorts of costumes on Halloween and whoever killed Dawn had probably been stalking her and maybe even followed her to the Halloween celebration and very likely even talked to her at some point. So he knew perfectly well who he was killing."

"He?" Pamela raised her brows.

"Clayborn always calls killers *he.*" Bettina reached for the sandwich half.

But Pamela wasn't ready to resume eating yet, though she leaned toward the straw protruding from the tall glass that contained the vanilla milkshake and sipped a long sip. Fortified by the cool, creamy sweetness, she went on.

"You told him Mary put a photo of the costume on her website? So anybody who visited *The Lyon and the Lamb* would know to look for Bo Peep at the bonfire if they wanted to kill her?" Bettina nodded, chewing. "And that it was just a last-minute thing that Dawn ended up in the Bo Peep costume and Mary was the sheep?"

Bettina swallowed and nodded. "Everything. I told him everything," she said. "He pointed out that *The Lyon and the Lamb* might not have the following that we imagine—especially among killers."

"Well, he *does* think they're all men." Pamela cocked an eyebrow and laughed a tiny laugh. She plucked the frilled toothpick from the other half of her sandwich and picked up the sandwich. Mayonnaise was the ideal accompaniment, she reflected as she bit into it. Anything more would disturb the perfect balance of the rye bread, Swiss, and ham.

For a bit, there was silence again as they alternated bites of sandwich with forkfuls of slaw and nibbles of pickle. But when the plates were bare except for a few crumbs and the empty paper cups that had held the slaw, Pamela spoke again. She'd just remembered the most curious aspect of the crime scene.

"What about the strands of yarn around Dawn's neck?" she asked suddenly. "Did you bring that up? It was like the killer had a plan, like he meant to tie them, but then didn't."

Bettina looked up from the glass that had contained her milkshake. She'd just used the straw to slurp the last few drops. "Of course I brought it up," she said, her good-natured expression softening the impatience implied by the words. "I'm as curious about that as you are."

"And what did he say?"

Bettina twisted her lips into a disgusted zigzag. "He said once the killer realized that the blow to the head had killed her, he realized he didn't need to strangle her."

"Did Detective Clayborn have any idea about why the weapon of choice—even if the killer didn't follow through with the strangling—was yarn?" Pamela asked as the server approached.

"I didn't ask him." Bettina looked slightly defeated. "You and I didn't talk about that." She glanced up and requested the check, and the server gathered plates, tableware, and glasses and carried them away all in one trip.

"You know what we have to do next, don't you?" Pamela said.

"What?"

"We have to talk to Nell again." Pamela leaned across the worn wooden table and lowered her voice. "Her neighbor is in danger. I'm convinced the person who killed Dawn thought the woman in the Bo Peep costume was Mary Lyon."

"Nell gets upset when she thinks we're getting involved in things better left to the police," Bettina said.

"We'll just have to convince her that this is really important. Mary's life is in danger and Detective Clayborn isn't going to do anything about it."

Chapter 5

"**I** know you walked here," Bettina said as they stepped out onto the sidewalk, "but I'm not walking up that hill to the Palisades, especially in these shoes." She extended a foot to display, below the hem of her chic pants, a suede pump in a dramatic shade of burgundy. "Anyway, my car is by the police station."

Pamela followed her friend through the narrow passage between Hyler's and the hair salon that offered a shortcut from Arborville Avenue to the town park, the police station, and the library. Yellow garlands of crime-scene tape still warned that the stand of trees where Dawn's body had been found was off-limits. And a charred circle at the left edge of the park marked the spot where the bonfire had blazed. Soon it would be raked and covered with topsoil, and grass seed would be sown in the spring.

Pamela and Bettina climbed into Bettina's faithful Toyota, and a few minutes later they were turning onto the hillside block where Nell and Harold lived. The neighborhood that Arborvillians called the Palisades was so named because the east half of Arborville was built on the slope formed by the backside of the cliffs that overlooked the Hudson River. Nell and Harold's substantial house was built of stones, rugged natural stones cleverly fitted together in no apparent pattern. A flight of steps that curved through thickly planted azaleas and rhododendrons led to its front door.

Bettina pulled up to the curb and parked, but there was no need to mount the steps to greet at least one of the Bascombs. Harold was standing in his driveway wielding a bamboo rake.

"The leaves are really starting to fall now," he said by way of greeting after they had climbed out of the car. Dried leaves like crumpled bits of brown paper littered the driveway and sidewalk. "Nell sent me out to tidy up."

"She's at home then?" Bettina offered a genial smile. Pamela smiled too, not the social smile she produced when she thought the occasion demanded a smile, but a genuine expression of the great fondness she felt for Harold.

"Two visits in two days?" Harold's answering smile was teasing. "And yesterday's visit, as I recall, touched on the fact that our neighbor, Mary Lyon"—he nodded toward the house across the street—"had implied on her blog that she would be present at the Arborville Halloween celebration wearing a Little Bo Peep costume that turned up instead on a murder victim."

The smile became more teasing as Harold went on. "I know," he said, "that Arborville's finest, under the guidance of the redoubtable Lucas Clayborn, are doing the very best they can to solve this crime. But something tells me that in certain circles his efforts are seen as falling short. Particularly because there's what might be construed as a yarn connection here."

"Can you read Nell's mind too?" Pamela asked with a laugh.

Harold laughed in response and he flourished the rake. "Not well enough to know that the driveway and sidewalk needed raking before she told me."

As they started toward the steps that led to the front door, he added, "She doesn't approve of your sleuthing, you know. But I do."

Nell met them at the door looking rather cheflike, in a white canvas bib apron that covered the front of her chambray work shirt and reached past her knees.

"Hello," she said. "What brings you two up here today?"

"We have something to discuss with you," Pamela said.

Nell had a look that was both probing and kind, a slight widening of her faded blue eyes coupled with a softening of her lips. She aimed the look at Pamela and then at Bettina. "Sounds important," she observed. "I've got something on the stove. Come on back in here."

They followed her down the long hall to the

kitchen. There, one glance made it obvious that an ambitious project was underway. A huge cookie sheet occupied the table. In the center of the cookie sheet was a mountain of pumpkin innards, the flat oval seeds tangled in the strands of fiber as in a moist net. On Nell's avocado-green stove, a large pot sat atop a burner turned high. The steam escaping from under its cover and the low, rumbling sounds suggested that intense cooking was taking place inside.

"The Halloween pumpkin," Nell explained. "We don't carve it—it's just as festive whole. And when the flesh is cooked"—she gestured toward the burbling pot—"it goes into the freezer and comes back out next month for pumpkin pie. Waste not, want not, as your Wilfred would say."

"And the seeds?" Bettina asked.

"I clean them off a bit and put them back by my compost heap. Harold and I could eat them, but the squirrels deserve their share too." Nell stepped over to the stove, picked up a long fork, and lifted the lid of the pot. She tilted her head aside to avoid the cloud of steam that escaped and probed inside with the fork. "Done!" she announced and turned off the burner.

Pamela and Bettina had slipped into chairs at the table as Nell checked on her pumpkin. Finished at the stove, she moved the cookie sheet with its cargo to the counter and joined them at the table.

"And now," she said, "the important thing? I hope it's not what I think it is."

"It might be." Pamela tried to muster a look she had cultivated while raising Penny, a look that had accompanied talks on the character-building value of difficult undertakings. "Mary Lyon's life is in danger," she said.

"Oh!" Nell's laugh was like an explosive sigh. "Surely the police—"

"*Not* surely the police." Bettina joined in, rising up in her chair. "The killer absolutely thought Mary would be wearing that Bo Peep costume and that's why he killed the person wearing it." The scarlet tendrils of her hair quivered as she bobbed her head decisively. "Clayborn is ignoring that fact, which seems quite obvious to me and to Pamela—and to you, I think."

It seemed to Pamela that Nell nodded the tiniest nod.

"The police are interviewing everyone who had an appointment at Dawn's salon during the past six months," Bettina concluded, with a twist of her lips that implied her low opinion of this strategy.

"And so you want me to . . . what?" Nell shrugged.

"We have to talk to Mary," Pamela said. "We have to first of all tell her to be careful, not to go out alone at night and like that. And we have to ask her about people who read her blog and might want to kill her."

Nell frowned slightly and looked as if she was about to speak, but Bettina spoke first. "You know her," she explained. "We don't, really. So why would she listen to us?"

"So we go across the street now?" Nell started to rise. "All three of us?"

"All three of us." Pamela nodded and they rose to their feet.

A few minutes later, Harold waved them on their way.

Unlike many people, Mary Lyon closely resembled the image posted on her website. She was not, in person, older or chubbier or less becomingly coiffed than her digital photo intimated.

She was a bit over fifty, Pamela imagined, though the years had been very kind to her. Her slender face was beautifully modeled, with high cheekbones tapering to a delicate chin. Her deep russet hair made her creamy skin seem all the creamier, and her blue eyes all the more striking. She was tall—even taller than Pamela—and thin enough that the leggings she wore didn't seem ill-advised.

"When Dawn Filbert was killed, she was wearing the Little Bo Peep costume you posted on your blog," Pamela said, once they'd been welcomed and offered seats in Mary's artistically furnished living room. She and Mary were occupying two armchairs upholstered in a nubby fabric featuring interlocking circles. Bettina and Nell faced them on the matching sofa. Between the armchairs and the sofa was a glass coffee table supported by a brass pedestal. A dramatic wall hanging dominated the fireplace wall.

"Such a shame," Mary said. "The killing, I mean. And Dawn was such a good hairdresser too." She raised a hand to smooth her lustrous tresses and explained that at her hair appointment Saturday afternoon, she and Dawn got to chatting about the Halloween celebration and Dawn said she hadn't given much thought to a costume.

"So you offered her Bo Peep?" Bettina supplied.

"Sure," Mary said. "Why not? It was a great costume, if I do say so myself, and she didn't want to be a sheep." She shrugged and managed to look sad without looking any less beautiful. "Now, of course, after what happened . . ." Mary stared at the coffee table for a moment, where a low pottery vase held giant golden chrysanthemums. As if the sight of the flowers cheered her, her expression brightened. "It didn't have anything to do with the costume, so I guess I don't need to feel bad."

"What if the killer thought that was you in the costume, though?" Pamela smiled to herself at the intent look with which Nell asked the question, as if she was determined to prove herself on her first foray into sleuthing.

"Why?" Mary opened her eyes wide and drew out the question.

"The wig and the hat made the costume a pretty good disguise," Pamela said.

A tiny wrinkle began to form between Mary's well-shaped brows. "Who would want . . . to kill"—she paused and laughed—"Brainard?" She laughed harder. "If they'd been after Bo Peep, they wouldn't have killed me. They'd have killed Brainard!"

"Brainard?" Pamela, Bettina, and Nell all spoke at once.

"We always dress as famous couples on Halloween, but we do it backward. Our friends think it's funny. Last year I was Sonny and old Brainy was Cher. But this year he was just a big spoilsport. So"—Mary made a gesture of wiping her hands—"nothing to worry about."

Pamela felt her eyes widen. Across from her, on the sofa, Nell just looked sad. Did Mary really not care that someone might have intended to kill her husband as long as she was okay? But she *wasn't*, actually, and that's what Pamela was about to explain before Bettina jumped in.

"You didn't make it clear on your blog who was going to wear what," Bettina pointed out, "and most people would think the woman was going to wear the dress."

Mary's reaction this time furrowed her lovely brow and disturbed the symmetry of her well-shaped lips. "You're right!" she exclaimed. "And I have tons of followers. But why would they want to kill me?" Her voice modulated to a thin wail.

"Most people probably have some secret enemy who'd be glad if they were gone." Despite the dire import of the words, Bettina's tone was encouraging.

"I just can't—I don't—" Mary stared at the chrysanthemums. As if addressing them, she went on. "Well, there was that knitting book 'author' . . . not books exactly, more like *booklets*. Like they sell at those hobby stores side by side with that cheap yarn in garish colors." Mary looked up. "I couldn't give them a positive review, could I? Ski hats with pompoms? Infinity scarves? Hello? Originality? So the husband of the 'author' shows up and offers me a bribe to revise the old reviews to make them positive and make the new ones positive in the future. And when I refuse the bribe, he threatens me." She shrugged and raised her hands, palms up. "I have standards. What could I do?"

Pamela didn't think infinity scarves and ski hats with pompoms sounded that terrible. Not all knitters wanted to take on projects requiring intense concentration and advanced techniques. And some people were grateful to find money in their budgets even for hobby shop yarn. But she—and Bettina and Nell—were saved from answering by the sound of feet drawing near.

A handsome man in a tweed jacket strode into the room.

"It's my husband, the Brain," Mary said with a lazy glance in his direction.

"Brainard Covington," Nell supplied. Looking up at him from her perch on the sofa, she said, "I don't think you know Bettina Fraser." She gestured toward Bettina, who was sitting next to her. "And this is Pamela Paterson." She nodded at Pamela, across the room.

"Delighted." He smiled a small smile. Then, displaying a bulging leather satchel and speaking to no one in particular, he announced, "I'm off to my seminar."

"I'm sure they're counting the minutes until you get there," his wife murmured

"What does Brainard teach?" Bettina asked as the front door closed behind him.

"Not much," Mary said. But then, apparently

sensing that she hadn't found an audience for her wit, she added, "Classics . . . Greeks, whatever. Old stuff. We moved up here from Princeton when he got the offer from Wendelstaff College and he's been there ever since."

"Did you meet at Princeton, then?" Bettina inquired in her sociable way.

"He was there and I was visiting someone. I'm not smart enough for Princeton, but he must have thought I was smart enough to appreciate how smart he was. Or maybe he just liked the way I looked." Mary laughed, but not as heartily as she'd laughed when contemplating the Halloween killer targeting Bo Peep and discovering he'd killed Brainard.

She stopped suddenly and raised a finger in the air, as if sensing that her audience's attention was flagging.

"Secret enemies! The llama farm! Don't let me forget," she exclaimed before carrying on with her earlier theme. "But anyway, men?" Even twisted by scorn, her features were beautiful. "That's all they want, isn't it? Somebody to admire them? Brainy's first choice was too smart for that." She flopped back in the armchair as if worn out.

"Llamas?" Nell inquired after a few moments.

Mary leaned forward again. "I'm supposed to do a post on llama wool, or whatever they call it—fur?—for the owner of some llama farm in Kringlekamack? *Please!* I said. *Hello?* It's 'Mary had a little lamb,' not 'Mary had a little llama.' "

* * *

"Sad," Bettina commented when they reached Nell's side of the street. "Just like you said, Nell. It's sad when couples can't get along." Bettina shook her head. "I wonder if she gets along with anyone. You consider her a friend, but . . ."

"A neighbor," Nell said with a raised eyebrow and a tilt to her head that suggested she was making a distinction. The three of them took a few steps in the direction of Bettina's Toyota.

Before leaving Mary's, they had suggested that she be very careful when she left her house, especially at night. Perhaps there was another explanation for Dawn's murder, one that didn't involve the killer's expectation of who would be wearing the Bo Peep costume, Pamela had told her. But perhaps there wasn't. And it didn't hurt to be careful.

"Mary has a son," Nell said as Pamela and Bettina began to climb into Bettina's car. "He's grown up now, but still . . ."

"They still love their mothers." Bettina paused and met Nell's gaze.

"And our little town certainly doesn't need another murder," Nell added.

Tuesday morning's *Register* didn't announce any arrests in what it was calling the "Arborville Halloween bonfire murder"—so presumably, Detective Clayborn and his associates were still at work interviewing patrons of Dawn Filbert's salon. Pamela wasn't sure whether the previous day's conversation with Mary Lyon had laid to rest her fears that the bonfire murderer would strike again—or heightened them.

Mary had enemies, yes, but how bent on murder could the recipient of the bad reviews be? Or even the woman's chivalrous husband? On the other hand, Pamela had once received a very frightening email from an author who figured out that Pamela was the editor who had given a thumbs-down to his article on the ecology of replacing caskets with funeral shrouds.

Then there was the llama farmer Mary had mentioned. People could be very protective of their animals. Pamela was protective of her cats. In fact—she jumped from her chair and took up a pad of the notepaper that, along with address labels, arrived in the mail without ever being requested. *Cat food*, she wrote as the first item in what was to be the shopping list for the Co-Op Grocery errand on that day's agenda.

She tipped her wedding-china cup to drain the last few swallows of coffee that was now lukewarm, rinsed the cup and the plate that had held her toast, and headed upstairs to get dressed and start her day. Catrina followed at the heels of her mistress's furry slippers.

Ten minutes later, wearing jeans and the same sweater she'd been wearing since Sunday, Pamela sat down at her desk, welcomed Catrina onto her lap, and pressed the buttons that would bring her computer to life. There was no message from her boss at *Fiber Craft* and she didn't expect one until she returned the work that had arrived the previous day. But there was an email from Penny, with a photo of her in her Halloween costume of a black velvet cape, scary makeup, and a witch's peaked hat. That message made her smile, not least at the fact that the note accompanying it contained no further reference to Dawn Filbert's murder.

She opened the attachment from her boss's Monday email labeled "String Skirt" and settled down to evaluate "The String Skirt as Puberty Marker in Bronze Age Cultures."

Chapter 6

A scarecrow lounged in a chair on Roland DeCamp's porch. The scarecrow's body was a pair of jeans and a plaid flannel shirt stuffed with straw, and a battered felt hat topped his jack-o'-lantern head. En route to the DeCamps' house, Pamela and Bettina had driven by other houses displaying acknowledgments of the holiday just past. Some homeowners' shrubs had been encased in webs produced by giant spiders that now sat atop the shrubs looking fearsome. At other houses, phalanxes of skeletons paraded across yards that had sprouted tombstones. Elsewhere, bedsheets rippling in the wind suggested ghostly shapes.

Roland and his wife, though childless themselves, lived in a neighborhood inhabited by numerous families with school-age children. Many of them were relative newcomers to Arborville, and the houses built on the land that the old-timers still called the Farm appealed to them because they were large and modern and had dependable plumbing and lots of closets. Arborville's old-timers, however, considered their own old-time houses historic and charming, and had yet to forgive the latest generation of Van Ripers, a Dutch family that dated back to before Arborville was Arborville, for selling their family's farm to developers.

Melanie DeCamp welcomed Pamela and Bettina at the door. She was Roland's wife, blond and elegant, not a member of Knit and Nibble but delighted that her husband had followed his doctor's advice and taken up knitting to offset the stress of his job as a corporate lawyer. Melanie motioned them in, and they saw that they were evidently the last to arrive.

Nell had settled into the substantial armchair Melanie always reserved for her—the other seating possibilities in the DeCamps' sleek living room, a low-slung turquoise sofa and matching chair, required legs as well-exercised as Melanie's own to rise from them once one was seated. Holly Perkins and Karen Dowling sat side by side on the sofa. They were both young marrieds and the best of friends, though Holly's dramatic good looks and outsize personality made her as unlike her shy blond friend as any two people could be.

Holly and Karen greeted the newcomers and moved closer together to make room for Pamela and Bettina on the sofa. From her armchair, Nell spoke up with her own cheery hello and resumed extracting yarn, needles, and a partially finished stocking from her knitting bag. She had already embarked on her annual Christmas project—dozens of colorful stockings to be filled with treats and distributed to the children at the Haversack women's shelter where she volunteered.

As Pamela and Bettina settled themselves, Melanie cocked an ear toward the kitchen, as if responding to a summons that only she could hear. "You know he always wants to bake the Knit and Nibble goody himself," she murmured, excused herself, and hurried toward the hall that led to the kitchen.

"We're all quite ourselves again after Saturday night?" Bettina surveyed the group, her eyes lingering on Holly. Pamela was glad Bettina's question made it sound as if this was the first time they were meeting again since the adventure they all, except for Karen, had shared on Saturday night. There was no reason to alarm Holly—or timid little Karen—with suspicions about the bonfire murderer's true target and thus the fact that the murderer might strike again.

"A few good nights' sleep did wonders," Holly said with a smile that stopped just short of activating her dimple. "Desmond is quite himself as well."

But Karen wasn't so upbeat. "I wasn't even there," she said with a delicate shudder, "and I've been having nightmares. When I saw the *Register* Sunday morning, I couldn't believe I was reading about something that happened in my own little town— the town where Dave and I thought we could raise our dear baby Lily in safety."

Nell's busy needles ceased moving and she raised her eyes from the stocking heel she was shaping. From the perturbed look she directed at Bettina, Pamela was sure a scolding was on its way. For all that she had been enlisted to help with the visit to Mary, Nell never approved of the lively discussions that community misfortunes often gave rise to, feeling that the impulse was more to titillate than to inform.

But before she could say anything, Melanie stepped back into the living room. "He needs to keep an eye on his creation for about ten minutes, but he wants you to go ahead and start without him," she said.

The aroma of something rich and sugary baking had begun to drift into the living room from the direction of the kitchen.

Bettina closed her eyes and sniffed, her brightly painted lips curving into a smile. "I'd say he's come up with a winner," she observed.

Melanie ventured farther into the room. "It's that ready-made cookie dough you buy at the grocery store," she whispered, her carefully manicured fingers shaping a rectangular package. "In the refrigerator case, and you form it into cookies and bake them." She smiled and held up a finger. "But don't let on I told you."

Holly and Karen returned to their projects, which they had set aside during the brief discussion launched by Bettina's question. Holly was making a stocking too. She was well past the heel and nearing the point at which the toe would be worked. She'd finished her ambitious color-block afghan a few weeks previously and had declared her intention to join Nell in the stocking project until inspired with an idea for her next creation. "Maybe Desmond would like a hand-knit sweater," she had said, "but I'm not sure." Karen's project was, for a change, not a garment for her daughter Lily, who had been born the previous Christmas, but a baby blanket for a friend who was expecting her first child.

Bettina's knitting reposed on her lap, partly hidden by an open magazine that contained the pattern for an ambitious Nordic-style sweater, navy blue with red ribbing and bands of snowflakes in red and white. It was destined for Wilfred and had been in progress for a year. She was frowning and tracing a line of the pattern with a finger as she murmured numbers to herself.

Pamela herself was engaged in an ambitious project, a sweater she intended to give her mother for Christmas. She'd spent a few weeks paging through pattern books and knitting magazines while satisfying the need to keep her fingers busy by joining Nell in her previous do-good undertaking— hand-knit infant caps to be donated to hospitals. At last she had settled on a design for a loose A-line cardigan with wide sleeves, and large buttons marching down the front. She had splurged on cashmere yarn in a cornflower blue and planned to use vintage silver buttons she'd come across at a tag sale. The back and one of the fronts was complete, and she was partway through the other front.

As she knitted, enjoying the sensation of the extravagant yarn against her fingers, the smell of baking cookies had become more intense.

"I think they're done," Bettina announced. She had been chatting with Karen about Lily's latest doings, but now she swiveled her head in the direction of the kitchen. "I hope he's paying attention," she added.

And, in fact, he was. A minute later, Roland

emerged. "Welcome, everyone," he said. "I apologize for my late entrance, but I was unavoidably detained."

Had he worn an apron for his cookie-baking? Pamela found herself wondering. He was dressed, as always, in a scrupulously tailored pinstripe suit, a starched white dress shirt, and a discreetly patterned, obviously expensive, tie.

He strode across his living room's luxuriant carpet, followed by a sleek black cat, and took his seat in the low-slung turquoise chair that matched the sofa. The elegant leather briefcase that served as his knitting bag sat ready at the chair's side. As soon as he had settled into the chair, the cat leaped up beside him and snuggled against his thigh. The cat, Cuddles, had been adopted by Roland from the same litter that included Ginger.

"Did you get many trick-or-treaters?" Holly inquired. "Or were all your neighbors at the parade and bonfire?"

Roland looked up from the briefcase, which he'd hoisted onto his lap. "If by trick-or-treaters you mean the children asking for handouts of candy," he said as he worked the latch, "they come around in the afternoon." The briefcase top sprang open.

"Ohhh!" Holly sounded genuinely heartbroken. "You don't get to treat them then, and they're so cute in their little costumes. Desmond and I miss most of them too, with our schedules at the salon."

Roland frowned. "I don't see the point of it," he said. He lifted a swath of knitting from the briefcase, along with the mate to the needle from which it hung, and a skein of camel-colored yarn.

"But you have a scarecrow on your porch—and a very nice one too," Bettina chimed in.

"That's Melanie's doing." Roland clicked his briefcase closed and lowered it back to its spot on the floor.

"People enjoy Halloween," Nell said, leaning forward from the depths of the armchair, "though I wish there was less emphasis on candy. Dressing up, however . . . it's a chance for people to exercise their imaginations and become somebody they're not."

"And dance around a fire like some kind of . . . of . . . barely civilized . . ."

"Barbarians?" Nell suggested, the tilt of her lips hinting at a smile.

"Yes!" Roland's lean face was intense. "Barbarians."

"No one was dancing." Holly's tone was that of someone calmly correcting a factual error.

"And you weren't even there anyway." Bettina's tone was less calm.

"I know they weren't really dancing," Roland snapped, sounding irritated that his description of the Halloween revelers had been taken literally. "But I didn't have to be there to know what it was like. All these people out roaming around in the dark, and nobody looks like who they really are, and Arborville's police force—which I support with my tax dollars—has to work overtime. And look what happened."

"Oh, Roland . . ." The hint of a smile vanished and Nell's voice faltered. "That was a terrible, terrible thing, but it didn't have anything to do with primal urges. Halloween is just fun for the children, as long as they don't eat too much candy, and the community so enjoys the parade and bonfire."

Roland grunted and began to study his project. "You haven't made much progress since last week," Bettina commented from across the room.

"I've made a lot of progress," Roland said, raising his eyes from the rectangle of camel-colored knitting he was pondering. "This is the second sleeve. Last week I was working on the first sleeve."

Holly directed a dimply smile in his direction. "The second sleeve!" she exclaimed. "You've really been busy—and Melanie is going to love her sweater."

"She should," Roland said. "She picked out the yarn and the pattern. But I haven't been any busier than usual. I'm just very efficient." He thrust his right-hand needle through the first stitch on his left-hand needle, caught up a twist of yarn with his right-hand forefinger, and soon was methodically creating a new row.

"That's a perfect color for her!" Holly wasn't giving up easily in her effort to engage Roland in conversation. "Melanie is always so elegant."

"She is?" Roland looked up with a puzzled frown. He thought for a minute as the frown deepened, then he said, "Yes, elegant. I suppose she is," and resumed his knitting.

Holly sighed, laughed to herself, and gathered her knitting to migrate across the room and crouch by the side of Nell's armchair. Soon the two of them were conferring about the steps involved in shaping the toe of Holly's in-progress stocking.

Next to Pamela, Bettina and Karen were comparing notes on babies—though the baby in question for Bettina was her Boston granddaughter. Pamela was happy to knit in silence for a bit, and grateful Roland's mention of Dawn Filbert's murder hadn't given rise to a more extended discussion.

Fifteen minutes passed. Holly had returned to her spot on the sofa and resumed her work on the stocking. Bettina had broken off her conversation with Karen to switch from the red yarn with which she'd been knitting ribbing to the navy-blue yarn of the sweater's body. The silence that had descended on the group was broken when Roland, consulting the impressive watch normally concealed by his aggressively starched shirt cuff, announced, "It's ten minutes to eight. I must excuse myself to prepare the coffee and tea."

He slowly rose from the turquoise chair, making sure not to alarm the cat cuddled against his thigh, set his knitting in the spot he had vacated, and headed toward the hall that led to the kitchen. Soon the aroma of brewing coffee began to drift in from that direction. Pamela was nearing the end of a row, and when she reached it she set her knitting aside. She was about to venture to the kitchen and offer to help carry things when Roland reappeared carrying a sleek pewter tray, which he set on the coffee table.

It held five steaming cups of coffee with their saucers and two empty cup-and-saucer sets. The cups and saucers were made of pale porcelain, unadorned, but all the more impressive in their elegant simplicity.

"Tea is coming," Roland explained, and hurried back toward the kitchen, this time followed by the black cat.

"We can help," Bettina called after him and started to rise. But Melanie had joined them.

She waved Bettina back onto the sofa and said, "He likes to do it himself. He's so proud of being in the group and he enjoys these meetings so much."

In the armchair, Nell suppressed a quizzical expression.

Roland returned bearing another tray, which he set next to the first one on the coffee table, aligning it so both were exactly parallel.

"Oh my goodness, Roland!" Holly exclaimed. "You got into the spirit of Halloween after all! These are just too cute!"

Besides a porcelain teapot and the cream-and-sugar set that matched the cups and saucers, as well as spoons and small napkins, the second tray held a heaping plate of cookies. They were chocolaty rounds studded with candy corn.

"They look divine!" Bettina reached for one. "What a clever idea! Chocolate and candy corn."

Roland had taken his seat and been joined by the black cat, which was once again cuddled against his thigh. A tiny close-lipped smile appeared as he absorbed Holly and Bettina's praise, but instead of looking at them, he looked at the carpet. "Well"—he cleared his throat—"I knew you'd all expect something . . . something seasonal, and so I . . . it just seemed . . . candy corn . . . is so . . ."

"So Halloween!" Nell said with a triumphant laugh.

"I can't imagine a better combination!" Bettina reached for a cookie and then a napkin, tasted the cookie, and pronounced it divine.

"Plates!" Roland exclaimed, springing to his feet and startling the black cat. He lunged toward the hall that led to the kitchen. Crockery rattled and a cupboard door banged shut, then he was back with a stack of small plates from the same delicate porcelain set. He placed them on the coffee table next to the plate of cookies and returned to his chair, calming the black cat with a gentle pat.

Melanie, standing behind her husband with her hands on his shoulders, smiled at the group, seemingly delighted by Roland's success as a host.

But he glanced around the room and suddenly leaped up, startling the black cat again, as well as Melanie. He turned back for a moment to stroke the animal, which looked up at him trustingly, then seized the porcelain teapot. He poured two cups of tea and placed one on the coffee table within reach of Karen. He carried the other to Nell and set it on the small table next to the substantial armchair that was always reserved for her.

"Now,"—Roland glanced around again—"does everyone have everything they need?"

"I'll take a cookie," Nell said, starting to rise. "Just one, though."

"Let me, let me—" Roland edged toward the coffee table where the plate of cookies waited, but he swiveled back to ponder Nell and said, "Cream and sugar too! You need cream and sugar for your tea!"

Nell was on her feet now. "Roland, really"—her voice was soothing—"everything is lovely. Please relax and sample your own treats."

He was about to return to the sleek turquoise chair when he noticed Melanie still on her feet. He waved her toward the turquoise chair with a courtly gesture and fetched an extra chair from the dining room. Soon everyone was settled, with coffee or tea sugared and creamed to their satisfaction and one cookie or more in reserve on a small porcelain plate.

Pamela didn't really like candy corn, though she acknowledged that it was as crucial to the rituals of Halloween as peppermint candy canes were to Christmas or foil-wrapped chocolate eggs to Easter. But she had to admit that the pairing of chocolate with candy corn was inspired. Sweet as the chocolate cookie was, its flavor still hinted at the slight bitterness of the cacao bean, and that bitterness tamed the excruciating sweetness of the candy corns studded here and there.

Melanie didn't usually join the group when Roland hosted Knit and Nibble, but perched in the turquoise chair, she seemed to enjoy the benign gossip and the chatter about babies and home improvement projects unloosed by Roland's expertly managed refreshments. She was happily nibbling on the cookies, though to judge from her lithe, well-toned body, such indulgences were rare.

Roland's discreet peek at his watch signaled that he, at least, judged the time had come to return to the knit component of the evening. Taking their cue from their host, people began tipping cups to capture the last swallow of coffee or tea. Murmuring that she really shouldn't, Bettina helped herself to one more cookie.

Pamela lowered her empty cup to its saucer and

picked up her knitting. She'd left off at the end of a row, so there was no need to ponder which direction she'd been heading when the group put their knitting aside to sample Roland's treats. Soon she was once again enjoying the steady rhythm of yarn-looping and needle-thrusting as, stitch by stitch, the blue cashmere sweater front continued to grow. Roland had made short work of cleaning up, loading the two pewter trays with cups, saucers, plates, and the rest, and allowing Melanie to help him by bearing one to the kitchen.

Next to Pamela, Bettina was advising Karen that Lily was plenty old enough to enjoy eating banana slices with her fingers. Holly had once more left the sofa to confer with Nell about the progress of the Christmas stocking. Back in the turquoise chair, Roland was contentedly at work on what he had made clear was the *second* sleeve of the camel-colored sweater destined for Melanie.

After some time had passed, Nell rested her knitting in her lap and raised a hand to muffle a yawn. "It must be nine, or nearly so," she said. "I don't usually get sleepy this early, but I still haven't quite caught up with my sleep after Saturday night."

"I'm ready!" With a flourish, Bettina completed the last stitch in a row. She reached for her knitting bag and tugged it up onto her lap.

After a brief flurry of activity, during which knitting was stowed in knitting bags and coats and jackets were retrieved, the Knit and Nibblers gathered at Roland's front door, congratulating him once again on his Halloween cookies. Nell had arrived with Holly and Karen because the walk all the way to the Farm was a bit far, even for her. But she was to be driven home in Pamela's car because Holly was stopping off at Karen's to look at swatches for a set of curtains Karen had in mind.

With a last round of thank-yous and goodnights, the five women stepped out onto Roland's porch, where the scarecrow's jack-o'-lantern grin, illuminated by the porch light, echoed their host's genial send-off. They made their way down Roland's front walk to their respective cars. Pamela, Bettina, and Nell climbed into Pamela's serviceable compact and, with a wave to Holly and Karen, set out for the Palisades and Nell's house.

Chapter 7

Pamela halted at the corner when she reached Nell's street. Even from the end of the block, it was clear that something untoward had happened in the vicinity of Nell's house. Intense lights—startling and brief as flashbulbs, but alternating red, white, and blue—dazzled from vehicles massed along both curbs.

"Police," Bettina said in a small voice from the back seat.

"Looks like," Nell agreed from her spot beside Pamela. Then, as if it had just occurred to her, she whispered, "I left Harold at home."

"Whatever it is, I don't think it's happening at your house," Pamela said soothingly. She turned and eased along until she was halfway down the block. "Look," she said, leaning over the steering wheel, "there's Harold standing in the street"— her headlights had illuminated his rangy figure—

"so he's okay for sure. And he's looking toward the Lyon-Covingtons' house."

"That's a relief," Nell murmured. "But what a reckless man! He always has to know what's going on."

"It's definitely something at the Lyon-Covingtons'!" Bettina exclaimed. "There are police in their yard."

The spasmodic flashes coming from the lights on the police cars made it hard to focus on anything beyond the range of Pamela's headlights. But Pamela stared hard toward the house that faced Nell's house across the street and made out two dark-clad figures emerging from the backyard.

Pamela started to open her own door, but Nell was already leaping from the car and dashing ahead. Before Pamela's feet even touched the pavement, Nell was halfway to Harold's side. She had reached him and tugged him several paces toward his own curb by the time Pamela caught up with her.

"They don't need your help, Harold," Nell was saying in a voice that sounded more frightened than angry. "But what on earth is going on?"

Pamela was curious herself. She blinked against the glare as the row of lights across the roof of the nearest police car flashed red white blue, red white blue in blinding sequence, straining to make out what the two dark-clad people, obviously police, were going to do next. And Bettina had joined them, clutching Pamela's arm and asking if she'd noticed whether Detective Clayborn was among the responders. Together, they took a few steps toward the dramatic scene as the Bascombs talked.

"More police," Bettina whispered, pointing to the Lyon-Covingtons' porch, where the porch light illuminated two officers who had just stepped out through the front door.

But they were distracted by Nell's sudden moan, and both turned. The streetlamp and the flashing lights on the police cars clearly revealed their friend's distraught expression. Barely resembling her own sturdy self, Nell stood with her hands clasped tightly against her breast and supported by Harold's arm. She moaned again, but this time the moan resolved into words.

"You were right, Pamela," she said. "You were so, so right, and we tried to warn her, but she didn't take our advice." She swayed toward Harold, he tightened his hold on her, and the words squeezed out through a tight throat. "Our little town didn't need another murder."

At the word *murder*, Pamela quaked, then froze. Bettina was talking, but Pamela felt like an onlooker watching a scene she herself wasn't part of—wasn't part of because it couldn't really be happening

How could there be another murder so soon after Dawn's just that past Saturday night? And if Pamela had been, as Nell put it, *so, so right*, that meant that this time the victim was—

"Mary Lyon," Harold was saying. In his long career as a doctor, Harold had often delivered unwelcome news. But after decades of experience, his voice and expression were no less sorrowful. "I was putting out the recycling," he went on. "A police car came careening around the corner and Brainard came dashing down the driveway yelling, 'My wife is dead! In the backyard!'"

"Oh, Pamela!" Bettina clutched Pamela's arm

again. Pamela tried to shake off the sense of unreality that had enveloped her. She gently freed her arm so she could wrap it around Bettina's shoulders. "Mary didn't take our advice," Bettina moaned. "She went outside in the dark and someone was waiting for her."

A police officer was approaching, Officer Sanchez, the young woman police officer with the sweet, heart-shaped face. "We need to clear the street," she said. "Are you residents of this block?" She scanned their faces slowly, from Harold to Nell to Bettina to Pamela.

"We are," Harold said. "Harold and Nell Bascomb, and we live right up there." He pointed to his and Nell's substantial house, with its shrubbery-filled yard and curving flight of steps.

"And you?" Officer Sanchez turned to Pamela and Bettina. Then she nodded toward Pamela's car. "Is that your car?"

After quick good nights and promises to get in touch the next morning, Pamela and Bettina parted with the Bascombs and soon were on their way down the hill. As they approached the intersection with Arborville Avenue, they passed the huge silver van with the logo of the county sheriff's department that signaled the arrival of the crime scene unit.

After retrieving the *County Register* on Wednesday morning, Pamela scurried even more quickly than usual back to the cozy haven of her kitchen. As if her sleep hadn't been disturbed enough by the grim discovery that Mary Lyon had been murdered, a cold front with winds that shivered the windowpanes and howled around the eaves had blown in overnight. She'd awakened at eight, feeling stiff and barely rested, but too on edge to roll over for another hour or two of slumber.

Besides, there were cats to feed. She had dispatched that task before starting water for her coffee, then she had fetched the paper, and now she was measuring coffee beans into her coffee grinder. She hoped these customary rituals would launch a day with few, if any, surprises.

Seated ten minutes later at her kitchen table, she hesitated before slipping the *Register* from its flimsy plastic wrapper. Perhaps it would be better to fortify herself with the slice of buttered, wholegrain toast that waited at her elbow, as well as a few sips of coffee, before discovering what the *Register*'s energetic reporter, Marcy Brewer, had done with what was sure to be the front-page story.

But her deliberations were interrupted by the telephone's ring.

"I knew your cell phone wouldn't be on," said an urgent voice.

The voice was right. Pamela had risen from her chair to lift the handset from the wall-mounted phone that had been a fixture of her kitchen ever since she and her husband moved in.

"Penny?" Among the tangle of thoughts that had vexed Pamela's waking and sleeping mind the previous night had been the knowledge that Penny, up in Massachusetts, would know as soon as almost anyone in Arborville did that Arborville had had another murder.

"Yes, Mom, it's Penny." Penny's matter-of-fact

tone was meant to suggest—what?—that after two murders in less than a week, calling home to discuss them had become a routine chore? "Lorie Hopkins texted me this morning and I looked at the *Register* online. So I know all about what happened."

"I was going to call you," Pamela said. "But I thought you'd be asleep, or in class, if I called now." She paused, but Penny didn't say anything. "There's no need for you to worry," Pamela went on.

"*Really?*" Penny sounded skeptical. "That woman who was killed had a yarn blog."

"Lots of people have yarn blogs," Pamela said. "The police will figure out who killed her. I have every confidence."

"You and Bettina won't try to help them?"

"Why would we do that?" Pamela tried to keep her voice offhand.

"*Mo-om!* She had a yarn blog. Hello? Knit and Nibble?"

"Penny! I'm not . . ." Pamela hadn't been sure what she was going to say next, so she was relieved when the doorbell's chime interrupted her unformed thought.

Still holding the handset, she stepped through the kitchen doorway and glanced toward the front door. Through the lace that curtained the oval window, she could see a figure garbed in a very seasonal color. Bettina's familiar pumpkin-colored coat stood out as a bright contrast to Pamela's lawn and the street and houses beyond.

"It's Bettina," she said quickly. "I have to go. Don't worry."

Bettina entered on a chilly draft of air. "Quite a change from the past few days," she pronounced. She'd added purple leather gloves and a purple beret to her ensemble, and her lipstick was the bright pumpkin shade of her coat. "Is that Nell?" she asked, noticing the handset Pamela still carried.

Pamela shook her head. "Penny. She knows all about the murder. Her Arborville friend, Lorie Hopkins, texted her, and she read the *Register* online."

"Did you read the *Register* yet?" Bettina advanced toward the chair that was the main piece of furniture in Pamela's entry and began to slip off her coat.

"I was just about to open it up," Pamela said, "and then Penny called."

"Marcy Brewer's article isn't very complete." Bettina smiled a secret smile. "The *Register* went to press before the crime scene people were through. But I've just been with Clayborn . . ."

"You'll tell me all about it. But what's happening with Nell?" Pamela asked as she led Bettina toward the kitchen.

"She called me," Bettina said. "She said she tried to call you, but your landline was busy and your cell phone just went to voicemail. I talked to her in my car on the way here."

"And?"

"She wants to know what we're going to do now."

"What *we're* going to do now? Meaning you and me?" Pamela laughed.

"Meaning you and me and Nell." Bettina felt the side of the carafe, then transferred it to a burner and lit a low flame under it.

"She didn't used to approve of amateur sleuthing." Pamela reached a wedding-china cup and saucer down from the cupboard and set them on the counter near the stove. Bettina, meanwhile, had stepped over to the refrigerator to retrieve the cream.

"She does now," Bettina said, peering into the refrigerator. "At least in this case." Bettina straightened up, holding a small carton, and turned toward Pamela, who was monitoring the progress of the coffee. "She feels guilty that she wasn't more adamant when we suggested that Mary be careful about going out alone at night. She wanted to know what Clayborn had to say, of course, and after I told her . . ."

Bettina broke off. Pamela had patted the side of the carafe to establish that the coffee was hot again and filled the cup destined for Bettina. Bettina claimed her coffee, as well as the sugar bowl and a spoon, and took her customary seat at Pamela's kitchen table. The *Register*, which was still tightly folded and encased in its plastic cover, remained on the table. Bettina pushed it aside. A wedding-china plate with an uneaten slice of toast remained on the table too.

"Your coffee looks cold," Bettina observed before commencing the sugaring and creaming that would transform her own coffee into the pale, sweet concoction she favored.

"It is," Pamela said. "And I never even had a

chance to take a sip." She poured it back in the carafe and lit the burner again.

Bettina looked up from her vigorous stirring. "I almost stopped off at the Co-Op after I left Clayborn," she said. "They have that pumpkin-spice crumb cake now. But I knew you'd be anxious to hear what he had to say."

"I am anxious"—Pamela raised the flame under the carafe and watched as a few small bubbles rose through the dark liquid—"very anxious." With the aid of an oven mitt, she tipped the carafe to refill her own cup, turned off the burner, and joined Bettina at the table.

After a long sip of coffee, Bettina spoke. "We already knew, last night, that Mary was dead and that Brainard discovered her body in the backyard," she said.

Pamela nodded.

Bettina rested her hand on the *Register*. "Marcy Brewer's article adds the information that, according to Mary's husband, Wendelstaff College Professor Brainard Covington, she had gone out to carry vegetable scraps to the compost heap at the far corner of the Lyon-Covingtons' property. It also adds the information that, according to the first responders, she had been struck on the forehead with a blunt object, breaking the skin."

"And the extra tidbits you got from Clayborn?"

"One tidbit." Bettina smiled the secret smile again. "But it's a good one." She paused, and Pamela could tell she was enjoying teasing her friend by drawing out the suspense. But Bettina changed the subject. "Is there more toast?" she asked, pointing to the plate with the uneaten toast. "Besides that cold piece?"

"Of course there's more toast," Pamela laughed, "but not until you—"

"Yarn." Bettina tapped her own neck. "Strands of yarn, just like when Dawn Filbert was killed.

"Oh my . . ." Pamela whispered.

"But this time"—Bettina paused for effect—"the yarn was tied. Tied in a bow."

"So . . ." Pamela rested her chin on her folded hands and frowned.

Bettina nodded, and the tendrils of her bright hair vibrated. "Definitely the same killer."

"And the killer knew that this time he'd really tracked down Mary—so he carried through with his whole plan: strike her on the head, which might or might not kill her but would knock her out, and then strangle her with the yarn." Pamela took a sip of coffee, and realized that—what with all the interruptions—it was her first sip of the day.

Bettina nodded again. "The ME will have to determine which thing actually killed her."

Pamela took another sip of coffee, determined not to let it get cold this time. "That's all, then?" she asked.

"Well," Bettina said, "that was all he had to tell me. But I had things to tell him." Without revealing the things, however, she rose from her chair.

"You told him about the llama farm?" Pamela watched as Bettina helped herself to two slices of whole-grain bread and slipped them into the toaster.

"Of course." Bettina didn't add the word *duh*, but her tone and her comical wide-eyed expression implied it. She let her answer sink in for a moment, then she gestured toward the toaster. "What can I put on the toast when it's done?"

"Butter? There's some right there on the counter."

Bettina wrinkled her nose. Pamela's fondness for black coffee and toast garnished with only a little butter was a source of great puzzlement to her. "Do you still have any of that Tupelo honey Wilfred brought back from the farmers market?" she asked.

"Help yourself," Pamela said with a smile. "It's in the upper cupboard to the left of the sink." She watched as Bettina staged butter, honey, and a plate near the toaster and pulled a knife from the silverware drawer. With a low *chunk*, the toast popped up, and Bettina wielded the knife to spread liberal amounts of butter and honey over its crisp surface.

Having sampled her toast and pronounced it delicious, Bettina was once more inclined to discuss her interview with Detective Clayborn. "I told him the ME, or forensics, or somebody should analyze the yarn the killer used," she said, "because it might be made from llama wool."

"I think I can guess what he said." Pamela's lips twisted into a rueful half smile.

"You can't!" Bettina slapped the table with one hand. The other held a piece of toast. "Because he didn't say anything. He just laughed. Even harder than when I told him about the llama farm."

"You explained that Mary had alienated its owner by refusing to feature the farm on her blog—and that she'd probably phrased the refusal in a very insulting way?"

"I did." Bettina licked a bit of honey from her

thumb. "And I told him about the author of the knitting booklets whose husband threatened Mary when she wouldn't accept a bribe to revise her negative reviews."

"And?" Pamela tipped her head forward and raised her brows.

"He didn't see how something somebody said or didn't say on a blog could be a motive for murder."

"So, does he have any leads?" Pamela asked.

Bettina sighed. "At least he admits that the same person murdered Mary as murdered Dawn—and that the person who killed Dawn probably thought he was killing Mary. The police have left off interviewing Dawn's clients at the salon. And they've interviewed Brainard."

"What?" Pamela had been in the act of raising her cup to her lips, but her hand paused on its journey. "He's the one who found her body!"

"It could all have been an act," Bettina said. "He kills her, then calls the police and pretends to be horrified. Based on what we saw when we were talking to Mary and he came in on his way to class, he could certainly have had a motive."

"But he certainly would have known Dawn wasn't his wife."

Bettina shrugged. "They fought that day and he refused to go to the parade and bonfire. So she says she's going anyway, but she doesn't say goodbye when she leaves, so for all he knows, she decided to wear the Bo Peep outfit herself."

After Bettina left, Pamela had browsed through the *Register* while finishing her coffee—though Bettina had reported the latest details on Mary's murder direct from Detective Clayborn, so there was no need to pore over the *Register*'s coverage of the case. Now, dressed in her usual jeans and a sweater, she was sitting at her computer, reading an article about images of cats in early American hooked rug design. The photographs alone—of rugs in the author's private collection—would have made the article worthy of publication, Pamela thought. But the analysis of the designs, which alluded to the cat's role as both pet and scourge of rodents, offered a fascinating glimpse into a typical eighteenth-century household.

She was just chuckling over a photo of a small hearth rug whose design featured a dozing cat surrounded by a border of cavorting mice when the doorbell's chime summoned her downstairs. For the second time that morning, the figure glimpsed through the oval window in the front door was Bettina, as revealed by her vivid, pumpkin-colored coat.

"Clayborn just called me," Bettina announced as soon as Pamela had pulled the door open far enough to make communication possible.

"Stop the presses?" Pamela swung the door all the way open and stepped aside.

"I hadn't had time to write anything yet, much less submit it for this week's *Advocate*." Bettina stepped over the threshold, and Pamela closed the door. A chilly draft had entered with her friend. "However," Bettina went on, "he wanted to make sure Brainard wasn't identified as a suspect in my article."

"You said the police interviewed him . . ."

"They did." Bettina made no move to tug off her purple gloves or otherwise make herself at home, but continued, her voice growing more excited with each word. "And Clayborn followed up with Brainard's alibi after I left this morning. Brainard was in the Wendelstaff library until a bit before nine Tuesday night. Then he left and drove home. He discovered Mary's body when he got out of his car—the garage is separate from the house, at the end of a long driveway. But Mary's body was already cold when the police arrived, suggesting she'd been killed a few hours earlier. So," Bettina concluded, almost panting, "how soon can you be ready to visit the llama farm?"

Chapter 8

Pamela blinked, and her mind scurried to catch up with Bettina's reasoning. Bettina watched for a moment, then let loose another flood of words.

"Clayborn doesn't have any other suspects at the moment," she said, "because he doesn't believe the enemies Mary made in connection with her blog could be a genuine threat. But we do, so we have to get busy and"—she pulled her smartphone from her purse—"I'll find the address of the llama farm. It's in Kringlekamack, Mary said . . ." Bettina's fingers, with their bright manicure, got busy on the device.

Pamela nodded. "I have to turn off my computer," she said as she headed for the stairs.

"I'll call Nell," Bettina sang out as Pamela reached the landing.

* * *

The llamas seemed used to having company. Most of them continued exactly what they were doing as Pamela, Bettina, and Nell approached the simple white fence, with its widely spaced horizontal slats, that contained them. Some ambled meditatively over the stubby grass, which was still a healthy shade of green. They stopped to nibble here and there, their long necks dipping gracefully toward the ground. Others, clustered around a wooden bin near the large shed at the back of their enclosure, were making a more substantial meal of hay. Only a few, perhaps bored with grass or hay, drifted toward the fence to examine the visitors who were examining them. The only sign of particular interest they exhibited was to tip their long ears forward.

Pamela had never explored the possibilities of knitting with llama wool, though she knew that various breeds of llamas produced wool that varied in fineness and softness. Gazing at the llama that now regarded her with gentle eyes, she admired the thick and shaggy coat that must have recommended the llama and its kin to the chilly mountain dwellers who first domesticated the creatures. This llama was the soft brown color of whole-wheat toast, though its confreres ranged in color from black through various shades of brown, all the way to white. And it was large—with its head raised, its long neck made it almost as tall as Bettina. But the enclosure contained llamas of all sizes, including a spindly-legged baby llama at that very moment standing beneath its mother having a meal.

"Lovely animals." Nell sighed. "Thank goodness

there's more interest in their wool than in their meat." As she spoke, wisps of steam marked her words in the chilly air.

Bettina was the first to turn away from the llamas. She'd had the foresight to wear her red sneakers, and the wisdom of her choice had become obvious when they pulled off the secluded road that led to the llama farm onto the parking area, half gravel, half muddy dirt, that served it. Now she led the way as the three of them made their way back to the parking lot and then along a rutted path toward a barn and a small stone house some distance from the llama enclosure. Beyond the house, fallen leaves under a glorious tree tinted the ground red.

As they approached the barn, a figure emerged from the shadows within. They'd come looking for Germaine van Houten—Bettina's smartphone search had yielded not only the address of the Kringlekamack llama farm, but also the name of its proprietor. But they were greeted instead by a young man wearing jeans that were more a work garment than a fashion statement and a sturdy pullover sweater exactly the color of the llama Pamela had been communing with. His abundant hair was gathered into a ponytail.

"In the market for a llama, ladies?" he inquired as they drew closer.

"I can see you're well-supplied"—Bettina accompanied the observation with a flirtatious smile—"and they're beautiful creatures. But I'm not sure Arborville is zoned for livestock."

"What can I do for you, then?" the young man

inquired with a flirtatious smile of his own. He was half Bettina's age, but few people could resist Bettina's charm.

"I'm a reporter," Bettina explained. "New Jersey has so many unexplored byways. Llama farms are certainly something most people would never dream existed just across the river from Manhattan."

Pamela and Nell looked at each other. Pamela was wondering why Bettina hadn't just come right out and asked if Germaine van Houten was around, and Nell's puzzled half frown suggested that she was equally curious. But Bettina had her ways. This young man, evidently an assistant, might reveal more about Germaine's whereabouts on recent evenings—and thus whether she had alibis for Halloween and Tuesday night—than Germaine would have been willing to do herself.

"I'm Jordan," the young man said.

"Bettina Fraser." Bettina offered her hand, then introduced Pamela and Nell. "My friends," she added, "are also curious about llamas. We're all knitters."

Jordan raised the plastic bucket he was carrying. "Come right along and get acquainted with the gang. I was just on my way to offer them some treats. Broccoli—that's their favorite. And some other stuff too."

He led the way as they proceeded down the rutted path toward the white-fenced enclosure, the plastic bucket swinging gaily in his hand and his ponytail bouncing against his sweater-clothed back.

"Germaine will be sorry she missed you," he commented as he loped along. "The llama farm is a big thing for her, a lifelong dream. Anything you can write about it will be great—she's always trying to get more exposure."

We knew that, Pamela said to herself.

But Bettina feigned ignorance. "It's not just a hobby?" She panted as she struggled to keep up with Jordan's long strides. She made a striking figure against the pastoral landscape in her red sneakers, pumpkin coat, and purple hat and gloves.

"Hardly," he called over his shoulder. "She inherited this land. It's been in her family for eons, and the house is a couple hundred years old. But she went into debt to launch the llama farm. The idea was to breed them to sell as guard llamas. It's a real thing—for sheep herds and like that. But New Jersey actually has a lot of llama farms, and competition is fierce."

"It is?" Pamela took over from Bettina, who had stopped to catch her breath.

"Fierce," he repeated. They were drawing near to the enclosure. The llamas, apparently recognizing that the ponytailed young man was bearing treats in his plastic bucket, had begun to range themselves along the stretch of fence that bordered the path, their long muzzles tilted in his direction. Jordan cut off to the side when he got closer and slipped around to the back of the shed. He opened a door, and in a minute he was stepping through a large opening in the front of the shed and joining the eager crowd of llamas that had turned away from the fence.

Pamela and Nell, meanwhile, had reached the enclosure and were watching from their side of the fence. Bettina was just a few yards away.

"Here you go, gang!" Jordan cried, dipping a hand into the bucket and tossing broccoli spears, apple halves, and carrots here and there. The llamas scrambled after them. A pleasant barnyard smell Pamela had noticed earlier seemed stronger now, with all the llamas in motion.

"They'll get a couple more buckets of treats and some grain," Jordan said as he stroked the shaggy neck of a nearby llama. "And I've got to fill their water trough, if you'll excuse me."

Bettina had joined Pamela and Nell at the fence by now. "Ask him about yarn," Pamela whispered as Jordan disappeared into the shed. In a moment, he emerged with a green rubber hose trailing behind him, water gushing from its nozzle. The water trough was next to the bin that supplied the llamas with hay.

Questions weren't necessary. Fond as Jordan seemed of his nonhuman charges, the presence of beings he could communicate with in his own language had loosened his tongue.

"So, anyway, where was I?" he shouted above the whooshing and gurgling sounds of water filling the trough.

"New Jersey has a lot of llama farms?" Pamela suggested.

"Oh, yeah!" Jordan dodged out of the way of a llama that seemed eager for a drink, the one that was the color of whole-wheat toast. "So—Germaine got the idea that she could sell the wool. But she didn't know anything about shearing them and whatever. And there's lots of high-quality llama wool out there online. People dye it with natural dyes, and it's a whole big deal. Hard to get into if you're starting from scratch."

"Your sweater kind of . . . matches that llama there," Bettina said, pointing to the llama at the trough.

"It should," Jordan said with a smile that Pamela imagined had charmed many young women. It revealed perfect teeth that looked all the whiter against the remains of a summer tan. He laid an affectionate hand on the llama's back. "We sheared her last spring as an experiment, and Germaine figured out how to card and spin the wool. My mom knit it." He stroked the sweater as affectionately as he had earlier stroked a llama.

Pamela searched her memory. The night of the bonfire, when Gus Warburton had aimed his flashlight at the body in the Bo Peep costume, what color had the strands of yarn looped around the neck been? She couldn't quite remember. The scene had been so shocking, and there had been so many things to look at.

"Ooops!" Jordan took a quick step backward. Water was sloshing over the rim of the trough onto the toes of his rugged boots. "Better turn this off." He dashed back into the shed.

A few other llamas had been standing off to the side, as if waiting for a chance at the trough. They ambled forward and joined the brown llama. The baby llama Pamela had noticed earlier came tottering after and looked up curiously, as if wondering what its elders found so appealing overhead.

"I'm not sure I've been a very good advertisement for Germaine's llama farm," Jordan said. He had emerged from the shed unencumbered by the hose and strolled over to where Pamela, Bettina, and Nell stood against the fence. "Like I said, Germaine will be sorry she missed you." He frowned, which scarcely detracted from his good-natured handsomeness, and turned to survey the llamas. Suddenly, he swiveled back and addressed Bettina. "Maybe you could come back! I know she'd like to talk to you."

Bettina glanced at Pamela and then at Nell, who had been watching the baby llama, her expression as soft as if she'd been studying a toddler on uncertain legs. Both nodded. Bettina said, "How about tomorrow?" and Jordan said, "Sure."

Nell's gaze returned to the baby llama. "I believe they're born ready to stand," she commented after a bit. "I saw a program on the Nature Channel."

"They have to." Jordan laughed. "Otherwise, no supper. Mama doesn't lie down to let them nurse." He pointed toward the baby llama. "That little guy is only . . . let's see"—he counted on his fingers—"three and a half days old."

"Born Saturday night?" Nell said.

"You got it!" Jordan's smile gave them another look at his perfect teeth. "Most inopportune too."

"How so?" Pamela, Bettina, and Nell all spoke at once.

"Nobody was around except llamas. I only come in during the day. Germaine lives in that house up there"—he tipped his head toward the small stone house near the barn at the end of the rutted path—"but she was out somewhere. Told me when

I came in Monday—she got home at midnight Saturday to find a new llama."

"It looks like everything turned out okay," Nell observed.

"Oh, sure! Mother and baby are doing fine." The baby llama was now nursing contentedly, standing under its mother and stretching its neck to reach the source of its meal. Jordan waved toward the pair. "Llamas certainly don't have humans helping them when they give birth in the wild. It's pretty cool—the females in the herd all cluster around the one that's in labor, just in case there's a predator in the neighborhood."

The llama that matched his sweater approached and began to nuzzle his shoulder. Jordan draped an arm over its neck. "They know they usually get more for lunch," he explained, "and this one is wondering where her grain and sweet potatoes are. They're all females, in case you're wondering, except for that big guy over there." He nodded toward an impressive pure white llama, then turned back to them. "So," he said, "I'll look for you to morrow, ladies, and I'll tell Germaine you're coming." With a smile and a half bow, he turned and headed for the gate.

The brown llama swiveled its long neck to track Jordan's progress up the rutted path toward the barn, but it lingered at the fence.

"Shall we go, then?" Bettina asked.

"I wouldn't mind warming up," Nell said, hugging herself. Bettina was wearing the fetching purple beret she'd started out in that morning, but Nell was hatless, and her white hair had been stirred into a disordered halo by the wind. "I'm not dressed as warmly as these guys." She nodded toward the llamas.

"Come along, then." Bettina slipped an arm around Nell's waist. "Let's hurry to the car." They took several steps, but paused when they reached the gravel that marked the beginning of the parking area. Bettina turned back. "Are you coming, Pamela?" she called.

"In a minute." Pamela had opened her purse, which dangled from her shoulder. She probed inside until she found her comb. Then she laid a soothing hand on the brown llama's neck and gently drew the comb through the woolly tufts of its fleece. A few hairs stuck in the comb. She nodded in satisfaction and tucked the comb back in her purse.

She reached the car and slid into the back seat in time to hear Nell protesting that she had done nothing particularly brilliant.

"But you did!" Bettina protested. Her profile, topped by a fringe of vivid scarlet bangs and the jaunty beret, was outlined against the windshield as she faced Nell, who was in the passenger seat. "If you hadn't noticed the baby llama and commented on it, we'd never have learned that Germaine was somewhere that wasn't the llama farm last Saturday night while Dawn Filbert was being murdered. You'll make a detective yet!"

"I agree!" Pamela exclaimed. "Otherwise we'd have come away from here with almost nothing useful . . . except—" She opened her purse once again and slowly drew out her comb, enjoying the mystified expressions on Bettina and Nell's faces. She held up the comb and pointed to the tiny tuft of hairs that had been captured by a few of its teeth.

"Llama wool," she announced. "From the same llama that contributed the wool for Jordan's sweater."

"The llama they sheared last spring," Nell whispered, excitement brightening her faded blue eyes.

"And Germaine spun the wool into yarn," Bettina added.

"So," Pamela explained, "you'll take a few of these llama hairs to Detective Clayborn and suggest that the lab compare them with the yarn from Dawn and Mary's necks. And you'll tell him that Germaine van Houten, who resented the fact that Mary brushed her off when she tried to interest Mary in blogging about her llama farm, may not have an alibi for the night of the bonfire."

Chapter 9

A remarkable scene greeted Pamela when she ventured out to retrieve the *Register* Thursday morning. Wilfred was standing at the end of his driveway in a plaid bathrobe, apparently having a conversation with a llama. The woolly creature, a creamy shade of white, stood on the strip of grass between the sidewalk and the street. Its graceful neck was extended to its full height and its long ears were tilted attentively in his direction.

"I'm Wilfred Fraser," he was saying, "but I believe you want to talk to my wife."

The llama seemed to nod. Parked at the curb was a narrow enclosed trailer of the sort used to transport horses, attached by a trailer hitch to a car that had seen better days.

Instead of continuing down the steps of her porch, Pamela hurried back into her house, turned off the kettle, and pulled on her warmest jacket.

The cold front that had arrived the previous day had settled in. A quick dash down the front walk could be managed in a robe and slippers, but a trip across the street to investigate who knew what kind of curious situation would require more protection from the chilly morning.

By the time Pamela reemerged from her house, Bettina had joined her husband. She was in a similar state of dishabille, in her case a pea-green fleece robe with a bit of white lace peeking out at the neck. Wilfred noticed Pamela first, and his relieved smile told her that her presence would be welcome. Bettina was doing the talking now, seemingly inquiring how the llama had found her address.

Upon crossing the street and joining Bettina and Wilfred, Pamela discovered that the situation wasn't quite as curious as it had first appeared. A woman was standing on the grass behind the llama. As Pamela had gazed at the scene from her porch, the woman was hidden from view by the trailer. She was sturdy and broad-hipped and taller than Pamela, with bold features and dark eyes.

"Not too hard," the woman said. "You told Jordan your name, and everything's on the Internet now. Ha, ha! I said to myself, somebody's interested in llamas. So"—she reached out and gave Bettina's hands a hearty squeeze (Bettina had been rubbing them together in an effort to get warm)—"you don't have to come to me. I've come to you!"

Without her makeup and with her hair in disarray, and doubtless in a pre-coffee state, Bettina scarcely seemed herself. She stared at the woman as if at an apparition and backed against Wilfred's reassuring bulk. He wrapped both his arms around her.

But Pamela spoke up. "Maybe we could talk in the house," she suggested, not wanting to lose the chance to learn more about Germaine van Houten— for that was undoubtedly who their caller was. The llama swiveled its neck to study the new arrival.

As if a spell had been broken, Bettina blinked, lifted her chin, and said, "Of course. We were just making coffee." She set off up the driveway in her pea-green mules, her matching robe billowing behind her.

Pamela started to follow, but she hesitated, turning to see what arrangement, if any, would be made for the llama.

"I could put her back in the trailer," Germaine offered, "but she was so relieved when we got here and she had a chance to stretch her legs. Weren't you, girl?" She bent close to the llama's face, and for a moment Pamela thought she was going to rub noses with the creature.

"A guest is a guest," Wilfred said, aiming a benevolent smile at the llama. "She can hang out in the backyard for a bit." He laid a guiding hand on the llama's neck, added a "Come along" directed at Germaine, and began to walk up the driveway.

A few minutes later, as the invigorating smell of brewing coffee promised to redeem a day that had started so abruptly, Pamela watched from Bettina's kitchen as the llama rounded the corner of the garage and ventured into the backyard, escorted by Wilfred and Germaine. Bettina's house was a Dutch Colonial, and by far the oldest on Orchard

Street, but she and Wilfred had added a large, modern kitchen with plenty of room for a table and chairs. Sliding glass doors opened onto a patio and gave a view of the backyard beyond.

The llama nosed the grass tentatively, then raised its head. Germaine leaned close to it and seemed to whisper something into the attentive ear it cocked in her direction. Wilfred, meanwhile, stepped onto the patio and motioned to Pamela to unlock the sliding door she was peering through. She could see he was shivering despite his flannel pajamas and woolly robe, but he waited chivalrously while Germaine crossed to the patio, then he stepped aside and motioned to her to enter first.

Germaine began to speak even before Wilfred followed her into the kitchen and the door slid closed. "When Jordan told me you'd come by, I said hallelujah!" she exclaimed, zeroing in on Bettina. "Because that very morning, I'd had my best idea yet! And now here was a reporter to bring it to the world!" Germaine's prominent eyes opened so wide that the irises stood out as dark rounds against the whites. She paused, her expressive mouth agape. Then, without stopping for breath, she went on, seemingly possessed by the idea she was about to articulate.

"Llama-rama cuddle-a-llama!" she cried. Her eyes darted from Bettina to Pamela to Wilfred. "People are starved for touch!" Pamela tried not to flinch as one of Germaine's large hands suddenly landed on her shoulder. "So here's the idea. Llamas are very touchable, soft, and they don't smell as much as some animals do. I'll charge by the hour, or maybe by the half hour. People can pick the llama they want, and I'll set up a few separate pens, and they can stroke the llama and cuddle it—and I guarantee their blood pressure will go down and they'll feel like they've just taken a mini-vacation. It will really catch on. I'm sure of it."

A session of knitting could have that effect, Pamela acknowledged to herself. And maybe part of the explanation was the yarn itself—the cozy feel of the in-progress swath in one's lap, the caress of the yarn against one's fingers as, stitch by stitch, the project grew . . . and what was a llama but a huge, walking heap of wool?

Wilfred, meanwhile, had retreated to the cooking area of the kitchen. He'd ranged four of Bettina's sage-green mugs along the high counter that separated the cooking area from the eating one and was filling them with coffee from a heavy Pyrex carafe. And Germaine had made herself at home, settling into one of the chairs that surrounded Bettina's well-scrubbed pine table. Bettina shrugged, motioned Pamela to sit, and took a chair herself. From Pamela's seat, she had a view of the llama nibbling Wilfred and Bettina's grass, its creamy white coat ruffled by the wind.

"Nice place you've got here," Germaine said, surveying the kitchen and then craning her neck to get a glimpse of the dining room. She turned back as Wilfred approached bearing two mugs of coffee. He set one in front of Germaine and one in front of Pamela, stepping away to fetch another for Bettina.

"Cream and sugar coming right up," he announced when he delivered the steaming mug.

"Do you have any llama milk?" Germaine asked,

then she quickly added, "Just kidding. Ha, ha!" with a wide grin that displayed her large teeth and emphasized her boldly modeled cheeks. "They do drink it, or did," she went on, "in the Andes. But I've only got one nursing mother now, and she needs all she's got for her cria, her baby llama—that's what they're called."

Wilfred waited, listening politely, until she finished, and then slipped behind the counter, returning with Bettina's sage-green sugar bowl, her matching creamer supplied with cream, and four spoons and napkins. Though she liked her coffee black, Pamela waited until Bettina and Germaine had availed themselves of sugar and cream and were ready for their first sip of coffee before tasting her own.

"I was going to make omelets." Wilfred spoke up from where he was standing near the stove. When Pamela first entered the kitchen, she'd noticed a carton of eggs, a stainless-steel bowl, and Wilfred's favorite skillet at the ready. Probably he'd expected to dash out for the paper and then return to the pleasant domesticity of breakfast with his wife—hardly imagining he'd end up, instead, playing host to a llama and her keeper.

"Oh, no, no, no!" Germaine hopped to her feet. "I couldn't impose! But I—you've been so kind and—what's this town? Arborville? Wait a minute! Mary Lyon lives here, doesn't she?"

She *did* live here, Pamela murmured to herself, after nearly choking on the extra-large mouthful of coffee she'd gulped in surprise. Was it possible that Germaine was so caught up in the world of llamas that she was completely out of touch with

the news? The *Register* was the county paper and
Kringlekamack was in the same county as Arborville—and Pamela was sure reports of Mary's murder had been on the radio and television as well.

"*She* isn't kind at all, I can tell you that." Germaine put her hands on her ample hips. "The
things she said to me about llamas!" Her voice
took on the mincing tone of someone parodying a
snob. "*It's Mary had a little lamb, not Mary had a little
llama.* Like she thought she was *so* funny. Ha, ha!
And when I brought one of my sweet llamas to visit
her, to show her how lovely their wool is—of
course, that was before I got my cuddle-a-llama
brain hurricane—she threatened to call the police."

Pamela's glance strayed toward Bettina, who was
sitting directly across the table from her. She was
sure the expression she saw on her friend's face
mirrored her own—eyes open wide as if to take in
and process this remarkable development, but lips
shut tight for lack of any suitable utterance.

At last, Wilfred spoke up, having first ventured
across the floor until he stood behind Bettina with
a hand on her shoulder. "You may not have read
the newspaper recently," he said. The fact that he
had tied an apron over his robe and pajamas detracted not one bit from his calm authority.

"Why?" Germaine looked startled, perhaps more
because of Wilfred's manner than his words.

"Mary Lyon was murdered on Tuesday night,"
Bettina blurted out, tilting her head to look up at
Germaine. She followed the announcement with a
vigorous nod that set the tendrils of her bright
hair aquiver.

"What?" Germaine seemed to stagger. She raised her large hands to clutch her head. "That can't be!" She bent forward to peer at Bettina, her eyes narrowed. "You're teasing me, aren't you? Trying to make me feel bad because I said bad things about her. I suppose she's your friend or something. Well—ha, ha!—joking about murder isn't very funny."

"It isn't a joke." Absent his usual cheer, Wilfred scarcely seemed himself. Pamela stared at his grim expression and relived the quake she'd felt when she, Bettina, and Nell first learned of Mary's death. Now, Bettina's kitchen floor seemed to shift beneath her chair, like an aftershock.

Germaine sank back into the chair she'd occupied. "Oh my goodness," she sighed. "I'm so sorry. What a terrible, terrible thing!" She folded her arms on the table and lowered her head until all that was visible was a mass of dark, wiry hair.

Pamela, Bettina, and Wilfred looked at one another. Pamela was the first to shrug. Puzzlement contracted her brows and tightened her lips. Germaine's display of amazement and then grief was as surprising as her apparent ignorance of Mary's death had been.

The mass of hair began to stir. Germaine raised her head, displaying large eyes brimming with tears. She mopped at them with the napkin Wilfred had supplied for her coffee and glanced toward the sliding glass doors. Beyond them, the llama was placidly helping itself to Wilfred and Bettina's lawn. She shifted her gaze from the llama to her hosts, who were regarding her seriously.

"I know what will cheer us up!" Germaine exclaimed, leaping to her feet. "I was going to suggest it anyway—for your article." She stepped toward the glass doors and slid one side open. Ignoring the sudden blast of cold air, she darted toward Bettina, pulled her to her feet, and began to lead her toward the open door. Bettina hung back, reaching for Wilfred with the hand that Germaine wasn't clutching.

"You'll like it!" Germaine urged. "You'll see how cuddly llamas are. Warm too! They have built-in sweaters. Ha, ha!"

Wilfred strode firmly toward the open door and slid it closed in one decisive motion. "I'm sure they're cuddly," he said, "but we're still in our pajamas and it's very cold out there." He watched Bettina until she had gotten settled back in her chair, then he added, "Let's all sit down and finish our coffee."

Germaine waved her hands as if to cancel out that idea. "I've intruded long enough," she said. "I see that, so I'll just take my llama and go"—she bent toward Bettina—"but I hope you'll still write the article . . . and . . ." She closed her eyes, furrowed her brow, and raised her hands in a gesture that almost looked prayerful. "I feel another brain hurricane coming. It's coming . . . coming . . ." She opened her eyes so wide, they seemed to be trying to escape their sockets. "Grief-counseling! Of course! Llamas as grief counselors!"

And with that, she slid the door open once more and slipped through. The three friends watched as Germaine guided the llama back around the corner of the garage and the creature and its mistress disappeared from view.

"Well," Bettina sighed, "that was certainly an experience." She picked up her coffee mug and took a long swallow, commenting at its conclusion, "The coffee is still quite warm."

"How about those omelets?" Wilfred inquired. "And some toast?"

Pamela had taken off her jacket and was sitting at the pine table in her pajamas and robe. She normally ate only toast for breakfast and, besides, she didn't feel she was dressed properly to accept an invitation to share a meal, even just breakfast. But the prospect of omelets and toast was so appealing—and besides, she and Bettina and Wilfred had so much to discuss—that she agreed with a vigorous headshake.

"Let me help," she added, starting to rise.

"No, no, no," Wilfred said from the post he had already taken up near the stove. "Please stay right where you are, and speak up if your coffee's too cold. There's some left in the carafe and I'm heating it."

Pamela sampled her coffee. The episode with Germaine had seemed to go on and on—but it had really only lasted about five minutes. In that space of time, her coffee had gone from scalding to just right and, sipping it now, she enjoyed the rich bitterness of the brew and its implication that the day was finally off to a sensible start.

From the cooking area of the kitchen came the clackety-clackety sound of Wilfred's whisk beating eggs in his stainless-steel bowl. Bettina stared out at her backyard, perhaps making sure the llama was really gone.

Pamela continued sipping her coffee, willing

the caffeine to do its work, to help her arrange the morning's events into some rational pattern. After a bit, she spoke, addressing Bettina's profile.

"Germaine was certainly odd, but she didn't seem like a devious person," she said.

"Devious?" Bettina turned to face Pamela. Her lips, bare of lipstick, were twisted into a puzzled zigzag.

"I don't think she was acting when she seemed not to know that Mary had been killed," Pamela explained, "or when she seemed so distraught after we told her. She seemed incapable of having a thought that she didn't blurt out immediately."

Wilfred spoke up from his post at the stove. "So that means she can't be the murderer."

"I think it does," Pamela said. She glanced in Wilfred's direction to see him tipping the stainless-steel bowl over his favorite skillet. A low, sizzling sound indicated that the beaten eggs had made contact with melted butter.

"But she was so odd." A little frown had settled between Bettina's brows.

"Odd," Pamela agreed, "but not a murderer."

"I'm still going to take the llama hairs to Clayborn," Bettina said. "And maybe he'll have something new to tell me about the case. Are you going to be home later?"

"I'm always home," Pamela said.

Woofus the shelter dog joined the group then, stepping timidly through the door that led to the dining room and aligning his shaggy body against the wall in his favorite napping spot. He was joined by Punkin, the ginger-colored cat that was the sister of Pamela's own Ginger. As Wilfred cooked, ex-

pertly shaping his omelets and keeping an eye on
the toaster as he cycled a few rounds of toast
through it, Pamela and Bettina began to chat about
topics more benign than murder.

Bettina enthused again over how cute her Arborville grandsons had looked dressed as Spider-
Man and Winnie the Pooh on Halloween, and
how fortunate it was that their parents had chosen
to go home after the parade and skip the bonfire.
Both agreed that Thanksgiving would soon be
upon them, not to mention Christmas. That topic
led to the cornflower-blue sweater, currently in
progress, that was to be Pamela's Christmas gift for
her mother. And then Bettina was reminded once
again of the tragic fact that the Boston children, as
she called her younger son Warren and his wife,
had declared that their daughter was to be given
no girlie gifts of any kind.

"Wilfred Jr.'s little boys," she concluded for-
lornly, in a lament Pamela had heard many times before, "are adorable, of course, but I always dreamed
of having a granddaughter . . . buying her wonderful dresses, and later we could go shopping together, and . . ." She broke off with a sigh.

She cheered, however, as Wilfred approached
bearing plates that he set in front of Pamela and
Bettina. The plates were from Bettina's set of sage-
green pottery. Centered on each was an omelet—
intensely yellow, glistening with butter, and folded
into an elegant half circle. Tucked alongside each
omelet were four triangles of buttered whole-grain
toast. He darted away and was back in an instant
with napkins, silverware, and a jar of blueberry
jam.

"Please begin, dear ladies," he said with a genial smile. Intermingled with the smells of toast and omelets in progress, Pamela had detected the aroma of more coffee brewing, and indeed Wilfred announced that fresh hot coffee would be available momentarily and that he would join them with his own omelet.

Chapter 10

Later that same morning, Bettina was herself again. Lipstick and eye makeup had been carefully applied, and the tendrils of her scarlet hair had been tamed to curve gently across her forehead and tickle her cheeks. Standing in Pamela's entry, she slipped off her pumpkin-colored down coat to reveal a chic forest-green jumpsuit accented by a chunky gold necklace that matched her earrings. Standing off to the side, Nell—who had entered with Bettina—was nearly invisible in her unassuming gray wool coat.

"I've been with Clayborn," Bettina announced, "and while I was uptown I stopped by the Co-Op." The telltale white bakery box had been transferred to Pamela's hands as soon as she opened the door, so the second part of the announcement was unnecessary, except that Bettina added, "It's some of their pumpkin-spice crumb cake. And," she went on, "I happened to run into Nell."

"*Not* at the bakery counter," Nell said sternly. "I was in the produce department." She slipped off her coat and laid it on the chair where Bettina had put hers. "I'll try a bit of the crumb cake, though— just a bit."

Pamela had been expecting Bettina to check in after her visit to Detective Clayborn, so when the doorbell's chime called her away from "The Persistence of Memory: Missionary Influence on Women's Dress in Raramuri Culture," she had closed her Word file and allowed her computer monitor to go to sleep.

"Come on into the kitchen," she greeted her guests, "and I'll get water going for coffee and tea."

Bettina fetched a chair from the dining room for Nell and then reached down a wedding-china plate from the cupboard. She removed the string from the bakery box, folded back the top, and used a spatula to carefully transfer the large square of crumb cake to the plate. "Ummm," she commented as she did so, "it smells just like pumpkin pie."

"Cinnamon, for sure"—Nell leaned close for a sniff—"and nutmeg . . . something else too. Allspice? I'll have to check my pumpkin-pie recipe."

The last word was drowned out by the clank and whirr of coffee beans being ground. Pamela started water boiling in the kettle, arranged a paper filter in the plastic cone that fit atop her carafe, poured the ground coffee into it, and measured tea into her special, one-person-size teapot, a squat, blue-glazed thrift-store find. Meanwhile, Bettina set out three of Pamela's wedding-china cups with their saucers and three small wedding-china plates, along with forks and spoons and napkins.

Pamela transferred the sugar bowl from the counter to the table, along with the matching cream pitcher, which she filled with heavy cream from a carton in the refrigerator. Then, with nothing else to do until the water boiled, she nodded at Bettina with brows raised and said, "Well?"

"Clayborn took the llama hairs," Bettina said. "I put them in a ziplock bag." She jumped up, fetched a knife from Pamela's knife rack, and laid it next to the square of crumb cake. "I think he just did it to get rid of me—because he didn't even ask me how I got them, or why. I told him anyway though. That is, I repeated the story we made up as a premise for visiting the llama farm—that I was doing some freelance work now besides the *Advocate* and pitched an article on llama farms to that glossy county magazine. And then I said it just happened to occur to me that if the llama hairs could be linked to the yarn wrapped around the necks of the murder victims—"

The kettle began to whistle then, and for a few minutes, everyone's attention was focused on steeping tea and brewing coffee and apportioning crumb cake among the three small plates. "Not too much for me," Nell protested as Bettina aimed a generous slice in her direction. Bettina redirected that slice to her own plate, and soon the three friends were seated cozily around the table, each supplied with the beverage of her choice and just the right amount of crumb cake.

Pamela teased off a bite and was delighted to discover that pumpkin-spice crumb cake married all that was delicious about crumb cake with much that was delicious about pumpkin pie. The hint of cinnamon normally found in crumb cake's buttery crumble topping had been enhanced with additional spices—surely nutmeg and allspice, perhaps ginger too. And the aromatic result evoked a pumpkin pie with the surprising texture of a sweet sponge cake. A sip of coffee to follow up supplied a pleasing bitterness that made the next bite of crumb cake taste all the sweeter.

"You were telling us about your meeting with Detective Clayborn," Nell said.

Bettina nodded toward Nell's plate, which despite her often-stated reservations about sugar, was nearly empty. She winked at Pamela, then turned toward Nell. "He did take the llama hairs, like I said," she explained. "And when I asked him if the Arborville police had any new leads, he was evasive. So if nothing else turns up in the way of a clue, he might explore the Kringlekamack llama farm angle."

Bettina's plate was nearly empty too, and she paused to scoop up the last bite of crumb cake and convey it to her mouth. A minute later, after following the bite of cake with a swallow of coffee, she went on, saying, "I made sure to remind him that there was plenty of reason for the owner of the llama farm—Germaine van Houten—I made sure he knew her name—to resent Mary. And that's when he told me that solving Arborville's crimes myself would not make my property taxes go down."

Pamela was aware that she was frowning. Yes,

Bettina had declared that she was planning to take the llama hairs to Detective Clayborn. And Pamela had been quite pleased with her own sudden decision to collect the hairs, and the ingenious way she'd accomplished the task with the only tool she had at hand—her comb. But . . .

"I guess you still think Germaine could be guilty," she blurted out a little more loudly than she'd intended.

Bettina had lifted the top of the bakery box and was peering inside, and she looked up with a startled expression that could have suited a person caught in the act of sneaking an unauthorized goody. But that wasn't what had startled her.

"I wasn't as convinced as you that Germaine wasn't acting," Bettina said. "And it was bad acting at that."

Pamela turned to Nell. "Did Bettina tell you that we woke up this morning to find a llama—along with its owner—on Orchard Street this morning?" she asked.

"She certainly did," Nell said, the skin around her eyes crinkling as a smile appeared.

"Do you still think she could be guilty?" Pamela asked.

"I wasn't there to judge the performance," Nell said, laughing. "But Germaine van Houten does sound like a very dramatic individual."

"She wasn't at the farm Saturday night," Bettina pointed out, "even though one of her llamas was due to give birth."

"So, no alibi," Nell commented.

"I wish we'd thought of a way to work something

about Tuesday night into the conversation this morning," Pamela said. "But even with the coffee Wilfred made . . ."

"I wasn't awake either." Bettina shook her head. "We could have brought up Saturday night too. Asked her if the llama farm gets many trick-or-treaters . . ."

With a gesture that suggested sudden resolve, Bettina folded back the top of the bakery box, revealing that a goodly portion of pumpkin-spice crumb cake remained. She picked up the knife and glanced back and forth between Pamela and Nell, who both shook their heads no. Pamela, however, hopped up and stepped over to the stove, where she launched a low flame under the carafe, which was still half full of coffee.

Bettina cut a slice of the crumb cake, talking as if to herself as she did so. "The medical examiner will probably analyze the yarn that was around the victims' necks," she murmured. "In fact, I'm sure she will." The cake was in transit now, on the spatula and heading toward Bettina's plate. "After all," she continued, "in the second case at least, the yarn was one of the murder weapons. So if it turns out the yarn was made from llama wool, she'll report that to Clayborn."

Cake in place and fork in hand, Bettina looked up with a smile. "And then he'll be glad he listened to me and that he has the llama hairs."

"I would be interested in learning more about the yarn the killer used," Pamela said. "And if it turns out to be made from llama wool"—her lips shaped a regretful half smile and she shrugged—"that would be pretty damning evidence as far as

Germaine is concerned. But I'd like to know more about the knitting author whose books Mary panned."

"I would too," Nell said. "The knitting author's husband actually threatened Mary—at least according to Mary."

Bettina suddenly sprang from her chair and darted toward the door that led to the entry, dodging Ginger, who had just wandered into the kitchen. The cat took advantage of Bettina's absence to leap onto the now-empty chair and rear up with her front paws on the edge of the table. She favored Nell with an unblinking jade-green stare.

"Ginger is used to having just me and Bettina sitting here in the morning," Pamela explained, advancing toward the table with the now-warm carafe. "She's met you before, of course, at Knit and Nibble, but she's wondering what's up now."

Nell reached out a wrinkled hand and caressed Ginger's head. Ginger leaned into the caress, closing her eyes, twisting her head this way and that, and folding her ears back to maximize contact with Nell's gentle hand.

Pamela refilled Bettina's coffee cup and her own, and made sure Nell's tea supply was adequate. She'd just deposited the carafe on the counter when Bettina reentered, absorbed in studying her mobile device. Ginger saw Bettina coming and vacated the chair by hoisting herself onto the table. From there, she hopped delicately onto Nell's thigh.

"I've got Mary's blog here," Bettina murmured, lowering herself back into her chair. Instead of sitting back down, Pamela stepped to where she could look over Bettina's shoulder at the small screen where Mary's photo and her website's banner, with the legend *The Lyon and the Lamb: Adventures in Woolgathering*, were visible.

Nell was still busy with Ginger's head rub, but she tipped her own head in the direction of Bettina's device as well. Bettina scrolled down rapidly, and Pamela blinked as words and images flew by.

"Here!" she said suddenly. "Stop right here!"

The text settled into place and Pamela began to read. "No reason to waste your money on Barbara Barrow's latest booklet for the hopelessly lame Craftfest imprint," Mary had written, "unless you fancy yourself in a ski hat with a pompom. (Even as a twelve-year-old, I knew that was a tacky look!)"

"Ooooh!" Nell shuddered. "I knew she could be prickly . . ."

"So—the knitting author's name is Barbara Barrow," Pamela said. "Now we just have to figure out where she lives."

"Probably not too far away"—Bettina's fingers were already dancing over the screen of her device—"because her husband came calling on Mary."

Pamela continued watching, and Nell gently lowered Ginger to the floor and joined Pamela at her post behind Bettina's chair.

"Here we are," Bettina announced after a few minutes of searching. "Barbara and Stuart Barrow, on Angler Road in Meadowside." She shut down her device and tucked it back into her purse. "I think," she said, turning to wink at Pamela and Nell, "I need to research an article on how Meadowside celebrates Halloween." She stood up. "I'll need help with my interviews, of course."

Pamela transferred the cups, plates, and silverware to the counter while Bettina put away the
cream and slipped the remaining piece of crumb
cake into a ziplock bag. Soon, the three of them
were tugging on coats and jackets in the entry. Catrina looked up from her nap in the patch of sun-
light that appeared predictably on the entry's
thrift-store carpet every morning and then went
back to sleep.

"Here's something else we should do," Nell said
suddenly, raising a finger. Pamela had been about
to reach for the doorknob but turned back. "Mary's
funeral is tomorrow," Nell explained, "and afterward, Brainard is hosting a reception at the Wendelstaff faculty club. Harold and I certainly plan to
go—Mary was our neighbor, after all. But the reception, especially, might be a good venue for a little sleuthing, no matter what interesting things we
learn today in Meadowside. And I'm sure the two
of you would blend in just fine with the other
mourners."

Chapter 11

The houses on Angler Road looked to have been built more recently than most of the ones in Arborville, and on smaller lots, for people with smaller budgets. The split-level designs evoked the fifties, but the houses had been carefully maintained and the neighborhood projected an aura of contented respectability. No house seemed without a door decoration, or a festive banner, or an amusing wooden yard sign. The Barrows' house was particularly noteworthy, with a bundle of Indian corn on the door, a bright orange banner with the word "Booo!" hanging from the porch roof, and a parade of skeletons marching across the lawn.

Bettina cruised slowly past the house, then nosed her Toyota into a spot at the curb a few hundred feet farther up the block. "We'll talk to some of the Barrows' neighbors," she said. "We'll ask whether Angler Road gets a lot of trick-or-treaters, and whether people give out a lot of candy. If any-body wonders why we care, we're writing an article for the *Arborville Advocate*."

"Clever idea," Nell commented from the pas-senger seat, "though I don't really condone lying. If the Barrows were at home handing out candy last Saturday night, they weren't at the Arborville bonfire killing Dawn Filbert because they thought she was Mary."

"It won't be lying if I really write the article." Bettina twisted her key in the ignition and the Toy-ota's engine rumbled to silence.

They decided to fan out, with Bettina taking the houses to the left of the Barrows' house, Nell tak-ing the houses to the right, and Pamela taking the houses across the street.

"We'll ring the Barrows' bell too," Pamela sug-gested, "though it's a weekday and they're proba-bly both at work. We might be lucky to find many people home at all, really."

"We'd better get busy then," Nell said, and she began to climb out of the car. "Though we really only have to find one person who can vouch for the Barrows being on Angler Road Halloween night."

The air was chilly but still, and the day was bright and cloudless. Lawns on Angler Road were still green, with fallen leaves like bright paint spat-ters here and there. Pamela and Bettina joined Nell on the sidewalk. Bettina pushed back her coat sleeve to consult her pretty gold watch and said, "It's exactly eleven thirty. Let's meet back here at noon and compare notes." Squinting into the sun-light, Pamela and Nell nodded.

They parted then, with Bettina heading for the nearest house and Nell heading in the other direction. Pamela stood near the car for a minute and studied the houses on the opposite side of the street. One had an elaborate Halloween-themed display on the porch—a whole family of pumpkins with faces painted on them, faces so realistic that Pamela wondered if they were meant to be portraits of the people who lived in the house.

Such enthusiasm for the holiday suggested that whoever answered the door—if anyone did—might talk willingly about Angler Road's trick-or-treaters. So Pamela made her way up the front walk to the porch and rang the doorbell.

She could hear the bell echo inside and tilted her head toward the door in hopes of also hearing footsteps. But there was just silence. She rang again and waited. More silence. Either no one was home, or the occupant didn't like to answer the door if no visitor was expected, or the bell was taken as a signal that a parcel had been delivered but could be fetched in at leisure.

Pamela retraced her steps down the front walk and tried the next house, a split-level whose construction combined brick and shingles. At this house, the door opened almost as soon as Pamela pushed the bell, but the woman who opened it took one look at her and said, "We're happy with our own church, thanks. Take your proselytizing somewhere else."

Pamela got only as far as "I'm not—" before the door slammed shut, causing the artificial flowers on the door wreath to vibrate.

As she once more retreated to the sidewalk,

Pamela noticed a woman emerging from around the far side of the next house. The woman was wearing baggy jeans and a down jacket that had seen better days, and she was carrying a pair of pruning shears and dragging a tall plastic bin. Leafy branches protruded from the top of the bin. The woman crossed the driveway, parked the bin at its edge, then stepped to the middle of the lawn and stared at the row of shrubs that softened the rather plain contours of the house.

After a few moments, she seemed to sense that she was being watched. She turned toward where Pamela was standing on the sidewalk in front of the house where she'd been taken for a missionary. Not sure how to interpret the look the woman was giving her, Pamela hesitated. She didn't know how she herself would react if she came out into her yard to do some pruning and found a stranger staring at her.

"What do you think?" the woman called suddenly. "Are they okay the way they are or do they look too shaggy?"

"I like shrubs to look natural," Pamela said, advancing along the sidewalk. "Not pruned into shapes a plant would never really have."

"I do too," the woman said. "Are you new in the neighborhood? I don't think I've seen you before."

"Actually I'm—" Pamela hesitated again. Bettina was such a better actress, and because Bettina genuinely was a reporter, this sleuthing errand wouldn't even draw very heavily on her acting skills. But Pamela wasn't sure she could sustain the ruse they'd concocted. She studied the shrubs for a moment, then her glance drifted to the woman's porch, where a very convincing witch stood sentry next to the front door.

"It looks like the residents of Angler Road take Halloween very seriously," she commented. "Almost everybody has some kind of great decoration up."

The woman smiled. "It's become quite competitive—like those people who cover their houses and yards with thousands of Christmas lights every year."

"Angler Road must get a lot of trick-or-treaters then," Pamela said.

"Do we ever! Our kids are all grown up now, with kids of their own, but we enjoy seeing the little neighbor kids in their costumes." The woman indeed looked rather grandmotherly, with salt-and-pepper hair cut in a wash-and-wear style and a rounded figure.

"Does everybody on the block get into the spirit of things?" Pamela asked, feeling encouraged at the direction the conversation was taking. "Buying candy for hundreds of children can get expensive."

"That it can!" The woman laughed. "But our kids always loved coming home with big bags full of goodies, so I can't begrudge this new generation of goblins." She laughed again, and then patted her stomach. "Of course, the challenge is buying just enough. My husband and I don't need to be stuffing ourselves with the leftovers."

"Some people just turn off the lights when they run out."

"We had to do that this year." The woman drooped her head in mock shame. "Word must have gotten around that Angler Road was the best place to trick-or-treat. The goblins kept coming and coming, and one by one houses went dark as people turned off their lights." She gestured toward the Barrows' house, with its parade of skeletons on the lawn. "Except for them. They don't have kids yet, but they really enjoy the holiday. They lay in a huge supply of candy and both dress up in costumes. They were mummies this year—really hilarious. He came out on the porch and just stood there with a basket of candy. The kids were coming in streams."

Pamela glanced across the street and noticed Nell making her way up the Barrows' front walk. She checked her watch. It was just noon, and when she shifted her gaze to Bettina's car, she saw that Bettina had already finished her canvassing and was sitting behind the steering wheel.

"I won't keep you any longer," she said, turning back to the woman she'd been chatting with. She couldn't just go and join Bettina in the car though. That would make it obvious she wasn't a new neighbor out for a stroll—especially when Nell joined them and they drove away. But that problem solved itself when the woman looked at her own watch and remarked that she'd done enough yard work for one day and it was time for lunch.

"It was nice talking to you," the woman said. "I'm Becky."

"I'm Pamela." Pamela smiled and dipped her head.

"See you around the neighborhood then," Becky said. And with a wave, she gripped the edge of the bin and began to drag it back across the driveway.

Pamela traveled several yards along the sidewalk, waiting until Becky had disappeared around the back of her house before she paused to look toward the Barrows' house. Nell had reached the porch and was standing at the Barrows' front door. She waited, perhaps hearing footsteps inside. But after a few minutes, she turned away, stepped off the porch, and headed toward the sidewalk.

"I found something out," Pamela announced as she climbed into the back seat of the Toyota.

Bettina was patting at her hair, which had strayed from its careful pouf despite the stillness of the day. "I wish I'd worn a hat," she said, tilting her head to catch her reflection in the rearview mirror. "But that's not as important as"—she swiveled in her seat to regard Pamela—"what did you find out?"

"Let's collect Nell and then drive a few blocks up the street before we pool our discoveries," Pamela said. "The woman who lives right over there"—she pointed toward the house with the exuberant shrubbery—"thinks she was just chatting with a new neighbor having a stroll and she might come back outside."

Nell arrived and settled into the passenger seat, commenting "No luck!" as she pulled the door closed.

Bettina twisted her key in the ignition and the Toyota came to life with a grumble that turned into a purr. They passed more of the tidy split-level houses, and when they reached a little park, Bettina nosed toward the curb and turned off the engine.

"Nobody was home," Nell said. "I even tried the

Barrows—though if they, or he, or she, or whoever came to the door, had said they were in Meadowside on Halloween night, I'm not sure that would have counted as a real alibi."

"I think they really were here though." Pamela leaned forward from her perch in the back seat. She recounted her conversation with the woman who had introduced herself as Becky.

"The last people on the block to run out of candy," Nell murmured, "not that children need all the candy they collect. But Dawn can't have been killed later than eight or eight thirty, because the bonfire hadn't been going too long before her body was found."

"The Barrows were certainly in Meadowside Halloween night, not in Arborville killing Dawn Filbert," Pamela said. "And from what Becky told me, it sounds like they wouldn't miss Halloween on Angler Road for anything. Not only do they make sure they won't run out of candy—they both dress up. This year they were mummies."

"They sound like nice people," Bettina chimed in. "I can't believe Stuart Barrow really threatened Mary the way she said. Their neighbors love them—at least the ones I talked to. And they love Barbara's knitting patterns and know all about that snotty Mary Lyon, who looked down her nose at knitting patterns ordinary people can understand—though it's a pity she was murdered."

"So," Bettina sighed, "I guess we found out something—but do we have any suspects left now?" She twisted her key in the ignition once again and they were on their way. "I, for one, could use some lunch," she commented as they cruised toward the intersection where they'd make the turn to head back to Arborville.

From Arborville Avenue, Bettina veered up the hill toward the Palisades and Nell's house. Harold was outside raking leaves and waved as Bettina pulled over and stopped. Nell got out and motioned him over to the car, and they made their arrangements for the funeral and memorial reception the next day, with Harold offering to drive.

The Toyota was halfway down the block when Pamela heard a voice calling, "Stop! Wait! Stop!" She twisted around to look out the window—she was still riding in the back seat—and saw Nell running after them, her gray coat billowing out behind her.

"It's Nell!" Pamela tapped Bettina on the shoulder. "She wants to tell us something!"

Bettina swerved to the curb and rolled down the window.

"I just thought of something!" Nell's face was pink with exertion. The words squeezed out in a breathless pant. She took a deep breath and then another.

"What?" Bettina stuck out her head. Pamela's view was of her friend's profile, frozen in an attitude of alarmed puzzlement.

"If the Barrows were both dressed as mummies"— Nell paused for a ragged breath—"how would anyone know they were really themselves?"

The drive from Nell's house to Pamela's was just long enough for the implications of Nell's question to sink in. As Bettina pulled into Pamela's driveway, driver and passenger both spoke.

"A mummy costume would be perfect for creating a fake alibi," Bettina exclaimed, her eyes bright. "Totally wrapped up from head to foot."

Pamela's comment was more measured. "They would have had to enlist accomplices," she observed, staring straight ahead without exactly focusing on anything. "It would be very clever though, almost the perfect crime. Your neighbors think you're at home dressed like mummies and giving out candy—but you're over in the next town killing someone."

"You'd have to really trust the people you recruited to be you," Bettina said.

"You would." Pamela nodded. "We have to think about this—but we can't cross the Barrows off our list of suspects yet."

"They *are* our list of suspects," Bettina pointed out. "Unless you want to retract your opinion that Germaine couldn't be the murderer."

Pamela reached for the door handle. Then she paused and raised an admonitory finger. "*One* of them could have been the mummy while the other was in Arborville committing the murder. That woman I talked to didn't say whether she ever saw two mummies at once."

"So we definitely won't cross them off," Bettina said. "I'd invite you across the street for lunch, but I'm babysitting for the Arborville grandchildren this afternoon and I've got to grab a quick bite and change my clothes."

Pamela climbed the steps to her porch, retrieved

her mail from the mailbox, and unlocked her front door. The sunny spot where Catrina took her morning naps on the carpet in the entry had vanished as the sun climbed toward midday. So there was no one to greet Pamela as she stepped inside. She shed her jacket and purse and, in a few moments, was studying the contents of her refrigerator.

She'd brought home a chicken from the Co-Op on Tuesday and roasted it with rosemary from the pot on her back porch. It had provided Wednesday's dinner as well, and would return again tonight. Pamela had always cooked real dinners, even after only she and her daughter were left. With Penny away at college, she still cooked real dinners—though a chicken could last a week, and its carcass could launch a pot of soup.

There was plenty of whole-grain bread left from Tuesday's fresh loaf, and plenty of the Co-Op's special Vermont cheddar. A piece of toast with a few slices of cheese and a fried egg on top would be a perfect lunch, she decided.

As she tended the egg in her small frying pan, watching as the white turned from translucent to opaque, she pondered again the question Nell had posed. Checking with neighbors to find out whether the Barrows had been at home Halloween night had seemed like such a good idea. But costumes, of course! Halloween was all about costumes. What better night to carry out evil deeds?

What was it Roland had said? People out roaming around in the dark, and nobody looks like who they really are? Maybe Halloween wasn't such a benign holiday after all.

Upstairs, Pamela awakened her computer monitor from its sleep. She'd expected to spend the morning evaluating the last two articles from the batch her boss had sent on Monday. But then Bettina and Nell had arrived and the sleuthing errand to Meadowside had been hatched, and now it was nearly one thirty.

She reopened the file she'd been working on that morning. Soon, she was immersed once more in the world of the Raramuri people of Chihuahua and their elaborate dresses, introduced by European missionaries in the 1600s but now cherished as a part of the Raramuris' own ethnic identity.

Chapter 12

"I wonder what Mary would have thought of her funeral," Pamela commented as Harold Bascomb maneuvered his Audi toward the exit of the church parking lot. The funeral had been held at St. Peter Martyr, an imposing Gothic-style edifice not far from the Wendelstaff campus.

"Some of the remembrances were awfully sentimental," Bettina said. "I kept imagining the coffin lid flipping open and Mary popping out with a sarcastic comment."

From the front seat, Harold snickered, but Nell twisted around to focus her kindly gaze on the passengers in the back seat. "Funerals are for the living," she observed, "not the dead. If those words comforted Mary's survivors, they served their purpose."

"Is anybody more familiar with the Wendelstaff campus than I am?" Harold asked. They'd already reached the campus's northern edge, where a vast parking lot stretched from the road they were traveling on to the bank of the Haversack River.

"There must be parking closer to the faculty club," Bettina said. "I hope so anyway. I'm not wearing my sneakers." In fact, she was wearing an elegant pair of slender-heeled pumps in a deep shade of purple. Her purple gloves, purple beret, stylish lavender coat, and violet and fuchsia cashmere scarf completed the ensemble.

"The faculty club is in the student union building," Pamela said. She visited the campus occasionally for craft-related events. "And the student union building is behind the quadrangle, near the river. There's a smaller lot after you pass the main part of the campus."

Soon, Harold had pulled into the smaller lot, which had a section marked "Visitors," and eased the Audi into an empty space. Around them, other people were climbing out of cars, most of them recognizable as fellow mourners by outfits more formal than those of the backpack-laden students milling about here and there.

Pamela guided her companions along a route that meandered past ivy-covered buildings, emerging at one end of the campus's central quadrangle. The quadrangle was a grassy expanse, still green, and crisscrossed with paths traversed by hurrying students. One of the paths led to the Wendelstaff student union building, whose modern design marked it as one of the college's newer structures.

A sign on a stand right inside the entrance read "Lyon-Covington Reception," and an arrow pointed to the left. They proceeded along a hallway until they could go no farther and had to turn left again.

Once they turned, an open door beckoned and a muted hubbub within suggested they'd reached their destination.

Looking rather at loose ends, but professorial in a tweed jacket, Brainard Covington stood apart from his guests, some of whom were investigating the buffet table and some of whom had equipped themselves with glasses of wine and formed small conversational groups.

The room featured floor-to-ceiling windows in the back wall, and the view was of the grassy slope leading down to the Haversack River and the river itself. On this bright day, the river looked its best. The water, murky at times, instead reflected the clear blue of the sky. And the tide was high—the Haversack eventually reached the ocean and thus was tidal—and so the detritus that sometimes marred its banks was submerged.

Brainard arranged his handsome features into a smile when he caught sight of the Bascombs, perhaps grateful for the soothing presence of his elderly neighbors. His handsomeness—characterized by deep-set eyes of the darkest brown, a classic profile, and a sensitive mouth—was of the sort enhanced by seriousness, and as if he realized this, the smile rapidly faded. He wasn't a large man. In the shoes she thought of as her funeral pumps, Pamela was as tall as he.

Nell advanced first, clasped Brainard's hand, and murmured a few words of comfort. Harold followed her, adding a gentle hand on Brainard's shoulder to the handclasp and murmured words he offered. Pamela and Bettina hovered in the background until Nell stepped aside and ushered them forward.

"You met Pamela Paterson and Bettina Fraser the other day," she explained. "They're fellow Arborvillians." Brainard nodded.

"I'm so sorry about Mary," Pamela said. "I know her blog will be missed," she added, after searching her mind for an appropriate comment.

"We're all knitters." Bettina reached out a comforting hand. "I hope you're doing okay . . . after such a shocking event."

Pamela studied Brainard's face as Bettina spoke. She and Bettina had considered the possibility that Brainard himself might have killed his wife—despite an alibi that Detective Clayborn had evidently accepted—and she was searching for some hint in his expression that contradicted his apparent grief. As he absorbed Bettina's words, his brow contracted and his eyes seemed to focus on something invisible a few feet ahead of him.

"Yes," he whispered. "It was shocking." After a few moments, he spoke again. "There's a coatroom," he exclaimed suddenly, as if recalled to his duties as host.

Nell began to unbutton her faithful gray wool coat.

"It's right over there." Brainard pointed to a door, slightly ajar, near the door through which they had entered. "And then"—he gestured vaguely toward the buffet table, which was parallel with the windows that looked out on the river view—"there's food, some kind of food. And people. Some other people from Arborville are here. And my son is here . . . somewhere." He squinted in the direction of a small knot of people clustered at the end of the buffet table where the wine was being served. "Obviously, not standing next to his father where he should be."

Bettina wasn't as resistant to being labeled nosy as Pamela was, and the seclusion of the coatroom offered a good opportunity for her to query Nell about the family dynamic Brainard's comment had hinted at.

As she divested herself of the lavender coat to display a form-fitting jersey dress in the same deep purple as her shoes, Bettina turned to Nell. "I guess Brainard and his son don't get along very well," she said.

"Hercules is a lovely young man." Nell handed her coat to Harold, who was standing at the ready with a coat hanger. "And he's following in Brainard's footsteps."

"Maybe more Brainard's idea than his own," Harold added. With his own coat hung up, his corduroy sports jacket, tattersall shirt, and knit tie had been revealed.

"I don't like gossip," Nell said primly. Freed of her coat, she headed back out into the main room.

Before Harold could follow his wife, Bettina planted herself in the doorway. "It sounds like you know something," she said, gazing up into Harold's craggy face.

"Herc is a graduate student in classics at Princeton," Harold said, "like his father before him." He shrugged. "I'm not sure that career path would have been Herc's first choice if left to his own devices."

Nell hadn't gone far. She was lurking a few yards from the door to the coatroom, and when she noticed that no one else had emerged, she backtracked and beckoned to Harold.

"I'm being summoned," he said with a wink at Bettina, who stepped aside. Pamela and Bettina followed the Bascombs as they proceeded toward the buffet table, where a few people more interested in food than drink were browsing, and servers who appeared to be students were stationed here and there.

"It's awfully early for wine," Bettina said, "but just the right time for lunch."

Nell and Harold had already picked up plates and were studying an inviting platter that featured raw vegetables arranged in bands of red, yellow, and green. Pamela and Bettina equipped themselves with plates and surveyed the offerings.

Besides the vegetables and their accompanying dip, there was a cheese ball surrounded by crackers, a chafing dish filled with meatballs in a creamy sauce, chicken tidbits on bamboo skewers, openfaced smoked salmon sandwiches on dark bread and garnished with capers, miniature crabmeat quiches, jumbo shrimp with a red dipping sauce, and several other tempting examples of food that could be managed with fingers or toothpicks.

Bettina passed by the vegetables and the cheese ball to head straight for the meatballs, adding three to her plate and moving on to the crabmeat quiches. Pamela took a meatball and a chicken tidbit and went on adding to her plate until there was no more space—though the plates, being intended for the use of ambulatory diners, were quite small.

When Nell and Harold reached the end of the buffet table, they had been hailed by some Arborville neighbors—people who lived on the same street as the Bascombs and Brainard—and were standing near the windows chatting with them. Pamela and Bettina surveyed the group, a mixture of Arborville people and academic types, who for the most part had gravitated toward their own kind.

Most of the Arborville people were middle-aged or older, dressed in the somber outfits that people of their generation considered suitable for somber occasions. Pamela herself had reached deep into her closet for a pair of brown wool slacks and a black-and-brown-striped jacket that she wore on occasions when jeans wouldn't suffice.

Brainard's Wendelstaff colleagues, however, represented a wider spectrum of ages, and their clothing represented a wider range of styles. Some of the men affected a traditional academic look, involving tweed jackets with leather elbow patches, and some of the women's grooming choices—hair allowed to go gray, minimal makeup if any—and ensembles—flat shoes, baggy trousers, and shapeless jackets—seemed intended to suggest that their minds were on higher things. Other colleagues, younger for the most part, resembled urban hipsters in their boots, skinny jeans, and flannel shirts.

Brainard was still standing apart, near the door, greeting a few late arrivals and bidding goodbye to people who perhaps had classes to get to or other demands on their time. Pamela nibbled at a shrimp as she watched him, half-hearing Bettina's exclamations of pleasure as she sampled her meatballs.

Brainard was really a very handsome man, Pamela

reflected, and Mary had been a beautiful woman.
And then—as if the thought had somehow summoned up the person who was the biologically determined result of such a pairing—a young man
whose looks combined a classic profile and a sensitive mouth with high cheekbones and russet hair
broke away from a group composed of hipster academics and made his way to Brainard's side.

The sight of the two together was so striking that
Bettina momentarily forgot her meatballs. "That
must be the son," she whispered, staring at the pair.
"Hercules."

Hercules—or Herc, as Harold had called him—
leaned toward his father and said something, but
it was impossible to make out his words from
where Pamela and Bettina were standing, especially in the echoing hubbub of the room. When
Brainard responded, his words too were inaudible.
His scowl, however, made it clear that Herc's words
hadn't pleased him.

Herc took a few steps toward the door, then piv-
oted and returned to his father's side. Father and
son stood together then, with matching scowls,
ready to greet guests, receive condolences, or
thank people for coming.

"I guess Herc decided to do his duty," Bettina
whispered. "He *should* be at his father's side for an
event like this, lending support—not to mention
that Mary was his mother."

"He might feel the loss more than Brainard
does," Pamela said and nodded.

Bettina picked up the last item on her plate, a
bamboo skewer with a morsel of chicken on it, and
glanced toward the buffet table. "Not too crowded,"

she murmured, "and one of the servers is just adding more meatballs to the chafing dish."

"Okay," Pamela said with a laugh. "I'll join you for seconds. This *is* lunch, after all."

"Oh my goodness!" Bettina's glance turned into a stare. "I certainly didn't expect to see her here."

"Who?" Pamela tilted her head in the direction Bettina was staring.

"The young woman from Hyler's, Felicity Winkle. We were talking to her the other day when we had the ham and cheese on rye."

In an apparent nod to the seriousness of the occasion, Felicity had chosen a simple navy-blue dress, and her fair hair was pulled back in the same low ponytail she wore for her job at Hyler's. Her only jewelry was tiny gold earrings.

"I guess she knew Mary from Hyler's," Bettina went on. "It was awfully thoughtful of her to come to this."

As they watched Felicity, she detached herself from the group she'd been talking to—some of the middle-aged Arborvillians who were likely patrons of Hyler's—and began walking toward the door. Bettina waved her down as she passed.

"I can't stay," Felicity said, pausing for a moment as Bettina took her hand. "I have to get to class." She looked around. "Not here," she added, with a twist of the mouth that suggested awe at her surroundings. "I'm at County Community, like I told you."

"Nothing to be embarrassed about," Bettina assured her with a comforting hand squeeze.

Felicity continued on her way, pausing again when she reached Brainard and Herc. Herc bent toward her as if acknowledging some expression of sympathy, but Brainard frowned and stepped back with a curt nod.

"Not very gracious," Bettina whispered. "I wonder what that's all about."

Felicity disappeared into the coatroom, re-emerged a minute later with a puffy down coat zipped over her dress, and stepped out into the hall.

All that remained on Bettina's plate was an empty bamboo skewer. She turned toward the buffet table, and Pamela turned with her. But while Pamela and Bettina had been talking with Felicity and then watching her awkward encounter with Brainard, a number of other guests seemed to have decided that their plates needed refilling too. So the two friends joined a line of people slowly making their way past the vegetable platter, the cheese ball, the meatballs, and the other offerings.

They advanced along the buffet table, waiting as a woman methodically spread cheese on one cracker after another and a man piled his plate with shrimp, leaving only two on the serving platter. When they stepped away at the spot where the food offerings gave way to the liquor, Pamela heard a familiar voice speak her name.

From a group among which Pamela recognized Marlene Pepper, one of Bettina's friends from Arborville, Nell stepped forward. "Pamela," she repeated, "and Bettina"—she beckoned them closer—"I'd like to introduce you to Mary's sister."

Pamela stared. The group included Nell, with her halo of white hair, and Marlene Pepper, the same size and shape as Bettina and dressed in an attractive skirt suit, and a woman Pamela recognized from Hyler's and the Co-Op, and a few other people. But no one seemed a likely candidate to be identified as Mary Lyon's sister.

Siblings could look very different from each other, of course. But could the stocky gray-haired woman in the shapeless trouser suit really be the sister of the ravishing Mary Lyon?

Pamela shifted her plate of food to her left hand to free her right hand for shaking as Nell explained, to the stocky gray-haired woman, that Pamela Paterson and Bettina Fraser were fellow Arborvillians, though not actual neighbors of the Lyon-Covingtons. "Martha Lyon," Nell concluded, and the stocky gray-haired woman extended a hand. Pamela took it, murmuring that she was sorry about Mary's death. When the hand was available again, Bettina took it and echoed Pamela's words.

Martha, it seemed, did not normally live in the Northeast. She taught classics at a college in the Midwest but had come east on a one-year sabbatical, subletting an apartment in Manhattan and doing research at libraries and museums.

As she spoke, Pamela studied her features, searching for some resemblance to Mary. Her mouth was less generous than Mary's, her eyes narrower and closer together. The strong bone structure and pronounced cheekbones that had given Mary's face its elegance just made Martha look stern. Earrings that were simple gold studs, a utilitarian watch on a leather band, and a small curiously shaped charm—to Pamela's craft-oriented eyes, it resembled a spindle—on a chain around her neck did little to mitigate her plainness.

"I never imagined my sabbatical research in Manhattan would coincide with attending my little sister's funeral across the Hudson," Martha was saying as Nell nodded sympathetically. "But I guess it was convenient that another family member was right here when it happened," she added, "for Brainard and Herc's sake."

"I'm sure they appreciate having you here." Nell's kind expression was even more comforting than her words.

"I'll be doing some organizing at the house," Martha explained. "It's painful for Brainard to see Mary's things every time he turns around."

"Not taking too much time from your research, I hope," said a masculine voice just behind Pamela.

Nell and Martha stared in the direction of the voice, both looking equally puzzled as to the identity of the speaker. Pamela stepped aside to see a pleasant-looking, middle-aged man in a tweed jacket.

"I'm sorry to intrude," the man said. "I'm Arnold Linden, one of Brainard's colleagues here at Wendelstaff." He glanced around the group, which now consisted only of Martha, Nell, Pamela, and Bettina. Marlene Pepper and the others had split off to form their own group.

"Martha Lyon," Martha said, extending a hand, which Arnold took, and she gestured toward Nell, Pamela, and Bettina in turn, mentioning their names.

Good memory, Pamela observed to herself. Probably comes of being a professor and keeping track of all those students.

"Brainard mentioned your sabbatical project to

me—before this sad thing happened." Arnold waved a hand around the room. "And now here you are. My field is art history, but there's so much overlap, especially in the ancient world, with art standing in for written documents and . . ."

Pamela's mind began to wander and she noticed Bettina glancing toward the buffet table, where several trays of petits fours had replaced the empty platters that had offered raw vegetables, salmon on dark bread, chicken skewers, and the rest. Harold appeared and drew Nell away to join him in talking to Herc.

Martha had taken several steps back, as if to acknowledge that discussion of her sabbatical project would not be of interest to anyone but her and her fellow academic, and Arnold had followed her. He had become quite animated, however, and snippets of the conversation drifted toward Pamela and Bettina as they made their way back to the buffet table.

". . . Princeton degree, of course, like yours . . ." This from Arnold.

"You must know Tigard Sanders, then," Martha responded.

". . . such an influence . . ."

Pamela handed her plate to a server and picked up a napkin and a delicate square pastry iced in pink and yellow.

Martha and Arnold's voices blended, occasional words popping out here and there. ". . . amphorae . . . Moirai . . . deconstruct . . . university press . . ."

At Pamela's side, Bettina was nibbling a chocolate petit four. "Such a shame Martha let her hair turn gray," she observed between bites. "Mary's was lovely, that russet shade." She paused. "Though I'd have gone a bit brighter if I was her." Bettina raised her free hand to touch her own vivid coif.

Chapter 13

It was nearly two by the time Harold turned onto Orchard Street and cruised to a stop in front of Bettina's house. Pamela and Bettina climbed out of the Audi and lingered at the end of the Frasers' driveway as Harold and Nell continued on up toward Arborville Avenue and the Palisades neighborhood beyond.

"Do you have plans for dinner tomorrow night?" Bettina asked as Pamela commented that she had chores waiting at home.

"You know I don't," Pamela replied with a laugh. "You and Wilfred and the knitting club are just about my whole social life."

"It didn't have to be like that." Bettina tipped her head toward the house next to Pamela's, of similar vintage to Pamela's, though hers was sheathed in clapboard and this house was shingled.

Pamela felt her lips tighten and a crease form between her brows. The inhabitant of the house

was an attractive single man named Richard
Larkin. He had wooed Pamela, in a low-key manner, starting shortly after he moved in a few years
earlier. She'd found him very appealing but had
resisted his overtures. Why, she wasn't sure, except
that her bond with her beloved husband had been
so strong that she couldn't imagine ever feeling
that close to anyone again. And the thought of trying, and then realizing that she was now messily
entangled in a relationship that wasn't what she'd
hoped, had made her reluctant to encourage him.

Bettina had lost few opportunities to talk up the
romantic possibilities of Richard Larkin—until
Pamela's lack of encouragement finally resulted in
his looking elsewhere.

"Bettina—please! I thought we'd agreed that . . .
that we weren't going to talk about Richard Larkin
anymore."

"I didn't say his name." Bettina raised her carefully shaped brows and smiled a close-mouthed
smile. "You did."

"I have to get home." Pamela turned away and
began to cross the street.

Bettina's voice floated toward her as she approached the opposite curb. "Wilfred is making
beef bourguignon," she called. "Come over at six."

That week's copy of the *Advocate* had arrived
while Pamela was out. She stooped for it when she
reached her driveway and then continued on
along the sidewalk and up her front walk. The Halloween murder had happened less than a week
ago, and Mary had been killed just the previous

Tuesday, so this would be the first issue of the town's weekly since those two tragic events.

As Pamela was turning her key in her front door's lock, she heard Bettina's voice behind her again, this time closer.

Coming to apologize for bringing up Richard Larkin? Pamela nudged open her front door but paused on the threshold, turning to watch as Bettina hurried up the front walk. She had apparently picked up her own copy of the *Advocate* and was now carrying its plastic wrapper in one hand and the newspaper, open to an inner page and flapping in the breeze, in the other.

" 'Pursuing all leads!' " she panted as she negotiated the porch steps in her high-heeled shoes. "That's a laugh! He has no leads at all except the llama hair, and of course he wouldn't say anything about that." She pointed to a column of text. " 'Assuring the citizens of Arborville that the police are doing their utmost.' This must be a press release from the police department, because I certainly didn't write it."

Pamela stood aside and waved Bettina through the door.

Hearing the front door open, Catrina and Ginger had come out to investigate. But when Bettina swept in waving the open newspaper, they both scurried away.

When both Pamela and Bettina were inside, Pamela extracted her own copy of the *Advocate* from its plastic sleeve and unfolded the paper. The front-page headline read, "Back-to-Back Murders Stun Arborville," and a quarter of the page was taken up with a large photo of the woodsy spot where Dawn Filbert's body had been found—minus the body, but plus crime-scene tape and seemingly taken after the sun had risen the next morning. Another quarter of the page was taken up with another photo, more dramatic, of the Lyon-Covington house with police cars clustered at the curb and police bustling here and there.

"This is my article right here," Bettina said, pointing to the text that filled the remaining space on the front page. "And I have another inside specifically about Dawn Filbert—I interviewed some of the people who work at her shop—and another specifically about Mary Lyon."

She began to fold the newspaper back up. "I'm going to keep on Clayborn about those llama hairs," she declared. "Germaine van Houten is still the only likely suspect I can see—unless those mummy costumes were disguising the fact that one or more of the Barrows wasn't really at home that night."

"I'll come tomorrow night," Pamela said as Bettina stepped toward the threshold.

"No more Richard Larkin." Bettina reached for Pamela's free hand and squeezed it.

No messages from Pamela's boss waited on the computer, and she'd met yesterday's deadline for returning the articles she was to evaluate. So she dedicated the rest of the afternoon to domestic chores: laundry, housecleaning, and preparing a shopping list for a Saturday morning trip to the

Co-Op. First, though, she set the carcass left from
Tuesday night's chicken simmering on the stove as
the first step in cooking up a pot of chicken soup.

As soon as she walked into her kitchen on Saturday morning, the grocery list fastened to the refrigerator by a tiny magnetized mitten reminded
Pamela of the first thing on her agenda. And the
cats that had trailed her down the stairs made it
clear that they expected their breakfast before she
even thought about hers.

Once Catrina and Ginger had been provided
with several scoops of chicken-fish blend, Pamela
set her kettle boiling for coffee. Before fetching
the newspaper, however, she added cat food to the
grocery list.

Back inside, she slipped the *Register* from its
flimsy plastic sleeve and unfolded it onto the table.
As the kettle began to whistle, she checked the
Local section for news about the two murders but,
as she had suspected, nothing had happened that
the *Register* judged worthy to report—and, in fact,
she suspected that nothing had happened at all.

Coffee and toast prepared, she settled down at
the table to read the paper more thoroughly. When
two cups of black coffee had been sipped from the
wedding-china cup and nothing remained of the
whole-grain toast but a few crumbs scattered across
the small wedding-china plate, Pamela rinsed cup
and plate at the sink and climbed the stairs to
dress.

Today, the sweater she chose to wear with her
jeans was a bulky turtleneck in a rich brown with an

interesting cable detail up the front. Back downstairs, she added a jacket and gloves to the ensemble—the turtleneck took the place of a scarf—and gathered a few of the canvas bags she'd used for her shopping ever since Nell convinced all her friends to renounce paper and plastic.

The bright but chilly weather was continuing, and Pamela enjoyed her walk up Orchard Street. The last few nights had been cold, cold enough that more leaves had traded the deep green of late summer for gold or vibrant red. And Thanksgiving-oriented arrangements of corn husks, ornamental squash, and chrysanthemums were replacing the sometimes macabre Halloween displays in yards and on porches.

Once she reached the Co-Op, she claimed a cart and headed toward the produce department. Browsing along the Co-Op's narrow aisles, she added celery, carrots, and two onions to the cart, as well as a baking potato. A few stalks of celery, a carrot, and an onion would go into the chicken soup, along with the egg noodles she already had at home. The chicken soup would be lunch for many days. The other onion would go into the meatloaf that would be Sunday's dinner, with a baked potato, and many dinners beyond that as well.

Emerging from the end of an aisle where bins piled high with fresh greens in leafy profusion flanked bins of lemons, limes, and oranges, Pamela steered her cart toward the meat department. Faced with lamb chops, rib roasts, tenderloins, and more—all from local farms—it seemed a shame to pick only a small package of ground chuck. But she would be enjoying the bounty of the Co-Op's meat department that evening in the form of Wilfred's beef bourguignon.

A detour down one of the Co-Op's central aisles was necessary in order to add several cans of cat food to her selections. Back on the store's periphery, she paused at the cheese counter where, instead of her usual Vermont cheddar, she requested a half pound of Swiss. The final stop was the bakery counter for a loaf of whole-grain bread. She pointed to a particularly appealing loaf—oval, gleaming, and just the right shade of toasty brown—and watched as it was sliced and tucked into a plastic bag.

Exiting with her groceries, Pamela waited at the light to cross Arborville Avenue. Directly across from the Co-Op was Borough Hall, Arborville's administrative center, a small, brick building dating from the early twentieth century. Two men from the town's DPW were at work now in front of the building—Pamela recognized them from the trucks that collected Arborville's garbage and recyclables.

Since mid-September, the small flower bed in front of the building, as well as the steps leading to the building's door and the landing in front of the door, had been decorated with materials evoking the harvest season. Dried cornstalks bearing dried ears of corn were lashed to the step railings with bright orange ribbon. More dried cornstalks bound into sheaves with more orange ribbon were stationed on either side of the door. In the flower bed, a bale of hay formed a seat for a scarecrow. Several jack-o'-lanterns kept him company.

Now the men were adding potted chrysanthemums to the display, and removing the jack-o'-

lanterns. Some had been nibbled by creatures and all had begun to collapse inward as their walls gradually decayed. Pamela had carried her own jack-o'-lantern to her compost heap several days before.

The light changed and the little striding figure that indicated it was okay to cross appeared below the signal. Pamela started across Arborville Avenue with a canvas grocery bag in each hand and her purse over her shoulder. She watched as one of the DPW men collected a maroon chrysanthemum from a handcart parked on the sidewalk, and then her glance strayed beyond the handcart to the bus stop a bit to the south of Borough Hall.

A couple, a young man and a young woman, stood together at the bus stop. A small wheeled suitcase was poised on the sidewalk near the young man's feet. Each half of the couple looked familiar, but until this moment the notion that the young man and the young woman might actually be a couple had not occurred to Pamela.

The young man was facing the young woman, displaying his classic profile to fine advantage when seen from halfway across Arborville Avenue. His russet hair glowed in the bright autumn sunlight. The young woman's fair hair was pulled back into a low ponytail and she wore the white shirt and black pants of a server at Hyler's. Then Herc Covington reached out a hand to caress the face of Felicity Winkle. Felicity raised her own hand to caress his.

By this time, Pamela had reached the opposite curb. But instead of continuing on past Borough Hall and thus past the bus stop and the young couple, she walked only as far as the south end of the flower bed with the hay bale and the scarecrow. There she paused, affecting a great interest in the refurbishing of the harvest display.

Herc was clearly on his way somewhere—probably into Manhattan to get a train or bus back to Princeton, and Felicity was clearly on a break from her job at Hyler's.

Pamela watched as one of the DPW men gathered up two of the rotting pumpkins. Behind her, she could hear Herc's voice saying, "We just have to be patient."

"Can't I come down there and live with you?" Felicity asked in plaintive tones. "I could get a job in Princeton just as well as here."

Yes! Pamela said to herself. *Why can't she?*

But young lovers must contend with the machinations of the old.

"He's got his pals in the classics department"— Herc's tones were equally plaintive—"and they're all spying on me. He'd cut me off without a cent."

The rumble of an approaching bus distracted Pamela from her study of the harvest display, where the other DPW man was now nestling a pair of chrysanthemums into the spots that had been occupied by the pumpkins.

"I love you so much, Herc!" Felicity raised her voice as the bus drew closer.

"I love you too," came Herc's response. "And when I'm done and I've got the degree and the job, I'll have my own money, and my father won't be able to keep us apart."

The bus wheezed to a stop. In the silence, Felicity's voice was loud, perhaps louder than she meant it to be. "I can't wait that long," she said. "We have to do something. I just can't wait that long."

As the bus pulled away, Pamela began to climb the steps leading to the door of Borough Hall, pretending that had been her errand all along. When she reached the top, she stepped in front of one of the cornstalk sheaves and turned back toward the sidewalk. Felicity stood at the corner, waiting to cross the east-west street that separated Borough Hall and the Co-Op from most of Arborville's shops and restaurants, including Hyler's Luncheonette.

Once Felicity had proceeded on her way—most likely heading back to Hyler's, Pamela thought—she descended the Borough Hall steps. She resumed her journey south on Arborville Avenue, turning onto Orchard Street at the corner with the stately brick apartment building. When she reached the spot halfway down the block where Bettina's house on the north side of the street faced hers on the south, she paused at the end of Bettina's driveway, even though the grocery-laden canvas bags were weighing heavy in her hands.

As she walked, she had been mulling over the conversation she had just overheard. Herc and Felicity were a couple—or hoped to be—but Herc's father, Brainard, objected to the match and was using his financial control over Herc to prevent the young lovers from realizing their dreams. That certainly explained Brainard's rudeness toward Felicity at the reception—as well as Herc's standoffishness on an occasion where one would expect son and father to console each other.

Bettina's Toyota was missing from its usual berth next to Wilfred's ancient but well-cared-for

Mercedes. Nonetheless, Pamela made her way up the driveway to the Frasers' porch, where she rang the bell.

After a few moments, the door swung back to reveal Wilfred, in his everyday garb of bib overalls and a plaid shirt. Before Wilfred even greeted Pamela, Woofus sidled up to his thigh, gazing at Pamela with a troubled expression that put his shaggy ears on alert. Wilfred rested a comforting hand on the huge animal's back, then turned his attention to Pamela.

"The boss lady's gone to the mall," he said.

"She'll be away for a couple of hours then, I guess." Pamela took a step back as Woofus edged closer to the threshold and extended his muzzle to sniff at the grocery bag that held the ground beef.

"At least," Wilfred said with a good-natured laugh. "But I was just about to pay a call on you, so let me—" He emerged from the doorway and relieved Pamela of the grocery bag that had interested Woofus. Woofus remained inside, looking conflicted about whether to follow his master on who knew what kind of mysterious errand or remain in the security of his own house.

Wilfred stooped toward the dog. "Come on, boy," he whispered encouragingly. "You know Pamela."

Woofus joined them on the porch, Wilfred pulled the door closed, and they set out along the little path that led to the driveway.

"What's on your mind?" Pamela inquired as they began to cross the street.

"Thyme," Wilfred responded.

"Time?" Pamela tilted her head to look up at his face and gave him a puzzled smile.

"Thyme," he repeated. "Fresh thyme. It's a crucial ingredient in my beef bourguignon recipe for tonight, and I recall seeing a pot of it on your back porch."

When Wilfred had been dispatched with a small posy of fragrant thyme sprigs, and a six p.m. arrival had been confirmed for her dinner invitation, Pamela put her groceries away. Then she checked her email, responded to a message from Penny, and settled down on her sofa. There, she gave herself over to the luxury of an afternoon with nothing to do but knit, and the prospect of a delicious dinner with her best friends.

Chapter 14

The Frasers' house was fragrant with the aroma of beef bourguignon—the savory richness of stewing beef enhanced by notes of carrot and onion and a piquant hint of thyme. Bettina met Pamela at the door, hung her jacket in the closet as Punkin watched from a favorite perch on the back of the sofa, and ushered her into the kitchen, where Pamela offered the bottle of burgundy she had brought.

"I know you bought burgundy for the recipe," Pamela said, "but here's a bottle for your wine cupboard or to drink tonight."

Wilfred greeted Pamela from behind the high counter that separated the cooking area from the eating one. He was wearing an apron over his bib overalls and his face was ruddy from kitchen heat. On the stovetop, a saucepan sat on a burner turned up high, its lid jiggling in a sign of the robust boil-

ing within. A half-full bottle of red wine waited on
the counter next to one of Bettina's sleek, Swedish
crystal wineglasses. Wilfred poured a few inches of
wine into the glass and handed it to Pamela. Then
he returned to his cooking duties and his own
glass of wine.

Bettina set the bottle Pamela had brought on the
high counter and picked up her wine. Whether by
accident or through calculation, her ensemble this
evening echoed the burgundy theme. She wore
wide-legged wool pants in a deep, rich red, paired
with a silky, bow-necked blouse in the same shade.

"You discovered something, didn't you?" she
said, regarding Pamela over the rim of her wine-
glass. "Something that has to do with the murders."

"I told her you came by while she was at the
mall," Wilfred explained from his post at the counter
near the stove. He was coring apples and standing
them upright in a ceramic baking dish. The apples
were bright red against the dish's creamy glaze.

"Maybe not something to do with the murders—at least I hope not," Pamela said. "But something to do with the Lyon-Covingtons, so that
means it complicates things."

"I'm all ears!" Bettina raised her eyebrows,
opened her mouth, inhaled, and froze, as if in the
grip of suspense.

"Herc Covington and Felicity Winkle are in love."

Bettina stared at Pamela for a moment. Then
she exclaimed, "The ring! Felicity's beautiful ring."
She went on, "That day we had lunch at Hyler's—
she wasn't wearing it anymore, and she told us all
about her boyfriend and the engagement being

broken off, and he's down in Princeton . . ." She broke off, a bit breathless.

"The boyfriend was Herc." Pamela nodded again. She went on to describe seeing the pair at the bus stop in front of Borough Hall and overhearing their conversation. "They see Brainard as the impediment to their being together," she concluded, adding, "and then, as Herc climbed on the bus, Felicity said they would have to do something."

"Like what kind of a something?" Bettina inquired, caught up in Pamela's story.

Pamela had taken a sip of wine after her long narrative. She swallowed, offered Bettina a shrug and a puzzled half smile, and said, "I don't know, but the something would be in the future, not the past."

"And the dead people haven't been Brainard—at least so far." Wilfred spoke up from his post at the counter, where he was now spooning an interesting mixture into the holes left in the apples when the cores were removed.

"Oh, dear!" Bettina shuddered. "At least so far? Felicity is such a sweet young woman. I wouldn't want to think—" She shuddered again.

Pamela was shuddering too, but inwardly. She'd had longer to ponder this new development than Bettina had, and she'd convinced herself—or at least tried—that a couple as appealing as Herc and Felicity would never contemplate something as horrible as murder. And a young man murdering his father . . . ? Of course, there was that Oedipus story . . .

She was relieved when Wilfred's voice, now cheerful, summoned her back to the comforting environs of the Frasers' kitchen.

"The stew is out of the oven and resting," he announced, "and the baked apples have gone in. I'll have the potatoes mashed in a trice, and then we'll eat."

Bettina was already bending into the refrigerator. She emerged holding a salad bowl carved from wood with a striking gnarled pattern. In the bowl, a tangle of curly arugula leaves was studded with cherry tomatoes. She set the bowl on the high counter and drizzled olive oil over the salad, tossed it with a large wooden fork and spoon, and added a sprinkle of balsamic vinegar to the now-glistening leaves. The finishing touches were a few grinds of pepper, a dash of salt, and another light toss.

"What can I do?" Pamela asked as Bettina headed for the dining room, bearing the salad before her.

"No need to do anything, dear lady," Wilfred said. "Too many cooks spoil the broth. But if you insist, you can fetch me a bowl for the mashed potatoes." He was energetically pumping his potato masher up and down in the saucepan where he'd boiled the potatoes.

Pamela opened the cupboard where Bettina kept the sage-green pottery dishes that were her favorite and lifted a medium-size oval bowl from a stack of bowls and platters. She stepped around to where Wilfred was working and watched as he exchanged the potato masher for an oversize spoon and added a goodly chunk of butter to the saucepan. He stirred the potatoes with the spoon as the butter melted, and then dribbled in milk until the texture changed from stiff to yielding. He lit the burner under the saucepan again and continued stirring.

"Got to make sure they're nice and hot," he explained. He stopped stirring for a moment to pour a bit of salt into his palm. "Just a bit," he said, tipping the salt from his palm into the saucepan and taking up the spoon again. "People can add more after they have a taste."

When the mashed potatoes had been heaped into the oval bowl, Pamela carried it to the dining room, where Bettina was refolding napkins, aligning flatware, and repositioning wineglasses, making sure that every detail of her carefully set table was perfect. After a satisfied nod, she lit the candles.

"I know it's just the three of us," she said. "But I so enjoy getting to use my pretty things."

The table was spread with a striped cloth in a loose, homespun weave, the stripes in various tones of blue and green that complemented Bettina's sage-green plates. Blue linen napkins were tucked beside the plates, along with knives, forks, and spoons in sleek stainless steel. Fresh wineglasses from Bettina's Swedish crystal set awaited wine from the bottle of burgundy in the stainless-steel wine coaster. Centered between pewter candle holders with modern Scandinavian lines was a squat turquoise pottery vase brimming with sunflowers. A salt shaker and pepper grinder, as well as butter in a shallow bowl, completed the preparations.

Pamela set the bowl of mashed potatoes to one side of the place setting at the head of the table where Wilfred would sit. To the other side, a large trivet marked the spot destined for the beef bourguignon. The salad bowl sat at the other end of the table, along with three small plates and three salad forks.

"Dinner is served!" Wilfred announced from the doorway that led from the kitchen. He was still wearing his apron and, with his hands protected by oven mitts, was carrying a casserole in a vibrant shade of orange. He'd left the casserole's lid in the kitchen, and a fragrant drift of steam rose from the stew. He set the casserole on the trivet and hurried away again, returning with serving spoons for the stew and the mashed potatoes.

They took their seats. "The stew is too hot to pass," Wilfred said, "so I'll serve." He reached a hand toward Pamela, who sat at his left, and she handed him her plate.

His ruddy face gleaming with satisfaction, Wilfred scooped a drift of mashed potatoes onto the plate and added a generous serving of the beef bourguignon as Bettina poured the wine. Wilfred went on to serve Bettina and himself. Then with a hearty "Bon appétit," he picked up his fork.

But before anyone could start eating, butter had to be passed for the mashed potatoes. Once she'd sculpted a little hollow into the peak of her mashed potatoes and slipped in a pat of butter, Pamela picked up her own fork. The cubes of beef, seared to a rich brown, were bathed in a gravy whose russet hue hinted at the red wine and tomato paste that had supplemented pan drippings and beef broth. Here and there among the beef cubes was a chunk of carrot, a mushroom slice, or a glossy little pearl onion.

Bettina took the first bite and, as she savored it, her expression reminded Pamela of the expression she sometimes observed on the faces of her cats when a head-rub was in progress—eyes closed and mouth curved into an ecstatic smile. With such an advertisement, Pamela eagerly sampled her own serving.

Wilfred had outdone himself. The beef was meltingly tender, savory, and meaty, infused with the flavors of carrots, mushrooms, and the subtly sweet onions—all melded together during the stew's long, slow cooking. Pamela was pleased to recognize in the gravy a fleeting note of the thyme she had contributed to the recipe. The mashed potatoes were the perfect complement to the beef bourguignon, with a flavor that didn't upstage and a texture that provided contrast—as well as a useful means of capturing extra gravy.

No one spoke for a time. The expression on Wilfred's face telegraphed his satisfaction with his afternoon's work in the kitchen, and Pamela contributed her own sounds of pleasure to Bettina's purring.

"A little more?" Wilfred offered when all that remained on the plates were streaks of the russet gravy and little dabs of mashed potatoes.

"The tiniest bit." Bettina handed her plate to her husband. Pamela requested a bit more too.

Wilfred served them spoonfuls of mashed potatoes and dipped into the casserole for cubes of beef. Then he helped himself to seconds as well.

After her first bite from the refilled plate, Bettina suddenly put down her fork. "I hope those sweet kids don't do something that will ruin their lives forever," she said, as if—with her hunger nearly satisfied—her mind had turned to other things.

"Do you mean Herc and Felicity?" Pamela looked up from her plate, where she'd been guiding a forkful of mashed potato toward a puddle of gravy.

"Of course." On Bettina's face, the cheer induced by Wilfred's meal had been replaced by an expression of distress that puckered her brow and erased her smile. "That conversation you overheard . . . with Felicity saying they had to do something . . ."

"Herc said they could wait . . . should wait," Pamela said, feeling her own cheer threaten to flee. "He'll get a good job when he finishes the degree. Just a few years, I'm sure. He seems industrious—and with Felicity so eager for them to be together . . . what better motivation?"

Bettina sighed. "From our perspective, it seems easy to wait."

"From our perspective *now*." Wilfred spoke up from the head of the table. "But when I was courting you, I was . . . impetuous. Faint heart never won fair maiden."

Bettina laughed. "Wilfred—you were forty when we met." In an aside to Pamela, she added, "I was only twenty-five."

"My dear, I was as eager as a boy. I couldn't wait for us to be together. And you're as beautiful now as you were then." Wilfred tipped his head to beam at his wife.

Pamela speared a cube of beef with her fork, but instead of raising her fork to her mouth, she studied her plate. She had no real reason to envy the bond the Frasers shared. They were generous in their affection for her. But their love for each other was the love of a man and wife, and she had lost that love when she lost her husband.

What would have happened, she suddenly wondered, if she had encouraged Richard Larkin's interest? Would the two of them be sitting here at Wilfred and Bettina's table, seeing the drama of their own courtship reflected in Herc and Felicity's romance?

So caught up was she in this reverie that she lost track of the topic whose conversational twists and turns had sparked Wilfred's revelation of his ardor and the adoring look he gave his wife. Thus, she was startled when Bettina responded to his compliment by saying, "What if she already tried once to 'do something,' but was confused about who Bo Peep was?"

As Pamela stared across the table, trying to fathom what Bettina meant, Wilfred said, "Do you mean Felicity killed Dawn Filbert thinking she was Brainard?"

Bettina nodded vigorously and her earrings, gleaming gold spheres on slender chains, swayed. "Herc could have told her that his parents' little

Halloween joke was to dress as famous couples, but with Brainard as the woman and Mary as the man."

Pamela dismissed the image of Richard Larkin beaming at her, which had popped into her head unbidden, and rejoined the conversation. "Felicity is an awfully delicate little thing," she said. "She hardly seems strong enough to imagine herself killing a woman, let alone a man."

"Brainard isn't a large man." Wilfred's tone was thoughtful, as if he was trying out Bettina's idea in his own mind.

"No, he isn't!" Bettina's nod set the earrings in motion again. "And that's all the more reason that Felicity could have mistaken Dawn Filbert for him—especially in the dark, back among those trees. But then, after she knocks him out, she bends over to make sure he's dead by strangling him with the yarn—"

"And she sees Dawn Filbert's face"—Wilfred completed the thought—"and leaves the yarn untied and runs away, probably hoping that her unknown victim—unknown to her at least—is just unconscious and not dead."

This was a great deal to think about. Empty plates sat in front of Wilfred and Bettina. On Pamela's own, a cube of beef and a pearl onion remained, in a tiny swirl of gravy. She quickly dispatched them and rose to her feet, saying, "Please let me clear away" and waving Wilfred back into his chair.

"Don't take the spoons," Wilfred advised.

Three trips to the kitchen sufficed, and Wilfred

joined her there on the third to remove his baked apples from the oven. When she returned from depositing the casserole on the stovetop, small plates and salad forks had replaced the plates and flatware she'd borne away. A mound of arugula sat on each plate, its fresh green bright against the dusky green of the plates. Peeking out from among the curly leaves were whole cherry tomatoes, glistening with olive oil.

Pamela sampled a few leaves. Their astringency was a perfect contrast to the hearty beefiness of the stew with its rich gravy.

With the salad course, talk once again turned to the food—the crispness of the greens, the way the cherry tomatoes concentrated the very essence of tomato-ness, and how olive oil and a touch of vinegar brought a salad to life. Then it meandered along familiar pathways: the doings of the Frasers' children and grandchildren, Penny's reports from college, and Wilfred's most recent craft project—a dollhouse modeled on a house in the Greek Revival style that was one of Arborville's most noteworthy.

When the salad plates were empty, Wilfred rose. "Dessert won't be a surprise," he said, "but I think it will be welcome. The Co-Op had apples direct from a farm in upstate New York. Red, but nice and tart—just right for baking."

He collected the salad plates and forks and disappeared into the kitchen. They heard the freezer door open and close. In a few minutes, he was back with a small bowl in each hand, which he delivered, one each, to Pamela and Bettina.

In each bowl was a baked apple, still rosy but

with skin crinkled from baking. Nestled against it was a generous scoop of vanilla ice cream, melting into creamy rivulets from the warmth of the apple. Wilfred fetched his own bowl, and for a bit no one spoke as they tackled the dessert with spoons that carved easily into the yielding baked apple flesh.

The mixture that Wilfred spooned into the hollowed-out apples had formed a sweet sauce as the apples baked. It tasted of brown sugar and butter and cinnamon, and chopped walnuts gave it a texture that contrasted with the soft apple flesh and melting vanilla ice cream.

"Delicious!" Bettina pronounced, and Pamela agreed as she maneuvered her spoon to capture apple, ice cream, and sauce all in the same bite.

"Do you think Felicity killed Mary too?" Pamela asked as they lingered over coffee later. In the silence induced by the delights of Wilfred's baked apples, her mind had circled back to the topic that had provided fodder for conversation on and off all evening.

Across the table, Bettina set her coffee cup back on its saucer. "Not on purpose," she said. "But she could have been making another attempt to get Brainard out of the way."

"You think she mistook Mary for her husband?" Pamela spoke without thinking, and she suspected that her expression signaled how ridiculous she considered that idea. Candlelight had created an elegant and relaxing atmosphere for the meal. She hoped the room's dimness also disguised her scorn.

Apparently, it had. Bettina continued unperturbed. "It was dark. Mary had probably put on some old jacket to carry out the compost. She was tall, even a little taller than Brainard. Maybe they kept an old jacket by the back door and shared it for grubby jobs in the yard."

"It's possible," Wilfred commented from his post at the head of the table. "Perhaps Felicity had been tracking Brainard and thought she knew his rituals—but didn't realize that he occasionally spent an evening in the Wendelstaff library."

"So, on Tuesday night, Mary had compost duty," Pamela chimed in. Perhaps Bettina's idea wasn't as outlandish as it had first seemed.

They sipped their coffee in silence. Pamela's cup was nearly empty and after one last swallow, she returned it to her saucer. "This was wonderful," she said, and started to rise. "Baked apples are a perfect autumn dessert."

Wilfred and Bettina rose too. "There will be more apples tomorrow," Bettina said. "Wilfred is going to the farmers market in Newfield."

"An apple a day keeps the doctor away," Wilfred interjected with a chuckle.

Standing at the open door, buttoned into her coat, Pamela hesitated before stepping over the threshold. "Felicity would have seen the face of her victim when she bent down to do the strangling. We're thinking when she realized she'd struck Dawn Filbert on the head Saturday night at the bonfire, she left the yarn untied because Dawn wasn't Brainard. But Tuesday night, the person who killed Mary tied the yarn to complete the job. If Felicity was the killer, why would she have done that when she saw clearly that she'd gotten the wrong person again?"

Bettina shrugged. "I don't know," she said.

Chapter 15

Leaves were starting to drop—though only some of the trees whose autumn displays were most glorious had turned their fall colors. On Pamela's trip outside to retrieve the newspaper the next morning, she realized that her black walnut tree had been shedding. Faded yellow leaves, small and shriveled, dotted the lawn and littered the front walk.

Thus, a few hours later, after she had breakfasted and dressed, Pamela fetched her bamboo rake from the garage and set about tidying her yard. Starting the first week of November, Arborville's DPW came around a few times a week to carry away leaves homeowners had raked into the street along the curbs.

Pamela was enjoying her labors. The day was bright and clear, with just the slightest breeze. People arriving for the Sunday morning service at the church next door were calling cheerful greetings to one another as they strolled past or climbed out of cars. She was nearly through, and almost wishing for another task to keep her outdoors longer—though today would be a good day for a rambling walk too—when she heard someone say her name.

"Pamela?" The voice was cheerful, if somewhat questioning. It came from the spot where the tall hedge that divided her property from Richard Larkin's met the sidewalk.

Pamela finished guiding a little pile of leaves toward the larger pile sitting near the curb and then turned toward the voice.

Framed against the glossy foliage of the hedge was an attractive woman, slender like Pamela, and as tall. But this woman apparently understood her natural advantages and had enhanced them with an outfit that featured skinny jeans, sleek leather boots reaching to the knee, and an equally sleek leather jacket. A scarf so soft it had to be cashmere, in a deep green that flattered her olive complexion, was twisted into an interesting knot at her neck. Her thick black hair was pulled into a fashionable messy-bun whose escaping tendrils called attention to her delicately modeled cheekbones.

"You *are* Pamela, aren't you?" the woman said.

Pamela nodded, aware of her baggy jeans, scuffed loafers, and ten-year-old jacket. The woman extended a hand that featured well-cared-for nails, though devoid of polish, and a few slender gold rings set with interesting stones.

"I'm Jocelyn Bidwell," she said as Pamela shifted her rake to her left hand and offered her right. "I'm so happy I'm getting to meet you at last," she added. "Rick has told me so much about you—

how helpful you were with his gardening—and your daughter and Laine and Sybil are such good friends."

The smile that accompanied this was warm and genuine, though also providing an opportunity to display perfect teeth. Pamela did her best to muster a smile of her own, her social smile at least.

"Hello," she said, then faltered. But Jocelyn was still smiling expectantly, and after a moment, Pamela rallied. "Yes," she went on, "having them next door— sometimes that is, when they visit . . . their father— has been wonderful for Penny and . . . and . . . How is the garden doing? I haven't seen it for a while because . . . there's the hedge, you know . . ."

"Not much left this time of year," Jocelyn said. "It will all come back in the spring, though. Rick credits everything he knows about perennials to you. He—"

She was interrupted by a familiar voice, Richard Larkin's voice. "Jocey?" it called from somewhere behind the hedge.

Jocelyn swiveled her head in the direction of the voice, then turned back to Pamela. "I guess he's ready." She laughed and pushed aside a tendril of hair the breeze had set adrift. "I have to run—but it was so great meeting you and talking to you. I hope we'll get to know each other better!"

And she was off.

Suddenly the clear, breezy day and the pleasant seasonal chore didn't seem as cheering. Pamela lurked near her side of the tall hedge until she heard the sound of a car engine. She peeked around the hedge and watched as Richard Larkin and Jocelyn set off for whatever Sunday outing they'd planned, thankful that their route took them up toward Arborville Avenue rather than past her own yard.

She quickly coaxed more leaves toward the large pile, in her irritated haste not caring that a few remained to speckle the grass. Then she stepped into the street to pull the piled-up leaves, rakeful by rakeful, over the curb. The task accomplished, she put the rake back in the garage and retreated to the house, where she settled at her customary end of the sofa and took up her knitting project—the cornflower-blue cashmere sweater destined to be her mother's Christmas gift.

Knitting in the middle of the day was a rare event for Pamela, one that puzzled the cats. But Catrina forsook her favorite sunny spot on the entry carpet and joined Pamela on the sofa, just as if—instead of its being not even lunchtime yet—dinner had been cooked and eaten and the day was winding down.

Pamela worked steadily at her task, thrusting the right-hand needle, looping the yarn with her finger, executing the needle dance that created a new stitch. As she worked, she willed the needles and the yarn to perform their soothing magic, but she sensed that the irritated knot between her brows had not smoothed away, the tension in her jaw had not eased, and the tight line of her lips had not relaxed.

Catrina was the first to sense a visitor. With her ears tipped forward, she raised her head and rested a paw on Pamela's thigh to gaze toward the front door. Then Ginger padded into the entry from the kitchen. When the doorbell chimed, both were already poised to greet Bettina, for that's who the visitor was.

As soon as Pamela opened the door, Bettina swept in, dressed in leggings, her red sneakers, and a cozy-looking, red-plaid poncho with fringe. "I thought you'd be on one of your walks," she exclaimed. "It's such a lovely autumn day. But I decided to check anyway—and here you are!"

She bent to bestow a quick head scratch on Catrina and coo, "Hello, kitties!" In her other hand she carried one of the canvas tote bags that were Nell's gifts to anyone she believed could be converted away from paper and plastic. The tote bag bulged with apples.

"I went to Newfield with Wilfred this morning," Bettina went on, "to the farmers market, and we bought apples, apples, and apples." She proceeded toward the kitchen, with Pamela and the cats following. "He gets so excited when the fall apple crops start to come in."

She set the tote bag on Pamela's kitchen table and began extracting apples. "This one's a Northern Spy, and here's a Macoun, and a Rhode Island Greening, and a Baldwin, and"—she held up an apple so dark it was almost black—"this one is a Sheep's Nose, and . . ."

Pamela nodded dully as the row of apples lined up on her kitchen table grew longer, some bright red, some green, some streaked red and yellow, some yellow with spots of blushing pink.

"What is it?" Bettina said at last, pausing with a reddish-purple apple in her hand. She studied Pamela's face and a small wrinkle appeared between her carefully shaped brows. "You seem a little . . . down. I didn't mean to barge in. Did I interrupt something?"

"I met Jocelyn." Pamela spoke looking at the floor.

"Ummm?" Bettina's expression barely changed, except the wrinkle went away.

"They were going somewhere today." Pamela continued looking at the floor, concentrating on one black tile in the black-and-white-checkerboard pattern.

"Oh?"

"Sometimes I wish I'd given him more of a chance."

"Hmmm."

Pamela abandoned her study of the floor to focus on Bettina's face. Bettina's expression was still bland. "Don't you care?" she blurted, hearing her voice thin out and start to break.

Instantly, Bettina's mobile face softened, and Pamela's friend was once again her caring self. "You made me promise not to talk about Richard Larkin ever again," Bettina said. "I was just trying to keep my promise."

"Oh, Bettina!" Pamela wailed. She sagged forward into the embrace that Bettina, still clutching an apple in one hand, offered.

"There, there." Bettina rubbed her back, and Pamela dipped her head and hunched over to rest her cheek on Bettina's shoulder. Pamela seldom cried, and she was startled by the gulping sobs and high-pitched moans she heard coming from herself. Burrowed against Bettina's shoulder, her face felt hot and slippery with tears.

Pamela wasn't sure how long they stood like

that. Eventually, the sobs became hiccups, and Bettina eased her into one of the chairs at the table where the two of them had seen so many happier times. After a final gentle shoulder rub, Bettina removed her hands and disappeared around the corner to the laundry room, where she knew Pamela kept a supply of fresh kitchen towels. She was back in a moment with a small towel that she moistened in cool water at the sink.

Gratefully, Pamela held the soothing towel to her face as its coolness calmed the feverish aftermath of her tears. She took slow, deep breaths. The breaths were ragged at first, but soon they smoothed out enough for her to speak.

"Have you met her?" she asked. Bettina had taken her usual chair and was studying Pamela from the other side of the table. Her expression was as mournful as Pamela imagined her own to be, but her eyes offered comfort and encouragement.

"Do you really want to talk about this?" Bettina asked, reaching for Pamela's hand, the one that didn't still hold the moist towel.

Pamela nodded. "I guess she's my neighbor now, at least part-time. She must have stayed there last night." She paused and dabbed at her eyes with the towel. "She's very . . . attractive."

"I've chatted with her a few times." Bettina shrugged. "Wilfred knows more."

"He does?" Wilfred *was* friendly, and his jaunts around the neighborhood with Woofus were often prolonged by his tendency to strike up a conversation with anyone willing to dally.

"Rick told him about her," Bettina said. "They knew each other long ago, in architecture school."

People did meet that way, Pamela knew. You'd find a kindred spirit if you were both studying the same thing. She and Michael Paterson had met in college.

"They've reconnected," Bettina added, somewhat unnecessarily.

"I guess it's too late then," Pamela murmured, half to herself. "There's nothing I can do."

Bettina hopped to her feet. "Let's put some of these apples in your nice bowl," she said. She took an apple in each hand and stepped toward the spot on the counter where Pamela's wooden fruit bowl, currently empty, reposed.

Pamela joined her, and for several minutes both focused on the constructive task of piling the apples, in the most artistic way possible, into the bowl. Then they stood back to admire their handiwork: a pyramid of apples, from deepest red to pink to striped to bright green, rising above the rim of the graceful hand-hewn bowl.

"*You* could date other people." Bettina said it in a musing tone of voice, as if the possibility had just occurred to her.

Pamela sighed. Was Bettina introducing a new theme? And would she become as insistent on this topic as she had been on the topic of Richard Larkin?

Pamela's face must have telegraphed her thoughts, because Bettina grabbed her hand and whispered, "It was just an idea."

Pamela lifted an apple from the top of the pyramid and rotated it so the slight blemish that had marred its otherwise gleaming skin was hidden. She sighed again, but this sigh reflected irritation at herself. She should have listened to Bettina earlier. Maybe she should listen to her now.

"I could," she said after a bit. "I could date other people. But how would I meet them? Arborville doesn't have that many . . . singles."

"You don't have to meet them in person, at first." Bettina was cheerful again, a mood that suited her vivid hair and makeup, and the multicolored baubles that dangled from her ears. "There's always the—"

"*Internet?*" Pamela hoped she hadn't sounded as horrified as she felt.

"Marlene Pepper's sister met someone very nice online. And she's almost sixty. They're going to have a Christmas wedding." Bettina was still holding Pamela's hand. She squeezed it.

"I'll think about it." Pamela returned the squeeze and then extracted her hand.

"You do that," Bettina said, locking her gaze into Pamela's. Pamela recognized the look as one she'd used while raising Penny. Its meaning had been, *I expect you to follow through.* Bettina collected her canvas tote and turned toward the door that led to the entry. "I'm off now," she said. "We're taking apples to the Arborville children and staying for lunch, then we're taking the boys up to the playground in the park."

Pamela followed Bettina into the entry. "Now, you take one of your walks this afternoon," Bettina said as they lingered at the front door. "It's too

nice a day to hide out indoors." Pamela nodded.
"And I'll be over tomorrow morning," Bettina
added, with her hand on the doorknob. "I'm seeing Clayborn first thing and I'll give you a full report."

She had taken a walk, and she had finished the
other front for the cornflower-blue sweater, and
she had baked the meatloaf. After dinner, she had
started a sleeve for the cornflower-blue sweater
and then dozed as a genteel British mystery unfolded on the screen before her.

Now it was the next morning and Pamela was
sitting at her computer as an email message made
its way to her inbox. When it finally arrived, she realized why it had taken so long. It was a message
from her boss at *Fiber Craft*, and it had brought
with it a whole string of attachments. "Please copy
edit these and get them back to me by next Monday morning," the message read.

She scanned the abbreviated versions of the titles
lined up at the top of the message, each marked
with a stylized paper clip and the Word logo. Her
work for the coming week would include articles
about ancient Roman dyestuffs, First Nations spindle whorls, Greek mythology, freestanding macramé
creations, and several other topics.

As she sat there, absentmindedly stroking Ginger, who had left her mother dozing in her favorite sunny spot to follow Pamela up the stairs,
another email popped into her inbox. She opened
it and was pleased to discover it was from Penny.

She postponed the decision about which article to tackle first and gave herself over to the pleasure of reading her daughter's note.

It was brief, but cheerful and informative. Penny's weekend had included an afternoon touring artists' studios in Fort Point on the occasion of the district's annual open studio tour. She'd gotten an A- on the research paper that had occupied her for the past month—a study of female artists connected with the Impressionist movement. And she'd returned to the thrift shop she'd discovered near the campus and come away with an amazing watercolor in a fancy frame.

Pamela sent a quick response, promising to write more later, and turned to the articles waiting for her attention. Freestanding macramé creations sounded interesting. And soon Pamela was immersed in the world of a pioneering woman artist, sadly now dead, who had used the techniques and materials available to her to fashion macramé structures that invoked the same awe accorded religious statuary. Pamela was just providing a dangling modifier with a proper antecedent when the doorbell chimed.

Bettina, certainly, just as she had promised, so Pamela saved her work and descended the stairs, with Ginger leading the way.

"I wouldn't say no to coffee," Bettina announced before she even stepped over the threshold. In a burgundy-gloved hand, she carried a white cardboard bakery box, suggesting that her contribution would be a sweet treat to accompany it.

Once inside, she handed the box to Pamela and slipped off her pumpkin-colored down coat, the gloves, and the burgundy beret she'd tugged at a jaunty angle over her bright coiffure. Under the coat was a pants and jacket ensemble in a striking wool plaid employing shades of yellow, orange, and burgundy. She had accessorized it with her sleek burgundy booties and amber and silver earrings.

In the kitchen, Pamela started water boiling in the kettle, smoothed a paper filter into her carafe's plastic filter cone, and measured coffee beans into her grinder. Meanwhile, Bettina opened the cupboard where Pamela kept her wedding china and arranged cups, saucers, and small plates on the table.

"I have interesting things to reveal," Bettina announced as she worked. Pamela turned, but was greeted with only a teasing smile. "First things first," Bettina said, and with a flourish, she slipped off the string that anchored the top flap of the bakery box. She flipped it back and tilted the box to display the contents. Inside were half a dozen doughnuts with the cakelike surface that marked them as the old-fashioned style.

"Pumpkin spice," Bettina explained. "This time of year it's hard to escape."

Pamela realized that the interesting revelations would not be forthcoming until she sat opposite her friend at the table with coffee and doughnuts at hand, so she returned to her task. She pressed down on the coffee grinder's cover and listened as, with growling and clattering, it reduced the beans to a fine grind. Then she tipped the grinder over the filter cone and watched its aromatic contents slide into the filter.

"Forks or fingers?" Bettina asked as she settled a doughnut onto each plate.

"Fingers, I think, for doughnuts," Pamela said.

Bettina added napkins to the table setting and a spoon for herself, then the cut-glass sugar bowl and cream pitcher, which she filled half full with heavy cream from the carton in the refrigerator.

The kettle whistled then, and the rich aroma of brewing coffee began to suffuse the small kitchen as Pamela poured the boiling water over the ground beans. And soon the wedding-china cups had been filled and Bettina had added sugar and cream to render her cup of coffee exactly the pale mocha shade she preferred.

"I wonder if these are as good as the Co-Op's pumpkin-spice crumb cake," Bettina murmured as she lifted her doughnut to her lips. She took a small nibble, then closed her eyes and chewed meditatively for a long moment. "I can't be sure," she pronounced, opening her eyes. "Try yours and tell me what you think."

Pamela left the doughnut where it lay. "Things to reveal," she prodded Bettina. "You said you had interesting things to reveal."

Bettina giggled, as if to acknowledge that she'd enjoyed prolonging the suspense occasioned by her announcement. Then she said, "The murder yarn wasn't llama wool." She waited with a slight smile, watching Pamela closely for her reaction.

"So I was right?" Pamela said. "Germaine van Houten isn't the murderer."

"Probably not." Bettina nodded.

"But Detective Clayborn *did* think it was worthwhile to have those hairs analyzed." Pamela took a cautious sip of her coffee. It was still very hot.

"Apparently so." Bettina nodded again. "He hates to admit it when he takes my advice about something, but sometimes he does take my advice." She sampled her coffee and smiled as she set the cup, which now bore the print of her bright lipstick on the rim, back on its saucer. "Perfect," she sighed. "But that's not all about Clayborn."

"He has a suspect of his own?" Pamela inquired.

"No." Bettina was obviously enjoying herself. "So he followed up our lead to the Barrows too."

"And?"

"He heard exactly the story you heard—that the Barrows, dressed as mummies, were giving out Halloween candy in Meadowside while Dawn Filbert was being killed in Arborville." Bettina picked up her doughnut and underlined her statement with an expansive gesture before raising it to her mouth.

"But remember Nell's idea?" Pamela sampled her coffee again and found that it was just right.

"Umm?" Bettina had taken a bite of the doughnut and was chewing.

"If the Barrows were dressed as mummies, how would their neighbors know they were really themselves? And my idea—that there could have been just one of them. In a mummy costume, neighbors wouldn't have known they were always seeing him—or her."

Bettina swallowed and took a sip of coffee before she spoke. Then she said, "I raised those points. I didn't tell Clayborn it was really Nell and you who thought of them."

"And he's still convinced the Barrows have alibis?" Pamela reached for her doughnut.

"The police talked to more people than we did," Bettina explained. "Some of the neighbors saw both out on their porch together, and parents chaperoning their kids heard the Barrows' voices."

"Well, that does it for the Barrows." Pamela's lips shaped a disgusted pout. "So who's left?" She bit into the doughnut, and the sweet cakelike texture, with its hint of pumpkin spice, momentarily distracted her from the serious topic of the Arborville murders.

"I could have told him about Felicity," Bettina said in a small voice.

"Umm?" Now Pamela was chewing.

"But the evidence is sketchy—just that conversation you overheard at the bus stop." Bettina shrugged. "And besides—"

She paused, and Pamela finished the thought. "It's hard to think that such a sweet young woman would do such horrible things."

"It is." Bettina nodded. "It really is."

"And if her intention was to kill Brainard, why would she have tied the yarn when she saw the person on the ground was actually Mary?"

With that, they gave themselves over to the full enjoyment of coffee and the Co-Op's pumpkin-spice doughnuts.

Chapter 16

"Oh, dear." The expression in Nell's faded blue eyes was bleak, and her normally cheerful mouth had gone slack. "So that means no progress at all has been made in figuring out who's responsible for the Arborville murders."

Bettina had just updated Nell on the previous morning's meeting with Detective Clayborn. But Pamela and Bettina had kept from her, as they'd done previously, the suspicion that Felicity might— just *might*—be the murderer.

Nell sighed. "I haven't been much help at all in your detecting, have I?" She sighed again.

The three were standing around the table in Nell's kitchen, where she had set out cups, saucers, plates, silverware, and napkins in preparation for that evening's meeting of Knit and Nibble. The air was infused with a hint of warm sugariness, and an interesting baked object in a rectangular Pyrex dish rested on the counter.

The doorbell chimed then, saving them from having to agree or disagree with Nell's statement. In a moment, they heard the door open and Harold offering a hearty welcome, followed by Roland asking if he was late.

"I had to drive all the way to the next block to find a spot on the legal side of the street," Roland said, sounding peevish. "I hope my car will be safe down there."

"I wouldn't give it another thought." Harold's voice took on the soothing tones of the doctor he'd been before retirement. "Your car will be fine."

By this time, Pamela, Bettina, and Nell had made their way past the gallery of travel souvenirs that decorated the hallway connecting the kitchen to the entry and the living room beyond.

"You're actually the first one," Nell said, "except for Pamela and Bettina, of course." She touched Roland on the shoulder.

"I'm not really the first one then, am I?" Roland surveyed the three women standing at the end of the hallway. "If they're already here. And *you're* here. That makes three. But then, you live here, so maybe you don't count . . ."

"No matter." Nell laughed, cheerful again. "Do go in and take a seat."

Roland transferred his briefcase to his right hand and lifted his left wrist to consult his impressive watch. "It's five after seven," he announced as he stepped toward the living room. "I *am* late, and two more people are still due."

"We're here! We're here!" Holly peeked through the gap between the door, which was still ajar, and the doorframe.

Harold had followed Roland into the living room, so Bettina tugged the door back open to admit Holly and Karen.

Soon the whole group except for Harold—who had retreated to his den—was settled in the Bascombs' spacious living room. Beneath a high, beamed ceiling, a comfortable sofa faced the natural stone fireplace. Roland had headed for the sofa and had been joined by Holly and Karen. Pamela and Bettina sat side by side on one of the small love seats, upholstered in faded chintz, that flanked the fireplace, and Nell sat on the other.

In summer, the grand fireplace held an attractive arrangement of dried flowers, but with the onset of cold weather, the fireplace reverted to its true purpose—evidenced by half-burned logs in a bed of extinguished cinders and ash.

For a few minutes there was silence, as people drew their knitting from their knitting bags—or, in Roland's case, his elegant briefcase—and pondered it, as one ponders the page of a book one has set down and then picked up again to recall exactly where one was. Pamela resumed work on the sleeve for the cornflower-blue sweater, and next to her Bettina took up the Nordic-style sweater that was to be Wilfred's Christmas gift. She'd gotten to the point where the navy-blue background was to be interspersed with a row of snowflakes, and she was studying the directions as she absentmindedly fingered the skein of white yarn that was about to be deployed.

As if determined to focus the conversation away from what was probably on everyone's mind, Nell spoke up once yarn was in play and needles were reliably clicking. "I've steamed and frozen my pumpkin," she said. "All ready for Thanksgiving."

"Pumpkin spice!" Holly's hands were busy with her knitting—another stocking for the children at the women's shelter. Otherwise, Pamela was sure the exclamation would have been accompanied by an enthusiastic hand clap. "I know you make your own pumpkin pies and I hope you'll teach me this year."

"Of course." Nell aimed a smile toward where Holly sat on the sofa.

"You don't have to wait till Thanksgiving for pumpkin spice." Pamela felt the love seat quiver as Bettina leaned forward. "The Co-Op has pumpkin-spice crumb cake now—and the other day they had pumpkin-spice doughnuts too."

"Pumpkin spice is one of the best things about fall," Holly said. "It's such a magical flavor."

Nell's smile grew indulgent. "It's just a blend of various spices, dear. You can mix it up yourself."

"Will you show me? When we make our pies together?" Holly's dimple appeared as her smile revealed her perfect teeth. Her dark hair was pulled into a casual bun tonight. Bronze-colored earrings that resembled tiny abstract mobiles dangled from her earlobes.

Before Nell could answer, a sound that was not exactly a word erupted from Roland. The sound apparently signaled displeasure, because Roland followed it up by saying, "I, for one, will be quite glad when Thanksgiving is finally over and we can stop hearing about pumpkin spice." He paused to gaze first at Nell and then at Holly, who sat next to him on the sofa. Next to Holly, Karen raised a délicate hand to her mouth, risking a dropped stitch as she abandoned a needle.

Ignoring Karen's alarm, Roland went on. "Of course, then what will it be?" he said in a disapproving tone that implied he knew the answer. "Peppermint? And the Christmas music has started already."

Holly's smile turned into a laugh. "No need to be grumpy," she said. "Most people like Christmas. And we're all thinking about it already, aren't we? So why not have the music? Nell and I are making the stockings for the children at the shelter, and Pamela's making the sweater for her mother, and Bettina's making the sweater for Wilfred."

"And *you're* making the sweater for Melanie," Bettina chimed in with a pointed look in Roland's direction. "So don't be such a spoilsport."

Seeming chastened, Roland addressed himself to his knitting as if it required the focus he might give to studying a legal brief, and no one said anything for a time. But the silence wasn't the meditative silence of knitters in thrall to the rhythm of their needles. It was an awkward silence, one in which perhaps a few knitters wished they had spoken a bit more gently.

So Holly lowered her knitting to her lap, leaned toward Roland, and tipped her head to study the swath of knitting hanging from his needles. "I really do love that camel color," she exclaimed. "You made a good choice."

"It wasn't my choice." Roland's busy fingers didn't pause. "Melanie picked it out."

Undeterred, Holly pressed on. "And you already

finished the sleeve you were working on last week! What is that? The back?"

"The front, actually."

"Are they different?" Holly raised her head to gaze earnestly at Roland.

"Of course they're different. It's a V-neck sweater."

"Melanie is going to love it, I'm sure." Holly resumed her previous posture and took up her knitting again. The stocking she was working on was bright red and she was just approaching the heel. "I've made up my mind," she said suddenly. "My next project is going to be a Christmas present for Desmond. A sweater, but I just have to decide what color." She leaned toward Roland again. "Maybe camel . . ."

Roland did set his knitting down now. And then he raised his left wrist and gave his arm a twitch to expose his impressive watch. "Eight o'clock," he announced. "I believe it's time for our break."

Pamela and Bettina were on their feet even before Nell rose. And the three motioned to Holly and Karen to stay put. As they headed for the kitchen, Pamela could hear Holly asking Roland if he thought camel would be a good color for Desmond's sweater. Or maybe navy-blue?

When they reached the kitchen, Nell spooned coffee from the canister on her counter into the basket of her ancient aluminum percolator. She added water, set the percolator on the stove, and lit the burner under it. On a second burner, she started water boiling for tea and then measured tea leaves into the squat brown teapot that waited on the table.

"You can serve the nibble," she said as she worked. "Pamela or Bettina. Knives are in the drawer to the left of the sink."

Bettina fetched a knife from the drawer and bent over the Pyrex baking dish on the counter. "This looks—and smells—yummy," she said. "But I'm not sure I know what it is."

"Bread pudding, of course," Nell said. "I hate to waste perfectly good food—and when leftovers of that nice bread the Co-Op calls country white go stale, bread pudding is the perfect thing to do with it."

"What else is in here?" Bettina was still bent over the baking dish.

The surface of the bread pudding was rippled. On looking closer, Pamela realized the effect was created by torn bits of bread. But the bits of bread had been bathed in a pale golden liquid which, on being baked, had shaded to a toasty brown around the edges of the baking dish. Here and there, raisins punctuated the ripples.

"Eggs and milk, vanilla and raisins." Nell stepped toward the table and bestowed a fond look on her creation. "A tiny bit of sugar, though it's hardly necessary with the raisins."

The teakettle's whistle summoned her to the stove then. She seized the kettle and edged back to the table, where she lifted the lid from the teapot and tipped the kettle over it. A cloud of steam rose as boiling water submerged the waiting tea leaves.

Bettina studied the bread pudding for a moment and tapped the knife blade along the edge of the baking dish, as if mentally dividing the bread pudding's length into six sections. Then she cut, and cut again crosswise, making twelve pieces. Pamela, meanwhile, had found a spatula in the drawer the knife came from.

The coffee had been perking for a few minutes at this point, contributing both a cheerful gurgle and a bracing aroma to the kitchen's atmosphere.

As Bettina held out the plates one by one, Pamela eased a square of bread pudding onto each one. Nell had set out seven plates, suggesting Harold would join the group for the nibble portion of the evening.

"Shall we serve them just like this?" Bettina asked, sounding a bit skeptical—though to Pamela, the bread pudding squares looked perfectly appealing, with the strata of bread layers interspersed with raisins visible on the cut sides.

"The bread pudding is still warm." Nell turned away from the stove, where she had just replaced the teakettle, and faced Bettina. "Maybe warm enough to melt ice cream"—a tiny closemouthed smile teased her lips—"but I don't know if anyone would be interested."

"I'll ask them!" Bettina exclaimed, and she set off down the hallway.

Meanwhile, Nell was filling coffee cups as Pamela checked the sugar bowl, with its stylized wheat-and-wildflower trim. It was nearly full, and Nell directed her to the refrigerator for cream to fill the matching cream pitcher.

Bettina returned with Harold in tow. She announced that everyone wanted ice cream with their bread pudding, and Harold fetched a carton of vanilla ice cream from the freezer. He and Bettina set to work adding scoops of ice cream to the squares of bread pudding and delivering the plates to the living room. Pamela made sure that everyone had napkins and silverware.

After many trips back and forth, Nell, Harold, Pamela, and Bettina took their places with the other Knit and Nibblers around Nell's large coffee table, which offered ample room for cups and saucers and plates of bread pudding. The sugar bowl and cream pitcher passed from hand to hand and soon everyone was settled, ready to sample Nell's frugal creation and with coffee or tea sugared and creamed to perfection.

"This is just awesome," Holly cooed. For her first bite, she'd carved off a forkful of the bread pudding and scooped up a bit of ice cream as well. "I honestly and truly have never tasted bread pudding before and now I've learned another amazing thing about cooking from Nell." She beamed at Nell, who had resumed her place on the love seat to the left of the fireplace. "Using stale bread! Who would think of such a thing?"

"Lots of people had to, dear," Nell said. "They had no choice." But she tempered the admonition with a smile.

Pamela had eaten bread pudding, but she suspected it was one of those dishes for which hardly any cook consulted a cookbook. Her grandmother had mixed up batches using a recipe known only to herself and which had perhaps been learned at the side of her own grandmother, who learned it from her grandmother before her.

So, she tasted Nell's bread pudding wondering if, like handwriting, it would bear the mark of its creator's personality. The texture, thanks to the egg and milk, was rich and smooth—as if the stale bread had been transformed into a dense cake. Sugar had been added, but not so much as to over-power the raisins, which were themselves sweet, and plump with moisture they'd absorbed from the milk. The flavor hinted at cinnamon too, and the vanilla Nell had mentioned.

"Very good," Pamela commented to no one in particular, because Bettina was perched on the very edge of the love seat and was leaning precipi-tously forward, the better to converse across the coffee table with Nell and Harold. The three were deep in a discussion of a topic Bettina was re-searching for the *Advocate*: Arborville's ongoing at-tempts to ban people seeking a shortcut to the George Washington Bridge from the town's resi-dential streets.

Pamela followed her taste of the bread pudding with a sip of coffee. The perked coffee was stronger and a little more acidic than the drip coffee she had come to prefer. But knowing it was the prod-uct of Nell's ancient aluminum percolator and drinking it in tandem with such a homey treat as bread pudding made it taste just right.

Snatches of the conversation about the bridge traffic drifted her way, but she was happy simply to listen as she alternated eating and sipping, enjoy-ing the way the vanilla ice cream smoothed out the aggressive flavor of the coffee.

On the sofa, Roland seemed content—perhaps even relieved—to be left to his own thoughts too. Dark head bent toward blond as Holly and Karen conferred earnestly about Karen's search for the perfect dining room table. Karen and Dave Dowling had furnished their fixer-upper house with Ikea and hand-me-downs initially and were gradually upgrading.

As Pamela added her empty plate to the others already on the coffee table, Nell half rose and surveyed the group. "Would anyone like more of anything?" she asked. "There's plenty in the kitchen."

"No, thanks . . . quite satisfied . . . delicious but full" came the responses, but Harold popped to his feet anyway. He hurried toward the entry and vanished down the hallway that led to the kitchen. In a moment he was back, bearing a large wooden bowl. As he approached the group and lowered it, Pamela could see that it was full of tantalizing foil- and cellophane-wrapped tidbits.

"Oh, Harold!" Nell exclaimed, half annoyed and half laughing. "You told me the trick-or-treaters took it all."

"All that we had out" —Harold tried unsuccessfully to hide a smile—"but I had some in reserve— in case we ran short." He tipped the bowl toward Roland and said, "Care for a piece?"

Roland dipped in a hand and took a foil-wrapped truffle. Harold continued along, offering candy to Holly and Karen and then edging between the end of the sofa and the love seat to extend the bowl to Bettina and Pamela. At last, he retreated toward the other love seat, where he'd been sitting with Nell, and lowered the bowl to the coffee table right in front of his wife.

But before it even made contact with the table's surface, Nell was on her feet. "We've all had quite enough sugar for one evening," she said, no longer only half-annoyed. "And you know perfectly well I don't want any candy. Please take that back to the kitchen."

"But our guests . . ." Harold waved a hand around the little cluster of knitters.

"Maybe just one more," Bettina murmured, reaching across the table for a mini candy bar.

"I'll collect a few plates then," Harold said, and Pamela leaned forward to help stack plates and consolidate silverware.

He headed for the kitchen with a small pile of plates, and Pamela followed with the rest. But as they passed back through the entry on their way to collect cups and saucers, they both stopped at once.

Harold stepped closer to the front door and cocked his head, as if listening. Pamela listened too. From somewhere outside came the muffled sound of someone shrieking. Harold opened the door, and the shrieking was suddenly much more audible.

Pamela glanced toward the living room to see if the sound now carried far enough to have piqued the curiosity of the other Knit and Nibblers. But no heads were turned in the direction of the entry, and the cheerful hum of conversation suggested that no one had noticed anything.

Harold stepped out onto the porch and Pamela followed. The shrieking was definitely coming from a woman, a hysterical woman. And from the direction of the sound, the confrontation—assuming she was shrieking *at* someone—was taking place in Brainard Covington's driveway. Brainard's porch light was on, but the light didn't reach that far. Besides, his car was parked at the end of the driveway, and it hid the figure—or more likely, *figures*—from view.

Pamela caught a word here and there. The diatribe seemed to be about love, love denied, and Brainard's ambitions for his son, coupled with resentment of both Brainard and his late wife. The voice strained and faltered, rising and falling in pitch. Pamela felt her own throat tighten in response.

Harold and Pamela looked at each other. In his gentle face, Pamela saw a mirror of her own feelings. How miserable this poor woman must be! Then, from behind them, came another voice—a practical no-nonsense voice.

"What are you two doing out there?" the voice said. It was Nell. She joined them on the porch, but before she could say anything else, a final, desperate shriek reached their ears. It resolved into words: "Your son should have had a different—" Father? Mother? The end of the sentence was muffled by sobbing.

"Oh my," Nell said. She clutched Harold's hand. "We should call 911. It was just last week that—"

But it seemed another murder was not in the offing. A shadowy figure emerged from behind Brainard's car and made its way to the passenger-side door. It opened the door, and a light went on in the car. It retreated into the deeper darkness and reemerged escorting a smaller figure, bundled in a coat and knit hat, sobbing more quietly now and with face buried in mittened hands.

The figure was docile as Brainard seated her—it was a *her*—in the car. A few moments later, he had taken his place behind the steering wheel, and the car was on its way down the street.

"No need to involve ourselves in our neighbors' business." Nell was her sensible self again. She went on, "We have knitting to tend to." She'd left the door slightly ajar, and now she seized the knob as she prepared to follow her own directive.

The door swung back a few inches, then stopped with a thump. From behind the door came a startled squeal. Nell peered around the edge of the door. After a moment, she eased it back to reveal Bettina and Holly, with Karen hovering a few paces behind Holly.

"We have knitting to tend to," Nell repeated, stepping over the threshold. Harold stood aside and waved Pamela through the doorway with a courtly gesture, then he followed her into the house. With Nell leading the way, the small group proceeded back to the living room, where Roland waited on the sofa.

Bettina fell in step beside Pamela and gave her a wide-eyed look that combined curiosity and alarm. *I heard most of it*, she mouthed soundlessly.

But Nell's manner made it plain that whatever had just happened across the street was not to become fodder for conversation. "I believe you were about to clear away the cups and saucers, Harold," she said as she lowered herself onto the love seat where she'd been sitting.

Pamela and Bettina had reached their seats as well, but Pamela stooped toward the coffee table for her own cup and saucer.

"No need, no need," Harold said cheerfully. He bustled about, attending to his chore as knitting resumed, though with a bit of discreet whispering between Holly and Karen.

Chapter 17

Pamela and Bettina saved their discussion for later. As soon as they'd climbed into Pamela's car, though, and even before Pamela had inserted her key in the ignition, Bettina spoke. "I could barely concentrate and I'm sure I dropped at least a dozen stitches," she said as she grabbed Pamela's arm. "Do you think that could have been Felicity? You saw things. I just heard them."

Pamela took a sharp breath, like a backward sigh. "She was muffled up in a coat and knitted hat—and mittens—and she was hiding her face in her hands . . ." She shook her head sadly. "So there was no way to identify . . . *her*."

"The voice was definitely a woman's," Bettina agreed. "But when you're shrieking like that, you don't sound like yourself."

"Who else could it be, though?" Pamela murmured. "The things she was talking about—*shrieking* about, really. Love being denied and it's Brainard's fault and Brainard's son should have had a different . . . it sounded like 'father.' "

"Or 'mother'?" It was too dark to see Bettina's face, but her voice conveyed the uncertainty that Pamela was sure her expression revealed.

"Why 'mother'?" Pamela thought for a minute, trying out the idea, even though Bettina hadn't sounded very certain about what she'd heard. "Maybe Felicity blamed them both," she said suddenly. "If Felicity *is* the killer, maybe Mary's murder wasn't a case of mistaken identity."

Bettina finished the thought, her voice confident now: "And that's why the yarn around Mary's neck wasn't left untied, like it was with Dawn Filbert."

"I guess Brainard took her home," Pamela said. "Maybe she'd been on the phone with Herc and he was saying they had to wait because of his father, and then she just exploded and showed up at Brainard's door and it all came pouring out."

"That *is* the most likely explanation."

"It doesn't necessarily mean Felicity is the killer, though." Pamela twisted her key in the ignition, and with a rough grumble, her car came to life.

"It doesn't?"

"She could blame both of Herc's parents for keeping her and Herc apart, but blaming and killing are two different things." Pamela shifted into drive and eased away from the curb.

The maze was designed to puzzle. Every few yards, a choice had to be made—to go left or right.

But which direction would lead to the exit and which would lead deeper into confusion? Pamela had a secret, though. She'd trailed a strand of yarn as she roamed the confusing passages, and now the same strand of yarn marked the way out.

She gathered it as she walked, absentmindedly rolling it back into a tidy ball. She was close to the exit, she was sure, because the ball had grown nearly as large as it had been when her journey into the maze began—and because the sounds and sensations of the outside world were imping- ing on her consciousness.

Notably, a telephone was ringing, and she was aware of a soft weight on her chest. When she opened her eyes, a pair of amber eyes gazed back at her, and Catrina's forepaws began a gentle kneading motion in the region of her collarbone. But the phone had to be dealt with.

Pamela grasped Catrina around her midsection, sat up, and deposited the cat back among the bed- clothes. Without bothering with slippers or robe, she hurried across the hall to her office and seized the phone.

"Pamela!" said an urgent voice. "Did I wake you?"

"Yes, no . . . what is it?"

It was Nell, though barely sounding like her usual serene self.

"Brainard is dead!" Nell said, her voice thinning to a squeak. "Landscapers—" The thought was in- terrupted by a moan, then a muffled thump sug- gested the phone had been dropped.

The next voice Pamela heard was that of Harold. "It's not a happy time up here," he said in tones that were nonetheless comforting in their gentle gravity.

"What on earth happened?" Pamela felt behind her for her desk chair and sank into it. "What did the landscapers do?"

"Leaf season," Harold said. "The Lyon-Covingtons had a landscaping service. The landscapers found Brainard when they ventured into the backyard this morning. He was lying near his compost heap."

"Are the police . . . ?"

"Just here now." In the background, Pamela could hear Nell weeping. Harold continued, "I was out getting the paper and one of the landscapers came running down Brainard's driveway, looking all frantic. He saw me and shouted something in Spanish. But luckily, I know a little Spanish. So I went back with him to see what had happened— and then I came home and called the police."

The weeping in the background subsided and Pamela heard Nell say, between hiccups, "The yarn, Harold. The yarn."

Harold responded to the cue before Pamela could say anything—and what he said was no surprise. Brainard had been knocked out and then strangled with several strands of yarn tied in a bow around his neck.

"The yarn was definitely tied?" Pamela said.

"I saw it with my own eyes," Harold confirmed. The weeping had started up again. "I have to go now," he added. "Someone's at the door and it's probably the police."

"Is Nell okay?" Pamela asked quickly. The sobs were alarming because Nell tended to be quite stoic in the face of adversity.

"She can't forgive herself." Harold sighed. "She thinks the murder is her fault because she brushed off the scene in Brainard's driveway last night. She keeps saying we should have called the police then."

"I'll be over," Pamela said just before Harold hung up.

She was shivering even though her nightgown was flannel, but instead of fetching her robe, Pamela keyed in Bettina's number.

Ten minutes later, dressed in jeans and a sweater, she stood at her front door watching through the lace that curtained the oval window as Bettina bustled up onto the porch. She opened the door before Bettina had a chance to ring and Bettina swept in. She'd tugged her purple beret over her bright hair and knotted a purple scarf at the neck of her pumpkin-colored coat, but her face was puffy with sleep and bare of makeup.

"What a thing!" Bettina panted. "What a thing! Poor Nell."

Pamela had fed the cats as soon as she descended the stairs, but there was no time for a human breakfast. She took her warmest jacket from the closet, and her own purple scarf—violet, really.

"We are absolutely not *walking* up that hill," Bettina said as Pamela buttoned herself into her jacket and wound her scarf around her neck.

"Of course not!" Pamela had almost said, "Why not?"—but their errand was too serious to tease Bettina about her aversion to walking.

As Pamela steered her serviceable compact up Orchard Street then up the hill that formed the Palisades, she filled Bettina in on what Harold had said. "And," she concluded, "Brainard was obviously killed sometime between when we overheard the shrieking in his driveway last night and early this morning when the landscapers showed up."

They were not surprised by the scene that greeted them when they reached the block where the Bascombs lived—though neighbors just stepping outside to collect their morning papers might have been. From the corner, Pamela and Bettina could see two police cars parked at careless angles in front of the Lyon-Covington house, the lights on their roofs flashing in sudden blazes like flashbulbs.

Pamela drove no farther than a few hundred feet after she made the turn. She parked on the Bascombs' side of the street, and she and Bettina finished their journey on foot. As they drew nearer, they saw that yellow crime scene tape already marked the Lyon-Covingtons' property as off-limits. It stretched along the front edge of the lot and across the mouth of the driveway, and then snaked toward the backyard. Pamela recognized a young officer she had recently seen arranging orange cones at the entrance to a street where an electrical wire had come down. He was now stationed on the driveway with his pleasant features struggling to look stern.

Pamela and Bettina made their way up the steps that wound through azalea and rhododendron bushes to the Bascombs' porch. Pamela rang the doorbell, and in a few moments Harold greeted them with murmured thanks and a grateful smile.

"The police just left," he explained as he led them down the hall to the kitchen after draping jacket and coat and scarves on the coatrack in the entry. "Just two of the uniform guys. Clayborn is across the street at the crime scene and I'm to talk to him down at the police station later this morning."

Nell seemed calmer than she'd sounded on the phone. She was sitting at her kitchen table wearing an ancient plaid flannel bathrobe and sipping tea, and she offered them a faint version of her usual smile as they entered. Their friend's improved state—plus the sunlight pouring through the window and aroma of fresh-perked coffee—had the effect of lifting Pamela and Bettina's spirits considerably.

Harold pulled out chairs for them and waited as they settled themselves. Then, without even inquiring, he set cups and saucers in front of them and reached for the percolator. The sight and smell of the coffee as it swirled into the cups lifted their spirits yet further. Cream and sugar sat waiting on the table in the wheat-and-wildflower pitcher and bowl.

Bettina began her ritual of transforming the dark and bitter contents of her cup into the pale and sweet concoction she favored, but Pamela took an eager sip, enjoying the jolt of the stronger perked brew.

The coffee loosened her tongue. "It's not your fault," she said, reaching for the wrinkled hand resting on the table and giving it a squeeze. "Calling the police when we heard the shrieking wouldn't have saved Brainard's life. The person shrieking at him on the driveway didn't kill him then—because we saw his car drive away. And the person didn't kill him when they got to their destination—because how would he have gotten back home?"

Nell acknowledged the comforting gesture by returning the squeeze. But her words suggested she wasn't convinced by Pamela's reasoning.

"But what if the person killed him en route, or when they got wherever they were going—and then brought the body back?"

"Why would the person do that?" Bettina looked up from her vigorous stirring.

"Yes, why?" Pamela agreed. "Suppose the person realized neighbors might have heard the shrieking? Why bring the body back then? Why not just hide it somewhere? The longer it took for anyone to discover Brainard was dead, the less likely the murder could be linked with the scene in the driveway."

Harold had not sat down. As Pamela spoke, she had been aware of something in progress behind her—a cupboard and a drawer opening, silverware jingling, and the soft clang of china against Formica. Now, instead of a response from Nell, the voice she heard was Harold's.

"How about bread pudding for breakfast?" he inquired.

Bettina had returned to her stirring. Now she looked up again with a surprised smile, but her expression soon turned hopeful. "I suppose it's too early to have it with ice cream?" she whispered.

"Yes, it is," Nell said, reverting for a moment to her familiar self. "Bread pudding is sweet enough."

"And there was plenty left from last night." Harold slid small plates containing squares of bread pudding in front of Pamela and Bettina. He followed up with a serving for Nell and then one for himself at the empty chair he would occupy. Once napkins and forks had been distributed, he took his place.

"This is how we ate our bread pudding when I was a boy," he said, winking at Bettina as he reached for the cream pitcher. Tipping the pitcher, he poured a goodly amount of cream over the pale gold cube, with its rippled top shading to toasty brown in spots.

Nell uttered a sound that resembled a discreet clearing of the throat, but she didn't say anything. With a fond but teasing glance at his wife, Harold passed the cream pitcher to Bettina, remarking, "Not that your delicious bread pudding requires any enhancement, my dear."

Bettina applied cream to her bread pudding and offered the pitcher to Pamela, who dribbled a bit on her own just to be sociable.

For a time, the silence was broken only by the clicking of forks against plates and the gentle chime of cups being returned to saucers. Then Pamela turned to Nell and waited until Nell looked her way.

"There's something we didn't tell you, even though you've been our partner in crime . . . solving," Pamela said. "And I think we should."

"What?" Nell's eyes widened and her mouth remained half-open.

Pamela shifted her gaze to meet Bettina's eyes.

"Felicity . . ." Bettina's voice trailed off, and after a moment, she added, "You explain."

Pamela described the conversation she'd overheard between Felicity and Herc at the bus stop, and then she backtracked to the day she and Bettina had eaten lunch at Hyler's and Bettina had noticed that Felicity was no longer wearing her engagement ring.

"The engagement had been broken off," Bettina interjected, "and she was so upset. But she said it wasn't Herc's fault."

"That voice in the driveway last night." Pamela couldn't bear to watch Nell's face, so she stared down at the nubbin of bread pudding that remained on her plate. "One of the things it seemed to say was that Brainard's son should have had a different father."

"Motive," Nell moaned. Then she touched Pamela's arm, and Pamela had to look at her. Surprisingly, Nell appeared more irritated than sad. "But, Pamela," she said, "you just tried to convince me that the shrieking person in the driveway couldn't possibly be the killer. So even if that was Felicity out there last night—"

Harold took up the thought. "We saw Brainard drive away with the shrieking person, and why would that person have killed him somewhere else and then brought the body back?" Summoning up the authority that had characterized his professional life, he tipped his head forward and locked eyes with Pamela. "Your own words," he said. "Your own words."

Pamela had to admit she was having trouble finding her way. If only there was a strand of yarn to follow through the twists and turns presented by this mystery.

"I was thinking out loud." Pamela shrugged. "But it's hard to deny that Felicity has a motive."

They all pondered that thought for a bit as Harold popped up and checked the percolator to see if any coffee was left. "A bit," he observed. "I can warm it up." Back at the table, he tapped the side of the teapot and peeked inside. "Plenty left in here," he reported as Nell reached for the teapot and refilled her cup.

"I'd like a splash of coffee." Bettina pushed her cup forward. Harold returned to the stove and soon the aroma of slightly scorched coffee, accompanied by a scalding sound, emanated from that direction. A few minutes later, he tipped the ancient percolator over Bettina's cup, and with a sizzle and puff of steam, the last few ounces of coffee surged from the spout.

Bettina hadn't even begun sugaring and creaming her infusion of coffee when she spoke. "I have to tell Clayborn about Felicity now," she announced suddenly, "about the conversation you overheard, Pamela, and about the shrieking last night. And you're talking to him today, Harold. You'll have to tell him what you overheard last night too. He'll interview her and he'll check on whatever she presents as an alibi and"—she raised a fastidiously manicured hand and crossed her fingers—"hopefully she has one and it proves to be legitimate . . . and she'll be in the clear." With that, Bettina reached for the sugar bowl.

"I certainly hope so." Nell's expression was somber. "I'm sure of it, in fact. Aside from the fact—a big fact—that Felicity is too small to kill Brainard, or even the others, if the shrieking person was Felicity and Brainard took her home, we're saying she walked all the way back up the hill just on the chance that he'd be taking out his compost at ten p.m.?"

"That's a good point," Pamela said. "Even if the shrieking person was Felicity, that doesn't mean Felicity was the killer."

Nell had been sipping her tea, and as if the fresh cup had provoked a fresh idea, she spoke up. "Maybe the killer was somebody else who was after Brainard the whole time and really was confused about who was wearing which costume. So maybe there's a Wendelstaff College connection."

Bettina nodded vigorously, and her bangs—her hair had been groomed more hastily that morning than was her habit—flopped over her forehead, grazing her eyebrows. Ignoring them, she nodded again. "Yes!" she exclaimed. "A Wendelstaff connection. Clayborn will think of it, if he hasn't already. A Wendelstaff connection is *much* more likely than to accuse that sweet Felicity Winkle. But we could look into it too. Sometimes the police put people off, or they don't ask the right questions."

"I am your partner in crime . . . solving." Nell emphasized the point by thumping the table with her fist. "I will go to the classics department at Wendelstaff and see what I can find out about department politics."

Bettina smiled. "This week's edition of the *Advocate* will cover Brainard's murder, of course . . . but aside from that, the contents will be a little sparse."

Her smile became mischievous. "Unless," she went on, "my editor would be interested in an article on the void that will be created in the Wendelstaff classics department by Brainard's death."

"I'm sure he would," Pamela said, and Nell echoed her words.

"Tomorrow morning, then?" Bettina glanced at Pamela and then at Nell.

"Tomorrow morning." They nodded in unison.

As Pamela and Bettina walked back to Pamela's car, a huge silver van with the logo of the county sheriff's department was just turning the corner.

Chapter 18

"You'd think Clayborn could have made time in his schedule yesterday for me, wouldn't you?" Bettina was revisiting a point she'd already made several times that morning, but Pamela murmured assent. "After all," Bettina went on, her voice shading from irritation to pride, "my reporting for the *Advocate* shapes Arborville's opinion of its police department."

"It does," Pamela agreed. "And you *will* be talking to him this afternoon."

"I certainly hope so—otherwise nobody will know anything about Brainard's death that they don't read in the *Register*." Bettina was panting slightly. In company with Nell, they were hurrying along one of the paths that crisscrossed the leaf-strewn grass of the Wendelstaff College quadrangle.

Nell spoke up. "But you'll do your article about

the void created in the Wendelstaff classics department by Brainard's death."

"We'll see what his colleagues say." Bettina had fallen a bit behind and raised her voice to be heard. "Maybe there is no void. Maybe they're glad he's gone."

"That would be a story too," Pamela said. "Wouldn't it?" She paused so Bettina could catch up, and Nell paused too. The three friends presented a study in contrasts. Nell was bundled in her faithful gray wool coat, Bettina was a vivid figure against the autumnal landscape in her pumpkin and purple ensemble, and Pamela wore jeans and a nondescript brown jacket. A brisk wind made her wish she'd added a hat and scarf to her outfit.

"I'm not sure the *Advocate* would print that." Bettina made a sound partway between a laugh and a pant.

"The classics department is in that building right ahead." Pamela gestured toward an impressive brick structure with white columns. "I checked online. It's the oldest one on campus, dating way back to the founding of the college."

The building's massive doors opened into a dim foyer, with hallways leading back from each side and a stairway rising up straight ahead. The ancient wooden floors creaked underfoot and the space smelled pleasantly of old wood. A directory indicated that the classics department was on the second floor.

Bettina led the way, after eyeing the stairs warily and taking a few minutes to catch her breath. Once they reached the second floor, a sign posted next to a door at the end of the paneled corridor they found themselves in identified their destination.

The floor creaked on this level too, and Pamela noticed she was walking on tiptoe as they approached the door that led to the classics department. They entered to find a small room that looked as if it had been furnished when the building was built and not touched since: wooden desk, wooden filing cabinets, straight-backed wooden chairs. The only signs that it was the twenty-first century were the computer monitor on the desk and the young woman sitting behind the desk. Her hair was bright chartreuse and she wore a stud resembling a tiny skull in her left nostril.

Bettina introduced herself as a reporter for the *Arborville Advocate* and explained her errand. Then she noted apologetically, "I know it's awfully soon to be asking about this, but the *Advocate* is a weekly and I have a deadline."

The young woman's lips, which were painted a deep maroon color, parted in an understanding smile, but she shook her head regretfully. "Dr. Stafford is in a seminar till noon," she said, "and after lunch"—she fingered her computer mouse and consulted the monitor in front of her—"he has a meeting of the faculty senate." She looked up. "Can you come back tomorrow?"

"It will be too late for my deadline," Bettina said. The young woman's expression was as dejected as the tone of Bettina's voice.

"Maybe another faculty member?" Pamela ventured. After all, the real purpose of their errand was to figure out whether any of Brainard's colleagues had hated him enough to kill him. A department chair might take a diplomatic tack.

"Maybe." The young woman nodded encouragingly. "The faculty offices are along the corridor"—she pointed to the door with a finger tipped by a maroon fingernail—"right out there."

But the door leading from the office opened of its own accord before Pamela could reach for the knob—or rather, someone opened it from the other side. A pleasant-looking young man burst in, nearly treading on Pamela's toes.

"I need to see Dr. Stafford right away," he announced.

"Greg!" The young woman smiled. "How are you doing?"

"Good," he said. "I hope, but I've got to get a letter from Stafford by tomorrow morning."

The young woman repeated the message she'd given earlier: seminar followed by faculty senate. "But," she said, "give me the information and I'll tell him."

Bettina and Nell began to edge toward the door, but Pamela lingered, feigning interest in a framed photograph that showed ornate columns silhouetted against a dramatic sunset. She caught enough of the conversation between Greg and the young woman to learn that he had an interview for a teaching job the next day, but the interview was contingent on a letter from his former employer.

When Pamela stepped back out into the corridor, she saw Bettina tapping on a door near the head of the stairs as Nell stood by. After a few moments, it was clear that no one was inside. Pamela

made her way across the creaking floor to join
them.

"We tried that one too." Bettina pointed at a
door closer to the office they had just left. "No
luck there either." The door they were standing in
front of seemed to serve in part as a bulletin board
for its occupant. Several cartoons involving characters dressed in togas were taped to its wooden surface, along with a clipping about an archeological
excavation in Italy, where the largest wine jug yet
found had been retrieved. In the margin, someone had written, "We always knew they liked to
party."

"I suppose most of the professors have classes in
the morning," Nell observed, "and if they don't,
there's no reason to come to the campus."

"He won't be in." The voice came from behind
them. "He's on sabbatical this term."

The owner of the voice was Greg, the young
man they'd encountered in the department
chair's office. He seemed older than the typical
student, but his face was unlined and his hair was
sandy and abundant, though neatly trimmed. His
eyes were a pale shade of blue that gave him a
guileless look, as did his rosy cheeks and gentle
mouth.

Bettina turned toward him and offered one of
her most flirtatious smiles. "I'm a reporter for the
Arborville Advocate," she said, "hoping to talk to colleagues of"—she tempered the smile—"the late
Brainard Covington. He'll be missed, I'm sure . . ."

"I can't help you," the young man said. "I'm not
his colleague . . . anymore."

Bettina's mobile face telegraphed her disappointment with a slight pout and a pucker of the forehead. Her hazel eyes searched Greg's face as if looking for comfort.

"You could try the faculty lounge," he suggested. "I'll show you where it is—there's usually coffee and sometimes even food." He pointed down the stairs. "It's this way. Just follow me. They won't all be from classics, but maybe you can get something for your article."

"If you're not his colleague," Bettina inquired as she fell into step beside him, "how come you know about the faculty lounge?"

"I taught here for seven years," he said. "Then"— he paused and rubbed his hands together, as if dusting them off—"no tenure, so poof! I'm out."

The faculty lounge was down the hallway to the right of the building's entrance. As they approached, they could see that the door was open invitingly and they could hear laughter. They stepped inside to see a room furnished with two long sofas and two easy chairs, all upholstered in faded green. Bookshelves, a small wooden table surrounded by four wooden chairs, and a wooden desk that seemed to fulfill the function of a kitchen counter completed the furnishings. The desk held a coffee maker, a hot plate with a kettle on it, the makings of coffee and tea, an assortment of ceramic mugs, and a package of disposable cups.

The room's occupants, who had been the

source of the laughter, were on their feet as Greg entered, followed by Bettina and then Pamela and Nell.

"Greg! How've you been?" said one of them, an elderly bearded man in a cardigan sweater. He paused for a handshake and glanced at his watch, explaining, "Class time," as he hurried out.

The liquid visible in the coffee maker's Pyrex carafe was the dark hue of coffee that had been kept warm for hours while growing progressively stronger, so they turned down Greg's sociable offer of a cup. And with no one else interested in refreshments, Nell didn't inquire about the possibilities for tea.

"Just make yourselves comfortable," he said, gesturing toward the closest sofa. "Some people are going to class but others are getting out, so you'll likely have somebody to interview soon."

They took seats on the sofa, but he remained standing. Then, with a friendly nod, he started out the door, pausing to say, "Good luck!"

"Wait!" Bettina jumped to her feet. She'd slipped off the pumpkin-colored down coat—it was very warm in the faculty lounge—to reveal an olive-green, fit-and-flare dress that matched her olive-green booties.

Pamela and Nell exchanged amazed glances, surprised not only by Bettina's action but by her agility. Pamela's helping hand was often required when it was time for Bettina to rise from a low-slung sofa.

Looking startled, Greg swung around to face the room again. Pamela wanted to know more about Greg too, but she hadn't been sure how to go about it. Apparently, neither did Bettina. She'd gotten his attention, but now she was stuttering and turning a becoming shade of pink.

"Um . . . I mean . . ." She offered him a smile that blended admiration with embarrassment. "It's just that . . . I was curious." Was she actually batting her eyelashes at him?

"Oh?" Greg took a few steps toward Bettina.

"You said you didn't get tenure here?"

He nodded.

"So what will you do?"

As Bettina waited expectantly, Greg looked puzzled—understandably so, in Pamela's view. Why should a woman who he had just met, and under the most casual of circumstances, be interested in his future?

Bettina answered that question. "It's just that you remind me so much of my son," she said with an apologetic laugh. "Up in Boston, and he doesn't have tenure yet . . ."

"Look for another job." He shrugged, raising his hands palms up. "What else can I do?" He stepped farther into the room and headed for one of the armchairs. Bettina sat back down and Greg lowered himself into the armchair, then leaned toward her, as if sensing a sympathetic ear. "It's complicated, though, because I want to stay around here."

"It's fun to live near New York City," Bettina said encouragingly.

"It's not that." Greg's lips twisted in a mournful smile. "I'd live anywhere. But my girlfriend got her

dream job teaching at Newfield State right when I
lost my job here." He described the upcoming interview Pamela had overheard him telling the
young woman in the department chair's office
about, then said, "It's not guaranteed at all—I'm
one of many they're interviewing, I'm sure—and if
I don't get that, I'll probably have to move away.
Somewhere, anywhere, that I can get a teaching
job."

Bettina had been making sympathetic mur-
murs, and Pamela was so moved by Greg's obvious
misery that she felt a catch in her throat—and all
the more as he went on.

"The ancient Greeks have been my lifelong pas-
sion," he said, staring straight ahead but not focusing on anything. "I used to build Greek temples
out of LEGOs when I was a little kid." Then he fastened his gaze on Nell, Pamela, and Bettina in
turn. "Do you know what it's like to have to choose
between the person you love and the subject you
love?" he asked plaintively, and slumped back in
his chair.

Bettina wiggled toward the edge of the sofa and
reached out to touch Greg's hand. "You'll get
something nearby," she whispered. "I'm sure of it.
Anybody who loves their subject that much has to
be a great teacher."

Greg pulled himself upright. "I've got a part-
time thing now, teaching humanities. But I can't
live on part-time forever." His expression cheered.
"I *do* have the interview, though, and Stafford always liked me. So he'll write a good letter." Greg

climbed to his feet and mustered a small smile, which he directed at Bettina. "Wish me luck!"

With that, he was out the door. But no sooner was he gone than someone else arrived—a woman dressed in a conservative wool pantsuit that suited her scholarly air. She was followed by a youngish man in more casual garb but bearing an over-stuffed leather satchel that marked him as a fellow professor. They nodded at Pamela, Nell, and Bettina, and seemed to find nothing odd about strangers turning up in the faculty lounge.

"Was that Greg Dixon?" the woman asked as she picked up one of the ceramic mugs. Did faculty members keep their own mugs in the lounge? Pamela wondered. Or did someone wash the whole collection every night?

The woman filled the mug with some of the lethal-looking coffee and stepped aside while the man picked up a mug and did likewise. "Sure was," the man said. "I wonder how he's getting on."

"It was a shame they let him go." The woman sampled her coffee. "It was all Brainard's doing."

Pamela smothered a startled yelp as Bettina poked her. From the other direction came Nell's soft, "Oh my."

"Really unfair." The man shook his head. "One person shouldn't have that much power."

"Brainard Covington was the head of the tenure committee." The woman shrugged.

"I guess Greg's gone back on the job market." The man sampled his coffee.

"What else can he do?"

The man laughed. "At least now if a job possibility calls here looking for a reference, Brainard won't be able to torpedo Greg's chances."

"This coffee gets worse and worse," the woman said. She headed for the other sofa. The man agreed about the coffee and followed her. Soon they were deep in a discussion of some upcoming lecture series.

"Shall we go?" Bettina whispered. Nell leaned past Pamela and cocked an ear in Bettina's direction. Bettina repeated the question. Pamela nodded and stood up, and soon the three of them were on their way down the hall toward the building's main door.

"We *did* discover things," Bettina said as the ancient wooden floor creaked in response to their footsteps.

Pamela nodded. "Probably more things than we would have discovered by asking outright."

As they approached the door, they almost collided with Greg, who was hurrying toward the stairway that led to the second floor. He was carrying his smartphone. "Just got a text," he said. "A guy I wanted to see today is back in his office now."

They waved him on his way and watched him climb the stairs. He was carrying his jacket, and its removal had revealed a sleeveless, V-necked sweater, obviously hand-knit from yarn in a natural brown shade, worn over a businesslike white shirt.

"I wouldn't have taken him for the sweater-vest type," Pamela commented as they lingered at the door while Bettina slipped back into her coat. "He seems too young."

Nell raised a brow and wrinkled her nose. "That

sweater looked like it was supposed to have sleeves," she said in a puzzled tone. "There wasn't any ribbing or anything around the armholes."

"Why would a person wear a half-finished sweater?" Bettina asked as Pamela pushed open the door.

Chapter 19

"I'm leaning toward lox and cream cheese on a bagel." The voice came from behind one of Hyler's oversize menus. "What do you think?"

"I'll join you," Pamela said as Bettina's scarlet fluff of bangs appeared over the top of the menu, followed by her hazel eyes.

"Made from sustainably raised salmon, I hope." Nell lowered her own menu. "Yes, I think I will have that too. And tomato juice."

The minute they'd walked in, Pamela had noticed that Felicity was on duty, serving a table near the door. They'd greeted her, but Pamela had purposely steered Bettina and Nell to a booth far at the back and on the opposite side.

It seemed inevitable that their conversation would stray to their morning's adventure at Wendelstaff, and Pamela was relieved when their server proved to be the middle-aged woman who had been at Hyler's forever. It would be best if

Felicity didn't overhear them discussing suspects and clues—or the grisly topic of murder in general.

Once they'd ordered and handed their menus back to the server, it took only seconds before Bettina leaned across the worn wooden table toward where Pamela and Nell were sharing the booth's other bench. "Why would a person wear a half-finished sweater?" she asked again, as if the question had been preying on her mind.

"Maybe it once had sleeves," Nell suggested. "When I was a girl, people often reused yarn or remade clothes. The Depression had taught them to be frugal."

"You think Greg took the sleeves off because he wanted the yarn for something else?" Bettina twisted her mouth into a skeptical knot.

"What if he"—Pamela paused for effect—"needed the yarn to strangle someone? Or several someones? Did you notice that Greg's sleeveless sweater was the same brown as the yarn we saw around Dawn's neck? And presumably the killer used the brown yarn later, though we didn't see those bodies in person."

Bettina added a frown to the skeptical knot, and Nell tipped her head sideways to give Pamela a curious stare.

But Pamela went on. "We know he had a reason—a *big* reason—to resent Brainard," she said. "Brainard was the head of the committee that turned him down for tenure." Pamela returned Nell's stare, then faced Bettina. She felt her lips form a tight smile. "Not only that, he had reason to want Brainard out of the way lest Brainard give him bad references in his new job search."

"Oh, Pamela!" Bettina's voice was a thin wail and her face resembled a tragic mask—though one with scarlet hair, bright lipstick and eye shadow, and dangly amethyst earrings.

The server was approaching, bearing three expertly balanced platters. But she paused about five feet from the booth, her expression nearly mirroring Bettina's.

"It's okay," Pamela said, beckoning her to complete her errand. And Bettina summoned up a smile and echoed Pamela's words.

As soon as the food had been delivered, however, and the server had departed in quest of their drinks, Bettina continued. "Greg was such a nice young man," she moaned, "and he reminded me so much of my own Warren. These young people trying to make it in the academic world have a hard time—especially when there are two careers to consider."

She cheered up somewhat as she inspected the contents of her platter. The bagel was a graceful circlet of golden-brown dough, with a surface that shone as if it had been polished. Bettina lifted the top half to inspect the filling. Layers of thin-sliced lox—pink shading to orange, gleaming, and nearly translucent—rippled over the bagel's lower half, nearly hiding it. The platter was garnished with a curl of lettuce and rounds of tomato and onion.

Pamela and Nell's platters were similarly tempting. Pamela added the tomato to her lox and replaced the top half of the bagel. She waited as the server delivered their drinks—a vanilla milkshake for Bettina and tomato juice for Pamela and

Nell—then lifted the formidable creation to her mouth and took a bite.

The bagel's dense texture resisted the teeth in a satisfying way, and its simple yeastiness was the perfect foil for the rich but delicate smoked salmon. Bettina's eyes grew wide as she sampled her own sandwich, gripping it tightly with both hands. After taking her first bite, she lowered it to her platter and beamed as she chewed. The pressure as she squeezed the sandwich to fit into her mouth had disarranged a few layers of lox, which were now escaping in translucent scallops from between the bottom bagel half and the top.

"Delicious!" she pronounced, and reached for the sandwich to launch another bite.

"It is a very good bagel," Nell murmured. "And the lox is quite healthful I'm sure." Her partly eaten sandwich reposed on her platter with several bites missing. "It's quite a bit more than I usually have for lunch, though. I'll take half home for Harold."

She picked up her knife and, with considerable exertion, managed to cut through layers of bagel and salmon, setting an un-nibbled half of the sandwich aside. Bettina, meanwhile, sipped at the straw jutting from the froth of foam that crowned her milkshake.

Nell had listened closely as, earlier, Pamela had laid out her case for Greg's guilt. And she'd watched sympathetically as Bettina reacted. But now she looked across the table at Bettina and said, "You *do* have to admit Greg would have had a motive for killing Brainard."

Bettina's eyes opened wide to regard Nell over

the sandwich, which she had picked up again and which was poised for another bite. She set the sandwich down and frowned. "I just can't believe that such a nice young man . . ." Her voice trailed off and she stared at the sandwich before speaking again. "Of course, losing his job would be hard . . . and with Brainard the head of the committee . . . and there's the complication of his girlfriend's job . . . but—" She brightened. "Why would Greg have wanted to kill Mary?"

Pamela spoke up. "He might have mistaken Mary for Brainard. We talked about that. Remember—the killer was confused enough to start out by killing Dawn."

A tiny moan escaped from Bettina's brightly painted lips. "But maybe the killer *didn't* mistake Mary for Brainard," she said. "Maybe the killer really did want to kill both of them. And why would Greg?" The question was as plaintive as if asked in defense of Bettina's own son.

Nell nodded sadly. "To punish the hated person by first depriving him of someone he loved?" She laughed, like a little cough. "Though in that case, the killer couldn't have known very much about the Lyon-Covington marriage."

Bettina picked up her sandwich again, and for several minutes all three women concentrated on their lunches.

With a last slurp, Bettina pushed her milkshake glass aside. As if responding to a signal, the server approached. Nell requested a container for the other half of her sandwich. "But not Styrofoam," she specified. And Pamela requested the check.

As the server retreated, skillfully managing all

three platters as well as the three empty drink glasses, Bettina reached into her purse for a mirror and her lipstick. She gazed into the mirror, lipstick in hand and ready to apply. But then she suddenly turned her gaze to Pamela and Nell. She was beaming.

"It can't be Greg!" she exclaimed. "At least not if we think he used the yarn from his sweater sleeves to strangle Mary and Brainard."

Pamela's "Oh?" overlapped with Nell's "Why not?"

"Yarn gets all crinkly when you rip something out," Bettina crowed. "I should know because I've had to rip out enough knitting." She gestured triumphantly with the hand that held the lipstick. "The yarn we saw—the yarn around Dawn's neck—may have been brown, like Greg's sweater, but it wasn't crinkly. We didn't see the other bodies, but we're assuming the same killer killed all three people. So the yarn would be the same yarn, brown but not crinkly."

Pamela nodded, but she said, "Ask Detective Clayborn if the other yarn was crinkly."

There was no chance to continue that discussion, however—at least not then and there—because Felicity Winkle had appeared at the end of the booth. She was dressed in the neat white shirt and black pants she wore for her job at Hyler's. But she wasn't visiting their booth on official business. She was carrying, not their bill, but a magazine. And as she lowered it and flipped it open to the page she was marking with her finger, it became clear that the magazine was a knitting magazine.

She laid the open magazine on the worn wooden table and smoothed the pages flat. The picture showed a young woman wearing a charming sweater, waist-length and with a modern boxy shape, worked in an interesting nubby stitch.

"I'm not good enough to join Knit and Nibble," Felicity said, blushing slightly. "But I really want to make this sweater." Her hand swept down a column on the opposite page, which was dense with abbreviations, numbers, and diagrams.

Bettina motioned Felicity to share the bench she occupied and Felicity slid in next to her. Bettina began to explain how to get started on the sweater as their own server approached with their check.

"I'm on my break," Felicity explained and the server smiled in acknowledgment.

Bettina pulled out her wallet and laid a few bills on the table, then went back to explaining. She finished up by giving Felicity her address and phone number.

Harold was standing at the curb guiding a pile of dead leaves into the street as Pamela steered her serviceable compact to a stop in front of the Bascombs' house. Letting his rake clatter against the sidewalk, he swooped forward to swing open the passenger-side door and extend his other hand to his wife. Nell accepted the hand and suppressed a smile at the exaggerated bow that accompanied the gesture.

"I brought you half of my lox and bagel," she

said, holding out the small white bag she'd left
Hyler's with.

"I am quite ready for a break, my dear, and a bit
of sustenance." Harold picked up his rake and
leaned on it in a pantomime of exhaustion. "But
before Pamela drives away"—he tipped his head
toward the car and waved at Pamela and then at
Bettina, who was in the back seat—"we're invited
to a funeral."

He explained that Martha Lyon had stopped by
the Covington house on some errand or other.
But seeing Harold working in the yard, she'd detoured to mention that Brainard was to be buried
on Friday and there was to be a reception afterward in the faculty club at Wendelstaff College.
"Déjà vu all over again, I'd say," he concluded.

"We have to go, though," Nell said. "After all,
they were our neighbors." She leaned back into
the car. "I think we should *all* go," she clarified,
and added—with a meaningful look—"and keep
our eyes and ears open."

Pamela waited until they had crossed Arborville
Avenue and were approaching the spot where her
house faced Bettina's across Orchard Street. Then
she put into words the idea that had been perco-
lating in her mind ever since they left Hyler's.

"Felicity is a knitter," she said. "We didn't know
that." She didn't take her eyes away from the road,
but she could sense that Bettina had turned toward her.

"No, we didn't," Bettina murmured.

"Are you thinking what I'm thinking?" Pamela asked as she nosed along the curb in front of Bettina's house and clicked off the ignition. Then she swiveled to study Bettina.

"Probably not," Bettina said with a puzzled frown. "I'm wondering if Wilfred is planning to cook tonight or if I'll be making baked salmon because it's Thursday. If so, I'll have to go out again. And I just had salmon for lunch."

Bettina had been a willing, if uninspired, cook throughout her married life, serving the same seven menus in rotation every week. But when Wilfred retired, he'd cheerfully taken over most of the kitchen duties.

"What *are* you thinking?" she asked, apparently sensing that Pamela had something important to say.

"We talked about how Felicity would have had a good motive for killing Brainard—and probably Mary too." Bettina nodded as Pamela spoke. "But we didn't talk about why Felicity would have used yarn."

Bettina's eyes slowly widened until Pamela could see white around her irises. "*Felicity is a knitter*," she whispered, echoing Pamela's earlier statement. "But—oh, dear!" She grasped one hand with the other and began twisting her fingers in a way that seemed painful. "Felicity is such a sweet young woman."

"Would you rather have the killer be Felicity or Greg Dixon?" Pamela asked.

"Neither!" Bettina exclaimed, slapping her hands against her thighs. "Neither! I'm sure it's somebody else."

"Are you going to tell Detective Clayborn what we found out about Greg Dixon?"

Bettina sighed. "I suppose I should." She sighed again, her expression mournful. But then she brightened. "Clayborn might already know about him," she said suddenly. "I'm sure he talked to Brainard's colleagues at Wendelstaff, and somebody must have told him about the tenure decision." She allowed herself a hopeful smile. "He might already have checked on an alibi and everything. And Greg hasn't been arrested! So . . ."

"But Detective Clayborn might *not* already know about him." Pamela felt mean. Bettina had been so relieved, but Felicity had previously been their only viable suspect, and she was such a sweet young woman. And a knitter! She went on to add, "The missing sweater sleeves . . ."

"The murder yarn wasn't crinkly yarn," Bettina said firmly, and she reached for the door handle.

Chapter 20

It was, as Harold had predicted, déjà vu all over again—except that when Bettina removed her lavender coat, the dress she revealed was not deep purple, but rather burgundy, and instead of deep purple pumps, she was wearing her burgundy booties.

Otherwise, the view of the Haversack River through the floor-to-ceiling windows in the back wall of the faculty club was the same as it had been the previous Friday. The elegant refreshments laid out on the white cloth that covered the buffet table were the same, including the meatballs, the chicken tidbits on skewers, and the bite-size crab-meat quiches. The servers were the same. The wine was the same. And the guests were the same—a mixture of Arborvillians in somber, conservative ensembles, and academics in garb that ranged (depending on their age) from urban hipster,

through tweed jacket with elbow patches, to
frumpy and even unkempt.

Divested of coats, Pamela, Bettina, and the Bascombs stood near the room's entrance surveying
the scene. Brainard had been the host the last
time, but Brainard was now . . . the departed. They
recognized Herc, in a slim dark suit, accepting condolences, melancholy lending his striking looks a
romantic air. Felicity was at his side, unabashedly
sharing the burden of grief, and dressed in black
this time, as if to openly acknowledge her bond
with the bereaved son.

Pamela recognized the man and woman who
had been chatting in the faculty lounge, the
woman blending with the other mourners in the
same wool pantsuit she'd worn the previous day,
though the man had replaced his casual garb with
a suit and tie. Standing near the bar and sharing a
discreet laugh with the bartender was the young
woman with the chartreuse hair and the maroon
lipstick from the classics department office.

As they stood there, a man detached himself
from a small cluster of people—academics, to
judge by the variety of their dress—and strode toward them with hand outstretched.

"I'm Ben Stafford," he said. "Brainard's department chair." Harold grabbed the hand first, then
Nell and Bettina and finally Pamela. The man surveyed them with a genial, though subdued, smile.
Though he was chubby, not too tall, and bald but
for a fringe of gray hair, he projected an air of confidence—enhanced by a scrupulously tailored
navy-blue blazer and gray wool trousers, a starched
white shirt, and a tasteful silk tie. The hand he had

offered for the round of handshakes was adorned with a gold ring bearing an impressive crest.

"Neighbors of Brainard's perhaps?" he inquired.

"Across the street." Harold and Nell spoke in unison as Pamela and Bettina nodded.

"Sad occasion." Ben Stafford sighed. "And so hard on the son—to lose both parents so shockingly, and in such a short period of time."

"Very sad," Nell murmured.

Ben Stafford extended an arm and gestured, as if to urge them farther into the room. "Please have some food, wine. I hope you see a few familiar faces . . . and Herc is here, of course, with his girlfriend."

He nodded toward where Herc stood with Felicity at his side, then his gaze drifted toward the door. Pamela glanced that way to notice a small group of people entering, colleagues just getting out of class perhaps. She checked her watch. It was ten minutes past one. Ben Stafford hurried to greet them.

"We should say something to Herc," Nell said. She led the way, and they joined the brief line of mourners waiting to pay their respects. When Pamela reached Felicity, she noticed that the young woman looked as if she'd been crying. Whatever Herc's relationship with his parents had been, they were still his parents. And as someone who loved Herc, Felicity must have been moved by his grief, if not by grief she personally felt. *But what if she was the one who killed them?* The thought jolted Pamela and for a moment she struggled for words.

At last she said, "This must be very hard for Herc." *Well, of course,* said a voice in her mind. But

Felicity responded to the spirit of the comment, overlooking its banality.

"Thank you for coming," she said, squeezing Pamela's hand. "We're managing." With a sad, fond smile, she nodded toward Herc.

As Bettina reached out to offer Felicity a hug, Pamela edged to the side and joined Nell and Harold, who were talking to Herc. "My aunt is here somewhere." He swiveled his head to scan the room, displaying his classic profile. "She's going to be helping me with the house. There's a lot of stuff. . . ." His voice trailed off, and Harold laid a comforting hand on his shoulder.

"We're right across the street," Harold said.

Herc nodded. "I'm going back down to Princeton Monday. But I'll be here again, on and off."

"Getting back to your studies will be a good thing." Nell's pale eyes seemed to darken as she studied Herc's face, as if dilated by some reflected grief. They all moved along then, relinquishing Herc to others with condolences to offer.

"I feel sadder than I did last week," Bettina commented to Pamela. "That poor young man."

Nell and Harold had been hailed by an elderly woman Pamela recognized from the Co-Op and had joined a small cluster of other Arborvillians. But Bettina was eyeing the buffet.

"It *is* lunchtime," Pamela said. "Past, even. We'll feel better if we have a bit to eat."

Bettina stepped up to the buffet table and took a plate. Pamela did likewise and followed her friend as Bettina made her way along the table, adding meatballs, jumbo shrimp, a bite-size piece of chicken on a skewer, and a ham-on-puff-pastry slider. She paused when she got to the cheese ball and turned to Pamela.

"I don't think they had these puff pastry sliders last week," she observed. "Do you remember?"

Pamela responded with a distracted "Umm?" and Bettina repeated the question.

"I'm not sure," Pamela said, and she added one to her plate as if to imply that a taste might jog her memory.

She hadn't been distracted by the tempting possibilities the buffet table offered, but rather by the sight of a woman standing near the bar, where the bartender and the young woman with chartreuse hair were now engaged in an earnest conversation.

She'd only spoken to Martha Lyon briefly the previous week, but she recognized the stern face topped by gray hair and the stocky body, so unlike Mary's long-limbed elegance. She even recognized the shapeless trouser suit and the simple jewelry.

"There's Mary's sister again," Pamela commented to Bettina.

"We should go over and talk to her," Bettina said. "She looks lonely."

So, with their plates filled, they made their way past a few clusters of chatting people to where Martha stood.

"I'm Bettina Fraser"—Bettina extended her free hand and Martha took it—"and this is Pamela Paterson." Pamela shook Martha's hand too. "We met you last week," Bettina went on, her mobile features shifting as a pucker of concern appeared in her brow and her cordial smile faded. "Your sister . . . such a tragic thing . . . and now this."

Martha seemed grateful for the attention. "I

don't know many of the people here," she explained. "I was talking to someone I met last week, but he had to go to class."

"You should eat something," Bettina said.

"I already did." Martha fluttered a hand to wave away the idea of food. "But you go ahead"—she nodded at Bettina and then at Pamela—"please."

A companionable silence descended on the small group as Pamela and Bettina worked their way through the tempting nibbles they'd borne away from the buffet. The meatballs glazed with creamy sauce were the perfect size to be eaten with toothpicks. And, with their tails still attached, the jumbo shrimp featured built-in handles. Pamela had dipped a few in their spicy red sauce before adding them to her plate. Martha seemed content to survey the comings and goings of the guests as her companions ate.

It was getting on toward two p.m., and more people were leaving than were arriving. A server came by to relieve Pamela and Bettina of their empty plates, and Martha consulted her nondescript watch.

"I've got a busy afternoon ahead," she commented. "I wonder if Herc is ready to leave."

"Going back to the city?" Pamela asked. "Your research must be quite demanding."

"It is." Martha's obvious delight in her work lent her plain features a hint of loveliness that evoked her kinship with Mary. But the hint of loveliness vanished. "That's not what the busy-ness is," she said. "Brainard had asked me to sort through Mary's clothes and take them away because it depressed him to see them. Now Herc wants me to go on with it, and more. Everything, really. So there's a lot of organizing to do."

"That's a huge job." Bettina leaned forward and squeezed Martha's hand.

"And a sad responsibility for a young man in his early twenties." Martha shook her head mournfully. "The house will have to be sold. So the sooner everything is gone the better. I'll get an appraiser to come in for the big things. Some of the furniture and art is quite good. But everything else . . . come by if you like. I'll be there all afternoon and for the whole weekend. Mary had a lot of craft supplies—*The Lyon and the Lamb* and all that. You might be able to use some of them."

Harold had driven the little group to the funeral and then to the reception afterward. Now Pamela and Bettina said goodbye to Harold and Nell as he dropped them both off in front of Bettina's house.

"Knit and Nibble at your house Tuesday, Pamela," Nell called as Harold pulled away from the curb. "So I'll see you both then, if not before."

Pamela hesitated before crossing the street. "I'm curious about the craft supplies Martha's going to be sorting through," she said. "Mary must have accumulated a lot of yarn and other knitting-related items."

"I imagine so." Bettina nodded. "*The Lyon and the Lamb* went on for a long time. People probably gave her things, hoping she'd feature them on the blog."

"Would it be ghoulish if we went up there this afternoon?" Even more exciting than tag sales and thrift shops, which Pamela loved, was the prospect of cast-off treasures that were simply being given away.

"Ghoulish?" Bettina laughed. "So what? Halloween is barely over."

Pamela suppressed her own laugh. "There could be things for Nell," she said. "Yarn for her do-good projects." Perhaps a charitable impulse would make her eagerness feel less ghoulish.

Bettina shrugged and consulted the pretty face of her gold bracelet watch. "I have time, but"—she lifted a foot encased in a chic burgundy bootie—"I have to get out of these shoes. And even then, I'm not walking up that hill!"

"Fifteen minutes?"

Bettina nodded. "Fifteen minutes. And I'll drive."

At home, Pamela fetched her mail from the mailbox and immediately transferred everything except the bill from the water company to the recycling basket. Upstairs, she changed her clothes, trading her brown slacks and black-and-brown-striped jacket for jeans and the same hand-knit sweater she'd been wearing for the past few days.

She was just descending the stairs when a flash of orange the shade of a pumpkin appeared behind the lace that curtained the oval window in her front door. She opened the door to admit Bettina, who stooped to greet Catrina with a head scratch as Pamela took her jacket from the closet, and soon they were on their way.

*　*　*

The crime-scene tape was gone and the Lyon-Covington residence—though neither resided there now—looked just as it always had: two stories plus an attic, gray shingles with white trim and black shutters, and attractive landscaping that featured azaleas, rhododendrons, and hosta. Only a few leaves littered the lawn, suggesting that the landscapers had continued to do their work despite having recently come upon the dead body of their employer.

They waited on the porch for several long minutes after Pamela gave a few resounding taps with the brass door knocker. Then Martha swung back the door and greeted them with a breathless hello. Instead of the suit jacket she'd worn earlier, she'd slipped a loose cardigan over her blouse.

"I was upstairs," she said. "That's where the clothes are, and Mary's craft room, and Brainard's study." She stood back and motioned them to enter. They stepped into the living room Pamela remembered from her first visit—the glass coffee table on the brass pedestal, the sofa and armchairs covered in the fabric with the interlocking circles, the dramatic wall hanging above the fireplace.

Martha had continued talking, more to herself than to them. ". . . so many books . . . a scholar's library . . . I'll take some . . . but . . ." She closed her eyes, shook her head with a spasmlike jerk, opened her eyes again, and blinked several times. "Too much to do." She sighed. "Come upstairs and I'll show you where the craft things are."

Four rooms, plus a bathroom, opened off the hall upstairs. Through the open door of one, Pamela glimpsed a king-size bed made up with elegantly coordinated bedding and decorative throw pillows. The door of another room was closed, but Martha pointed to it and said, "This one was Herc's when he was growing up." She took a few steps toward another open door and added, "And here's the craft room."

They stepped inside. Open closet doors revealed shelves upon shelves containing folded lengths of cloth, plastic bins of buttons, bundles of knitting needles, stacks of magazines and pattern books, and of course yarn—balls and skeins in every color and texture imaginable. To the right, an oak library table held a sewing machine. Scattered around on the table's surface were pincushions, scissors of various sizes, lengths of ribbon and rickrack, jars of pins, and a cloth doll body wearing only a camisole. A huge chest of drawers occupied the opposite wall.

"I'll leave you to it," Martha said. "Help yourselves. Just pile up what you want and . . . and you can take it home in pillowcases. There are plenty of those too."

Pamela and Bettina looked at each other. Pamela already had her own backlog of yarn, yarn she'd bought with no specific project in mind but just because she couldn't resist it. It filled many plastic bins. And when she visited tag sales at the homes of deceased knitters, she imagined poor Penny struggling—hopefully far in the future—to find takers for all the yarn her mother had left behind.

Bettina too had her backlog. And at the rate she was progressing with the Nordic-style sweater for

Wilfred, Pamela knew it would be ages before her friend was ready to tackle a new project.

But all this yarn shouldn't go to waste. She advanced toward the closet and began to examine it. Was there enough of any one particular yarn to actually make a garment? she wondered. Or were these all leftovers? Or samples offered by people hoping for a favorable word in *The Lyon and the Lamb*?

In many cases, there *was* only one skein. But Nell could use those, for the Christmas stockings or the knitted caps for newborns. Pamela began lifting skeins one by one—red mohair, lavender in a fine-gauge wool, soft acrylic in blush pink . . . Infant caps couldn't be wool, so the acrylic would be good for those . . .

Meanwhile, Bettina had taken a stack of pattern books and magazines from a shelf and was sitting in the sewing machine chair, paging through one of them.

Pamela continued with her task, happy to have a goal that would narrow her focus. Otherwise, how to deal with such bounty? Here was a rugged yarn in an austere shade of taupe . . . but this soft yellow would be nice for an infant cap . . . and the powder blue, and—

Footsteps in the hall, then Martha's voice, intruded on her thoughts. Pamela turned away from the shelves she was exploring to see Martha standing in the doorway, holding a sheet of paper in one hand and a pair of glasses in the other.

"Someone wants to buy this house," she said. She returned the glasses to their position on her nose and tipped her head toward the sheet of paper, frowning as her eyes traveled down the page. She looked up again. "And whoever it is sounds angry. Or something."

She advanced to the middle of the small room and extended the sheet of paper toward Pamela, who stepped forward to meet her.

"Mary never mentioned anything," Martha commented as Pamela scanned the paper.

The handwritten letter read,

> *I am writing to you yet again to tell you I want to buy your house because in actuality, it is <u>my</u> house. My parents built it and I grew up in it and I lived there for three decades with my mother after my father passed at the age of 55, and when my mother passed I would have owned it except for bad luck and trouble. Well, now my luck has changed and I have $$$$ again. And I've told you that I can pay to get my house back and ten times over, and you have ignored me and ignored me, for too long. I've written letter upon letter. And my patience is really running out. You know where you can reach me. This is your last chance.*

"Angry, or something, yes," Pamela said. "Kind of disturbed." She handed the sheet of paper to Bettina, who was still sitting in the sewing machine chair.

"Do you think I should show it to Herc?" Martha asked. "He *will* be selling the house."

"There's no letterhead or phone number or email address," Pamela pointed out. "Not even a signature. How would Herc get in touch?"

"There were other letters—apparently. This one sounds like a last-ditch attempt to get a response." Martha twisted her pale lips into an unhappy smile and lifted a shoulder in a shrug. "The person says, 'You know where you can reach me.' But Brainard and Mary might not have kept the other letters."

"*I* wouldn't." Bettina shuddered and handed the sheet of paper back to Pamela. "Whoever it is sounds like a complete nutcase."

"If they're so interested in the house, they're probably aware that its owners are dead now," Pamela observed. "The *Register* has given the story quite a bit of play: 'Tragic Sequel to the Halloween Bonfire Murder—Arborville's Woes Continue' and like that."

Bettina gave a scornful sniff. "Sometimes the *Register* is no better than the tabloids. The *Advocate* would never run that kind of headline."

"Well," Martha sighed, "I'll keep the letter and maybe let Herc know that someone might contact him before the house actually goes on the market." She edged back toward the doorway. "It looks like you're finding things." She nodded at the small cluster of skeins Pamela had set aside on the floor. "You can come back," she added. "I'll be working here all day tomorrow and Sunday."

Chapter 21

Pamela awoke later than usual on Saturday. By eight a.m., the white eyelet curtains at her bedroom windows usually glowed with early morning sun, but today they hung in shadowy folds. Even Catrina and Ginger had dozed longer than was their custom—though in their cozy nest beneath the covers, mornings were never bright.

Pamela felt a slight motion at her side, then an elongated softness made its way over her chest. In a moment a heart-shaped face covered in silky black fur emerged from beneath the sheet's edge. A few seconds later Ginger joined her mother, blinking her jade-green eyes as she surveyed Pamela.

Pamela's brain had been busy while she slept. But the complicated pattern woven by her dreaming mind had begun to unravel even before she opened her eyes. Just a few threads remained, fading and vanishing. She reached for them in vain. Something about the dream had seemed important, but what? And she couldn't linger in bed, courting their return. It was nearly nine a.m., and there were cats to be fed.

Having no need to don robes and slippers, Catrina and Ginger reached the head of the stairs before Pamela. She followed, tugging her fleece robe around her and looping the tie at her waist.

In the kitchen, she opened a fresh can of their favorite chicken-fish blend and transferred it to a clean bowl, using the serving spoon to break the larger chunks into appealing morsels. As she worked, her brain grappled with the sense that something had seemed obvious in the fuzzy moment between sleep and waking—something important.

She set water to boiling in the kettle, slipped a paper filter into her carafe's plastic filter cone, and ground a generous few scoops of coffee beans. Maybe coffee would help recapture the elusive dream. Then she braved the chilly morning in only her robe and slippers to dash down her front walk for the *Register*. By the time she returned to the kitchen and slipped the newspaper from its flimsy plastic sleeve, the kettle was whistling.

A few minutes later, she was sitting at the table with coffee in a wedding-china cup and a slice of whole-grain toast on a wedding-china plate. She put off paging through the newspaper until the toast was gone and she'd sampled the coffee. When she did begin to read, she was not surprised to find no column inches at all devoted to the Arborville murders after the dramatic story that had appeared the day after Brainard's body was found. She already knew from Bettina that Detective Clayborn had made no progress on the case.

She finished her browse through the *Register* at the same time that she drained the last drops from her first cup of coffee. Before refilling her cup, she closed her eyes for a moment and tried to will herself back into the nearly-awake-but-not-quite state she'd been in when the tantalizing dream, or whatever it had been, retreated. But it was no use.

She refilled her coffee cup, set the paper aside, and fetched a pen and one of the little notepads that came unbidden in the mail. The pages of this one, in acknowledgment of the season, were decorated with a border of tiny pumpkins linked by a spiraling vine.

She'd last shopped for groceries the previous Saturday, and a trip to the Co-Op was due. Catrina had wandered back in from the entry. With the overcast sky, there was no sunny spot to bask in on the entry rug. Flourishing her pen, Pamela bent toward Catrina. "More chicken-fish blend?" she inquired. "Or would you prefer a change this week?"

Getting no answer, she began her shopping list with *Cat food—chicken-fish blend.*

Bearing a canvas shopping bag that contained yet more canvas shopping bags, and with her purse over her shoulder, Pamela headed up Orchard Street toward Arborville Avenue. More trees had begun to show their autumn colors, and the vivid reds and golds were bright against the moody sky. The day was still, but crisp enough that the violet scarf Pamela had only recently brought out of its summer retirement provided a welcome coziness at her neck.

When she reached the stately brick apartment building at the corner, she paused and detoured briefly to check for interesting discards behind the discreet wooden fence that hid the building's trash cans. But there was nothing of note. After she turned the corner and walked a block, however, she paused again.

Interspersed among apartment buildings and garden apartments along Arborville Avenue were a few single-family dwellings. And in front of one of them, a nondescript brick two-story, was a Realtor's sign announcing that it was for sale.

For sale, Pamela murmured to herself. And with a suddenness that jolted her, the errant thought that had fled upon waking was back. *Of course*, she murmured, stamping her foot in irritation. It was so obvious. As Holly would say, *Duh*.

Someone had been angling for ages to buy Brainard and Mary's house, someone whose prose style suggested a mind not at ease. And that someone might finally have theorized that if the house's owners were dead, the house would go on the market.

The llama woman and the Barrows had been eliminated as suspects, and it was too sad to think that sweet Felicity could have murdered her potential in-laws. Greg Dixon had seemed possible—though Bettina had had a point. Two points, really. Detective Clayborn had undoubtedly learned about Greg Dixon—and the fact that he had a very legitimate grudge against Brainard—when he interviewed Brainard's colleagues. But for some reason—probably a credible alibi—he hadn't followed up. And the murder yarn hadn't been crinkly, so it hadn't come from Greg's missing sweater sleeves.

Pamela would do her grocery shopping, but as soon as she got back home, she would confer with Bettina about this new possible suspect, the letter writer. Detective Clayborn would have to be told.

Pamela took a cart from the small cluster right inside the Co-Op's automatic door and steered it over the ancient wooden floor toward the produce department with its leafy and bulbous offerings. She added greens, a few sweet potatoes, and a carton of cherry tomatoes to the cart, suddenly nagged by the recollection that a huge bowl of heirloom apples waited uneaten on her kitchen counter at home. But then she recalled that Knit and Nibble was meeting at her house on Tuesday. She'd make something with the apples then, but something different. Not a pie, a crumble, or an apple cake.

Co-Op fish was always fresh, and eating it the day it was bought took advantage of that fact. So shopping day often concluded with fish for dinner. Pamela steered her cart toward the fish counter and browsed among the offerings. She ate salmon so often—maybe it was time to branch out a bit. Displayed on the bed of crushed ice behind the counter's glass was an overlapping row of hand-length fish with gleaming silver scales and bright, clear eyes. "Sea Bass" the sign said. When the fish man turned to her with the jovial greeting that was his custom, she requested a sea bass, and waited while it was descaled and filleted.

At the meat counter, she added a pork tenderloin to her cart—it would be dinner for several days. A detour down one of the narrow aisles that occupied the center of the Co-Op's space took her to the cat food section. After a stop for a pound of Vermont cheddar, she wound up at the bakery counter.

Ranged along the top of the counter was an assortment of loaves—every shape from baguette through oval to round, and every color from burnished gold to deepest brown. Some were crusty with dramatic slashes, others were smooth or studded with seeds. Pamela requested a loaf of her favorite whole-grain bread and waited while it was sliced and bagged. Tucking her list back into her purse, she wheeled the cart toward the checkout station with the shortest line.

She emerged onto the sidewalk five minutes later, quite weighed down by three canvas tote bags full of groceries. The walk south on Arborville Avenue was thus not nearly as pleasant as her earlier stroll to town had been. She paused at a bus stop to rest her bags on a bench, then continued on, and was relieved when she finally reached the corner of Orchard Street. In just a few minutes she would be home.

But as she waited to cross Arborville Avenue, she heard a voice calling her name. The voice was coming from behind her, from the hill that sloped up to the Palisades. She turned, and when she recognized the owner of the voice, she lowered the tote bags to the sidewalk and waited.

Nell was a block away, but hurrying toward Pamela, her white hair floating around her face.

"What is it?" Pamela asked, feeling her forehead wrinkle. Nell's tone had sounded so urgent.

"Nothing desperate, dear. Don't look so worried." Nell slowed to a walk, panting. "Just a bit curious. But I was going to call you, and then when I saw you—" She had reached Pamela's side. From her arm hung a canvas tote that was the twin of one of Pamela's. It bore the image of a panda munching on a stalk of bamboo and an exhortation to save the panda's habitat.

"I'm all ears." This corner featured a bus stop too, and Pamela picked up her groceries and led Nell to its bench.

"It's Brainard and Mary's house," Nell said as she took a seat beside Pamela on the bench. She was still panting slightly. "Someone—very ghoulish, if you ask me—wants to buy it. He was hanging around this morning, taking pictures of it, and he started chatting with Harold when Harold went out to fetch the newspaper. He asked if the heir or heirs lived locally and had been around."

"Oh, Nell!" Pamela tightened her lips into a distressed grimace. She described the letter that Martha had found the previous day. "It could be the same person," she added. "What was he like?"

"I didn't see him," Nell said. "He only talked to Harold. And Harold didn't know about the letter, so he didn't think that much of the encounter— not enough to give me a detailed description of the man."

"But Harold probably remembers what he looked like," Pamela murmured, then, in a more excited voice, she added, "and anyway, the man will come back if he's so eager."

"I'm going to tell Martha about him," Nell assured Pamela with a vigorous nod. "She just hasn't shown up yet. Herc will be interested in a possible buyer and—"

"Nell!" Pamela grabbed Nell's hand, which was resting in her lap, clutching the canvas tote bag. Nell reared back and stared at Pamela with her eyes wide. "He could be the murderer!" The pitch of Pamela's voice rose in an uncharacteristic way.

"What?" Nell's other hand landed on top of Pamela's and squeezed. She paused and frowned. "You could be right," she said at last. "From what you said, it sounds like the Lyon-Covingtons were completely unresponsive to this man's letters. Even if they didn't want to sell, they could have been sympathetic enough to talk to him. A childhood house can really mean a lot to a person."

Pamela nodded. "I'm going to Bettina's right now. Detective Clayborn listens to her—sometimes—and he should definitely be told about this development."

"When I get home from the Co-Op, I'll ask Harold what the man looked like," Nell said as she and Pamela untangled their hands and Nell renewed her grip on the tote bag. "And I'll tell Martha to find out everything she can about him if he comes back."

"Good." Pamela rose from the bench, commenting, "This could be the breakthrough." She took up her grocery bags and she and Nell parted, Nell heading north toward the Co-Op and Pamela crossing Arborville Avenue and continuing on down Orchard Street.

The Frasers' front door opened before Pamela

had a chance to ring, and from the other side of the threshold, Woofus stared up at her in alarm. The shaggy creature edged back in confusion, and the door swung open farther to reveal Wilfred bundled in a warm jacket and a voluminous scarf.

"Pamela!" he said as a smile creased his ruddy face. "What a pleasant surprise! Woofus and I are just going out on an errand, but the boss lady is in the kitchen. I'm sure she'll be happy to see you." He stepped back and bent to give Woofus a comforting pat and a reassuring word as Pamela entered.

"Is that Pamela?" Bettina had appeared in the arch between the living room and the dining room. She was dressed for the day in one of the tunic and leggings outfits she wore when she was scheduled to babysit for her Arborville grandchildren. This outfit was a rich indigo color that contrasted strikingly with her bright red sneakers, and she'd added a necklace of large red beads with matching earrings.

"There's still some coffee," Bettina added. "Come on back in the kitchen, put those grocery bags down, and have a cup."

"I will," Pamela said, "but I've got something really important to tell you—about the case."

"I'm all ears." Bettina turned and led the way to the promised coffee.

"There's a sequel to that letter Martha found," Pamela explained as she followed Bettina through the doorway that led from the dining room to the kitchen. Once she was comfortably settled at Bettina's well-scrubbed pine table with a mug of coffee in front of her, she relayed Nell's story about the early morning visitor asking about the Lyon-Covingtons' house.

"This could be the breakthrough!" Bettina clapped her hands and smiled a red-lipped smile. "I will call Clayborn right this minute." She jumped up and scurried from the room to fetch her phone. In a moment, she was back. "I'm sure he'll take me seriously and he'll be really glad to hear this," she commented breathlessly as she tapped at the phone with a red-nailed finger. "He hasn't had anything new to tell me about the case, and I'll bet that annoying Marcy Brewer from the *Register* has been getting impatient. *And*"—she looked up, and her smile grew wider—"this means the killer won't turn out to be that sweet Felicity Winkle or that nice Greg Dixon."

Bettina lifted the phone to her ear, listened briefly, and then said, "Hello, this is Bettina Fraser from the *Advocate,* calling for Detective Clayborn." She listened again, and as she did so, the cheer that had brightened her expression faded. When she spoke again, her voice took on a pleading tone. "It's really important," she said. "It's a clue about the murders." After another pause, she lowered the phone and poked at its screen to end the call.

She raised her eyes from the phone to gaze mournfully at Pamela and moaned, "He's at a conference and won't be in till Monday. And apparently, the person who answered the phone doesn't know who I am."

Pamela sighed. She wrapped both hands around the coffee mug, enjoying for a moment the warmth it radiated, and then took a consoling sip.

"I'll call again first thing Monday morning," Bettina said. "It's all we can do. And I'm sure Nell will let us know if the man comes back to talk to Martha."

Chapter 22

Back in her own house, Pamela put away her groceries, leaving the cheddar out on the counter because lunchtime was drawing near. She'd have a grilled cheese sandwich and an apple—and thinking of apples reminded her that she still hadn't decided what to make for Knit and Nibble with the bounty of apples Bettina and Wilfred had given her.

She pondered that topic as she buttered the last two pieces of whole-grain bread from the previous week's loaf, laid one buttered side down on her griddle, and topped it with sliced cheddar and the other piece of bread, buttered side up. Maybe an apple trifle, she thought as she watched the sandwich carefully, looking for signs that the cheese was melting. When a few melted cheese dribbles began to appear at the joint where the top slice of bread joined the bottom slice, she flipped the sandwich and waited until a check of the sandwich's underside revealed that it had reached the ideal golden-toasty hue.

After she transferred the sandwich to a plate and set an apple on the table next to it, but before she sat down to eat, she selected a cookbook from the bookshelf at the counter's end and laid it on the counter for future reference.

Work for the magazine awaited. Of the articles her boss had sent at the beginning of the week for her to edit, five remained, and the whole batch was due back Monday morning. After lunch, Pamela climbed the stairs to her office and spent the next two hours among the textiles in the Musée du quai Branly in Paris. She learned that, as an ethnographic museum, its collections spanned many different cultures, and the photographs that accompanied the article made the esthetic value of the holdings clear. But English was not the author's native language, so Pamela's copyediting skills were called upon many times per page.

At last, she clicked on "Save," and when a quick check of her email showed nothing that needed a response, she allowed her monitor to lapse into sleep. Deciding to exercise her body after the workout the *Fiber Craft* article had just given her brain, Pamela devoted the rest of the afternoon to laundry and housecleaning.

As she worked, scrubbing floors, vacuuming rugs, dusting her collection of thrift-store treasures, she couldn't help reflecting on the curious new suspect in the Arborville murder case—someone who had grown up in Brainard and Mary's house and had wanted desperately to buy it for a long time. Did he think he could thus recapture the happiness he knew as a child? Had recapturing that happiness made killing three people—one by accident—seem worthwhile?

Pamela's own house was over a hundred years old, quite a bit older than Brainard and Mary's. With vacuum cleaner in hand, she paused in the middle of the entry. The ancient carpet, with its pattern of stylized foliage, covered an even more ancient parquet floor. Many generations had lived in this house before she and Michael Paterson bought it. People had been born, died, fallen in love, gone off to war . . .

By six p.m., living room, dining room, and entry smelled of lemon oil, and the cushions on the sofa had been fluffed and straightened, with the needlepoint cat turned right side up. Fresh towels hung in the bathroom and powder room, and both rooms had been thoroughly scrubbed, along with the kitchen floor. The sheets on Pamela's bed had been washed and put away, replaced by a set fragrant with lavender sachet.

As the Co-Op sea bass baked in the oven and a pot of brown rice simmered on the stove, Pamela studied the recipe for apple trifle she'd found in *Traditional Recipes from the British Isles*. Many steps were involved, including making one's own custard and stewing the apples—and she'd need a return trip to the Co-Op for ladyfingers. But the house was clean now. She'd have plenty of time on Tuesday to prepare the evening's nibble.

* * *

Seated at her computer later, Pamela took a moment to check her email before opening the Word file for "Was Royal Purple Really Purple? Experimenting with Ancient Roman Dyestuffs." The first message that popped up caused her to smile—a note from Penny was always welcome. But as she read it, the smile became tremulous and then disappeared altogether. It wasn't that harm had come to Penny. The message read,

> Hi Mom!
> Everything is good here and I hope things are good in Arborville and you and Bettina are still leaving it to the police to figure out who killed those people.
> I'm looking forward to my trip home for Thanksgiving. Laine and Sybil will be in Arborville then, and Laine said Jocelyn will probably be there too, so it's a good thing they really like her. Have you met her yet? Laine said Jocelyn's clothes are great and their father seems really happy.
> Love,
> Penny

Pamela stared at the computer screen. What with the housecleaning, and finding the perfect recipe for apple trifle, and the thought that maybe if Detective Clayborn tracked down the man who wanted to buy the Lyon-Covingtons' house he'd capture the killer, she'd been feeling that all was right with the world.

But now . . . *their father seems really happy* . . .

Pamela left "Was Royal Purple Really Purple? Experimenting with Ancient Roman Dyestuffs" unopened and swung her chair around so her back faced the computer. All was not right with the world. The only solution was to sit down with her knitting needles and yarn and let the rhythmic motions of the needles and the caress of the spun wool work their soothing magic.

Catrina and Ginger leaped eagerly onto the sofa as soon as Pamela had settled into her customary spot and taken up the in-progress sleeve of the cornflower-blue sweater. The British mystery unfolding on the screen before her, with its refined accents and tastefully appointed interiors, was nearly as soothing as her knitting. With the climax drawing near, she was nearing the end of the first sleeve as well. She yawned and closed her eyes for a moment, and the next thing she knew, the characters in the mystery had been replaced by cats.

Ginger cats, to be precise. Unfortunately, both Catrina and Ginger had long since fallen asleep, one against Pamela's right thigh and the other to her left on the arm of the sofa. But as the cats frolicked on the screen, a narrator whose tone was as portentous as if his topic was the rise and fall of empires explained that for every eight ginger males there were only two ginger females and it all had to do with the X chromosome.

As he spoke, Pamela recalled the dashing ginger tomcat who had for a time frequented Richard Larkin's yard and who was responsible for Ginger's existence. Against all probability, Catrina had given birth to three black males and three ginger females!

On Sunday morning, Pamela had a call from Nell before she had even taken her first sip of coffee. "He came back again this morning," Nell announced with no preamble. But Pamela recognized Nell's voice and understood at once who the *he* was.

"Detective Clayborn is at a conference and won't be back in Arborville until Monday," Pamela said. "But if you got a good description and found out where he's living now and maybe even his name—"

"I got his business card," Nell answered, sounding curiously unexcited.

"His business card?" Pamela laughed. "Well, he's certainly not trying to hide his identity. He doesn't sound like a very clever murderer."

"He's not," Nell said. "That is, he's not a murderer. He's a real estate agent."

Pamela moaned. It wasn't unheard of for real estate agents to prospect for listings in Arborville. The town was charming, and Pamela herself had received phone calls asking whether she was interested in selling.

"He seemed quite nice," Nell added, "aside from the fact that it's awfully soon to pounce on an heir whose parents have both just been murdered." In the background, Pamela could hear Harold commenting, "And he has a client who's dying to live in Arborville." Then she heard Nell's voice, somewhat muffled as if she'd turned away from the phone—but not so muffled as to obscure its scolding tone—saying, "That is not funny."

"So who wrote the letter?" Pamela asked, quite aware that there was no way Nell could have an answer.

"We might never know. But this man isn't him," Nell said.

"We'll get the letter from Martha"—Pamela nodded, even though only the cats were present to witness her determination—"and we'll pass it along to Detective Clayborn. The police have ways of tracing things like that. There could even be DNA."

"Yes," Nell said. "That's what we'll do. Something has to happen soon to solve this case. Our little town just isn't the kind of place where these kinds of things should happen."

It wasn't, Pamela reflected as she hung up the phone. And if the real estate agent actually got the listing, would he hope potential buyers hadn't followed the story of the "back-to-back murders" that had "stunned Arborville," as the *Register* had put it?

Pamela had more articles to edit for *Fiber Craft*. They were due the next morning, and with the sky a moody gray, the prospect of staying indoors doing useful work appealed. So after breakfast, Pamela climbed the stairs to her office, got dressed, and sat down at her computer.

It came to life with its usual chirps and hums, and soon Pamela was untangling the convoluted syntax of an article on the economics of the modern hemp industry. Because it was so durable, Pamela read, the hemp fiber had been adopted by clothing designers aiming for sustainability. The author, in fact, was a designer herself—and quite a crusader for sustainability—and Pamela did her best to tone down the article's polemical tone.

It was a relief, then, when she turned to "African American Designers Discover Traditional African Textiles." The photos that accompanied the article didn't need to be copyedited, of course, but Pamela lingered on the images of chic cocktail dresses sewn from vibrant prints featuring stylized animals and plants or angular abstractions.

One article remained when Pamela's stomach reminded her that a slice of whole-grain toast and a few cups of black coffee did not satisfy for too long. Catrina had wandered in partway through the article on African American designers and African textiles and installed herself on Pamela's lap, creating a zone of warmth as welcome as a lap rug. Pamela leaned back in her chair and raised her arms over her head in a luxurious stretch. Then she lifted the cat for a cuddle, set her on the floor, and together they proceeded down the stairs.

Half an hour later, Pamela was back at her computer, with Catrina once more on her lap, tackling an article called, "Art Reflects Life: Clues to Ancient Greek Textile Creation in Images of the Fates." Unfamiliar words abounded—the Fates were the Moirai, it seemed, three goddesses. One spun the thread of life, one measured it out, and one snipped it off at life's end. If you knew what they looked like, or could read the little Greek inscriptions that often accompanied their images, you could recognize them on vases and bas-reliefs. And here was a photo of a Greek vase, and another, and another. And yes, the same three figures appeared on each, one with a spindle, one with a thread, and one with shears.

Pamela worked methodically, adding a semicolon here, subtracting a comma there, as another part of her mind began to enjoy the author's erudition and the way he teased such interesting insights from his material. After a few pages, though, she stopped and scrolled back to the top of the article.

Frowning, she leaned closer to the computer screen and reread the pages she had already read. A connection was begging to be made. But what was the connection?

Suddenly, she knew. She thrust her chair back from her desk and spun around until she could reach her phone. Catrina looked up in alarm and leaped to the floor.

She punched in Nell's number and waited, holding her breath as her heart lurched in her chest and she counted off the pulses of the ringing phone. At last Nell answered, sounding puzzled at Pamela's obvious agitation and even more puzzled when Pamela asked her to recall the details of a conversation about the Lyon-Covingtons that had taken place one day as she and Pamela and Bettina sat at Nell's kitchen table.

But Nell's memory was sharp, and she confirmed the crucial detail that Pamela had thought she herself remembered. She also mentioned that Martha had shown up that morning and was hard at work with her task of sorting out the Lyon-Covingtons' belongings.

Pamela swiveled back toward the computer screen, saved her work, and closed Word. Catrina watched her, as if wondering whether a lap was going to be available again. But when Pamela popped up from her chair and hurried toward the door, Catrina chose the next best alternative. She leaped nimbly onto the vacated chair and thence to the computer keyboard.

Pamela tugged on her jacket as she ran across the street, and she arrived panting on Bettina's porch with finger already extended toward the doorbell. Bettina's car was in the driveway, but Wilfred's wasn't—hopefully, the two hadn't gone out somewhere together.

Pamela pressed the doorbell once, twice, three times, and heard it echo inside. Then Bettina was at the door, her expression modulating from welcoming smile to alarm, undoubtedly startled by her friend's intensity.

"We have to look at all the pictures the *Advocate* photographer took at the Halloween bonfire," Pamela exclaimed by way of a greeting. "I think we can get into the *Advocate*'s archives with your password."

"Of course." Bettina backed away, looking flustered, and Pamela stepped over the threshold. "Why?"

"Grab your phone and I'll explain," Pamela said. "It has to do with the murders."

As they sat side by side on Bettina's sofa, Pamela described the puzzle piece that had fallen into place as she read the article about the Greek Fates. "And then I called Nell," she said, "and that was another puzzle piece, and I remembered the shrieking person. I understand that too. Now we just have to . . ."

Bettina's fingers were busy on her phone's screen, swiping through photo after photo. The two friends, their heads close together, bent toward the phone and stared as they relived the evening that had started as a pleasant community ritual and ended in the discovery of a murder. The photographer's lens had captured zombies and witches, princesses and gremlins, even Pamela in her not-very-convincing cat costume, and—

"There," Pamela exclaimed with an excited lurch that jolted the sofa. "That's the costume! In the background. See—there!" She pointed at a small figure garbed in flowing draperies, silhouetted against the dancing flames of the bonfire. "Keep going. Maybe there's a close-up."

Bettina stroked the screen with her forefinger and a child dressed as Batman appeared, then a very recognizable Harold in his vampire costume. But in the next photo, the figure in the flowing draperies returned, still in the background but facing the camera.

"Look," Pamela said. "Look where she's standing now, and look closely at her face. Isn't that . . . ?"

Bettina lifted the phone to within a few inches

of her eyes, then held it out at arm's length. "You're right," she said slowly. "So . . ."

"She's up there now." Pamela rose to her feet. She was still wearing her jacket.

"We're not walking, though." Bettina jumped up and hurried to the closet for her coat.

"Don't leave your phone behind," Pamela advised as Bettina reached for the doorknob.

Chapter 23

"We just got to wondering how Martha's doing with the clean out," Bettina said after they'd climbed the curving steps that led to Nell's front door and Nell had greeted them with a puzzled hello. "I'd hate to think she was throwing away yarn that could make infant caps or Christmas stockings," she went on. "You should come over with us. Mary really had accumulated an amazing amount of stuff."

Nell tipped her head and narrowed her eyes, giving them a look she had probably perfected while raising her children. "That's all you're after, then?" she said as a half smile threatened to sabotage her attempt at sternness.

"It's up to you," Pamela answered with a half smile of her own. "If you don't mind missing out."

Nell's glance traveled from Pamela's face to Bettina's and back to Pamela's. Her faded eyes were sharp in their nests of wrinkles. "I have a feeling there's something you're not telling me," she said. "I'll get my coat."

"More yarn? Sure." Martha led them up the stairs to the craft room, which looked much the same as it had on Friday. The closet doors stood open, revealing the sewing and knitting supplies, and the magazines and pattern books—minus only the yarn that Pamela and Bettina had carried away in pillowcases. The oak table's surface was still cluttered, and the drawers in the huge chest that dominated one wall were doubtless still brimming with linens . . . or blankets . . . or out-of-season clothes.

With a cordial repetition of Friday's *I'll leave you to it*, Martha was on her way out the door. But Pamela nodded and Bettina recognized her cue. She hopped forward and touched Martha on the arm.

"It's you," she cried. "What a coincidence!" She pulled her phone from her purse and said, "I've just been going over the *Advocate* photos from Halloween, trying to identify people for an article." She tapped at the phone for a second and then displayed the photo where the figure in the flowing draperies was looking right at the camera, tilting the phone so Martha could see it clearly. "I want to use this photo, but it needs a caption."

Martha frowned. "Didn't the *Advocate* already cover the parade, and the bonfire . . . and the murder? I think I found that issue out in the driveway last week."

Bettina smiled. "Our motto is 'All the news that fits'—at least, that's what people in town say. There wasn't room for all the pictures in one issue."

Martha took a step back and waved the phone away. "Well, it's not me," she said. "I wasn't even at the bonfire. Why would I be?"

Bettina held up the phone and glanced back and forth between it and Martha, as if comparing the photo with the real-life person. "I'm sure it *is* you," she insisted. "And the Greek outfit—aren't you a classics professor, just like Brainard was?"

Martha closed her eyes and tightened her lips. She continued to retreat, waving her hand more rapidly—flapping it, almost. She seemed to be trying to cancel out the scene unfolding before her.

Pamela stepped close to her and took her by the arm. Martha halted and opened her eyes. "Is there some reason you wouldn't want it known that you were at the bonfire?" Pamela asked. Her voice was calm, like the voice of a friend concerned about Martha's evident distress.

"Of course not," Martha said quickly. She frowned, which made her look quite formidable. "What would I have to hide?"

Pamela tipped her head toward the curious charm on the chain around Martha's neck. As if she was just noticing it for the first time, she said, "Why do you wear the spindle charm?" She waited a moment, as Martha's expression changed from irritated to pleased. But before she could explain the spindle's significance in terms of her research project, which was perhaps what she meant to do, Pamela spoke again.

"You should really wear the shears," she said.

"You cut the thread of life and tied it around your victims' necks."

Suddenly, Martha was transformed. Her expression—brow furrowed, eyes wide, mouth gaping—might have suited a Greek Fury. She wrenched herself out of Pamela's grip and plunged across the room toward the oak table that held the sewing machine. She seized the most lethal-looking of the various scissors lying on its cluttered surface and turned to face Pamela, waving the scissors menacingly.

Pamela retreated a few steps, but she continued talking as Bettina and Nell watched from behind Martha's back, at a post near the open closet. "You never got over the fact that your sister stole the man you loved," Pamela said.

Martha made a choking sound, and the hand waving the scissors faltered.

"But why wait all this time to do something about it?" Pamela asked. "Over twenty years, a generation?"

"I thought I'd recovered." Martha's voice had become small. "And I had the chance to spend a year out here—the libraries and museums in Manhattan have exactly the research materials I needed. I thought if I lived near Brainard and Mary, we could all just be friends. But then, to see the way she treated him—like she didn't even care for him, and she'd stolen him away from me and ruined my life. Then after she was . . . gone, I threw myself at him."

Nell and Bettina looked at each other, their faces brightening.

"That was you shrieking outside that night, wasn't it," Nell said, not unkindly.

Martha nodded, and her head remained bowed. "I said awful things. I told him his son would have turned out smarter, and wouldn't have been attracted to such a low-class girl, if he'd married me. He tried to calm me down, and he drove me back to the city. But I came back later that night, and you know the rest."

Martha's arms had been hanging dejectedly at her sides as she spoke, but now her right arm jerked at the elbow and she aimed the scissors straight at her own throat. "I have nothing left to live for," she moaned.

Bettina jumped forward and grabbed Martha's right arm. Martha twitched, and the scissors fell to the floor with a clunk.

Then Bettina raised her phone and tapped in 911.

Chapter 24

Pamela's favorite cut-glass bowl sat on the kitchen table, a layer of ladyfingers already in place on its bottom. She picked up a giant spoon and began adding a layer of the stewed apples she had prepared the previous day. The soothing rhythms of cooking had been a welcome distraction from reporters' telephone calls and visits.

Bettina watched attentively. She had dressed for the evening's meeting of Knit and Nibble with her customary flair, in an outfit that paired wide-legged pants in a vivid mustard shade with a fetching waist-length jacket in large black-and-white checks. Her antique amber and silver earrings dangled from her earlobes. The two friends had already discussed Sunday's adventure, agreeing that there was no harm in letting Detective Clayborn believe that they'd visited the Lyon-Covington house on Sunday with the sole purpose of rescuing yarn that might otherwise go to waste.

"Martha had a very guilty conscience," Bettina repeated for the umpteenth time, and Pamela nodded.

There was probably a great deal of truth in that statement. Yes, they had paid their call on Martha with the express purpose of eliciting a confession—but Martha had been more than happy to oblige. And when the police responded to Bettina's 911 call, Martha had repeated nearly verbatim the sad tale of her love for Brainard, her sister's perfidy, and the desperate measures to which she had resorted.

"Which apples did you use?" Bettina asked suddenly, glancing at the wooden bowl on the counter, which still contained a goodly number of the heirloom apples from the farmers market.

"The firm, sour ones are best for this," Pamela said, "so they don't get too mushy when you cook them. I picked out all the Rhode Island Greenings, and I added a little sugar, but not too much."

"Clayborn is relieved the murders have been solved, of course." Bettina returned to the previous topic. "I didn't think it was necessary to remind him that poor Dawn Filbert was killed only because the borrowed Bo Peep costume caused Martha to mistake her for Mary—even though I suggested that possibility right from the start." She watched as Pamela returned the giant spoon to the bowl of stewed apples, and her gaze followed the bowl as Pamela set it aside.

"Could I just . . . do you think . . . ?" Bettina's voice was apologetic, but hopeful.

"Of course." Pamela laughed. "Help yourself to

a spoon from the drawer and tell me what you think."

Bettina furnished herself with a spoon and sampled the stewed apples, pronouncing them yummy as Pamela retrieved from the refrigerator the bowl of custard that would form the third layer. She spooned an inch of custard over the apples and then covered it with more ladyfingers, laid in concentric circles like pale, delicate brickwork.

"When does the whipped cream go in?" Bettina asked.

"At the end," Pamela said. "It's not one of the layers. It goes on top, and I'll whip it just as soon as Roland looks at his watch and reminds us it's time to nibble." She continued with the layering, spooning apples over the ladyfingers and then spooning custard over the apples.

"Shall I get out cups and saucers?" Bettina scanned the kitchen to check whether this task had been anticipated.

"It's done." Without looking away from her careful work, Pamela nodded toward the door that led from the kitchen to the dining room. "And bowls too. Bowls are better than plates for trifle."

Bettina swiveled around to glance into the dining room, where Pamela had spread a lace tablecloth over the table and arranged seven each of cups, saucers, and bowls from her wedding china, along with spoons and carefully pressed linen napkins.

"Oh!" Bettina's bright red nails flashed as she raised a hand to her mouth. "Seven people—yes,

Felicity is coming, but there's to be an eighth. I forgot to tell you."

Pamela laughed. "Whenever we debate about adding more members, we usually decide six people is a perfect number. I know Felicity is moving down to Princeton when she finishes her semester at County Community and just wants to get some momentum going with her knitting. But who is this other person? And does she—or he—want to join for real?"

"It's Greg Dixon's girlfriend," Bettina said. "He's that nice young man who reminded me so much of my Warren."

"And it turned out he really is a nice young man and didn't kill anyone." Pamela took up her rubber spatula and used it to coax the last bits of custard onto the trifle. "But why is his girlfriend coming here tonight?"

Bettina started to answer, but both were distracted by the doorbell's chime. Pamela checked the clock over the kitchen sink. It was only ten minutes to seven.

Bettina hurried toward the entry, the words "I'll get it" trailing behind her.

The trifle was complete now, except for the whipped cream, and it would wait in the refrigerator until eight p.m. But Pamela left it on the kitchen table for a moment and stepped close to the doorway to listen.

The front door opened, and a cheery—but unfamiliar—voice responded to Bettina's greeting. Pamela took a few steps into the entry.

A young woman who looked to be of the same generation as Holly and Karen was slipping out of a casual wool jacket as Bettina held a canvas tote bag from which knitting needles protruded.

"This is Gwen," Bettina explained. "Greg's girl-friend, Gwen Talbot."

"I guess I'm a little early." Gwen glanced toward the living room, with its unoccupied sofa and chairs. "I wanted to be sure I could find the house." She was attractive in a pleasant sort of way, with light brown hair styled in a wash-and-wear bob and bright, eager eyes.

"You're very welcome." Pamela gestured toward the living room. "I'm just finishing up in the kitchen, but you and Bettina can—" At that moment they heard a light tapping and then the door, which Bettina hadn't closed all the way, swung inward. Nell's face appeared, and then her whole body, as she stepped over the threshold.

"Hello, hello," Nell said. "The door was ajar, so I didn't ring"—she turned back toward the porch—"and here comes Roland, right behind me." Nell advanced farther into the entry and stood aside as Roland joined her, briefcase in hand.

Bettina introduced Gwen to Nell and Roland, and Pamela urged them all to make themselves comfortable in the living room. Nell and Roland obeyed, and Nell beckoned Gwen to follow her, but Bettina tagged along when Pamela returned to the kitchen.

"As I was about to say," Bettina said, speaking to Pamela's back until they had both resumed their previous positions at the table, "Greg Dixon emailed me at the *Advocate* yesterday."

Pamela had picked up the bowl containing the trifle, but now she put it down again. "Why?" she asked. Out in the living room, Roland was insisting that the hassock was perfectly fine for him and the ladies should take the sofa.

"He saw the article in the *Register* about Martha confessing," Bettina explained, "and how you and I and Nell were there and prevented her suicide and called the police—and he wanted to let me know he was glad everything had been resolved. And he also wanted to let me know that he was offered the job he had that interview for. I guess he could sense my motherly interest."

"And he mentioned that his girlfriend was looking for a knitting club?"

Bettina smiled and shrugged. "I commented on the hand-knit sweater with the missing sleeves when I emailed back. One thing led to another. But she doesn't want to join. She's moving closer to her new job soon."

The doorbell chimed again, and once again, Bettina hurried toward the entry.

"Felicity!" Pamela heard her exclaim, then, "You're wearing your beautiful engagement ring. I'm so happy for you and Herc."

Pamela slid the trifle onto a shelf in the refrigerator and then set about preparing her carafe for the coffee-brewing, filling the kettle, and grinding coffee beans. When those tasks were complete, she took her best teapot from the cupboard and measured in enough loose tea for six cups. Perhaps

Gwen or Felicity would turn out to be a tea drinker like Nell and Karen. Then she added one more cup, saucer, bowl, spoon, and napkin to the arrangement on her dining room table.

The doorbell chimed once again, and when Pamela finally joined her guests, Nell, Gwen, and Holly were lined up on the sofa. Karen was almost lost in the comfortable embrace of the big armchair while Roland perched on the hassock, immaculate in his pinstripe suit, starched white shirt, and lustrous tie. Bettina had brought in two chairs from the dining room for her and Felicity, and they'd saved the rummage sale chair with the carved wooden back and the needlepoint seat for Pamela.

Holly greeted her by saying, "Of course, we're all brimming with curiosity," accompanied by one of the smiles that showed both her perfect teeth and her dimple to advantage. Her luxuriant hair flowed in loose waves to her shoulders, with her trademark colored streak—bright orange tonight— accenting her pretty forehead.

Nell's voice came from the sofa. "Nobody believes we just *happened* to be visiting Martha when she decided to confess and then turn a pair of scissors on herself." A secret smile played about her lips. "I think they all know you too well, Pamela."

Roland was already hard at work on his project— evidently a new section of the camel-colored sweater he was making his wife for Christmas. "I certainly take everything I read in the *Register* with a grain of salt," he observed without looking up. "But I *am* surprised that Lucas Clayborn didn't try to take credit for solving the mystery. The police do little enough that's useful, considering what I pay to the town in taxes."

Pamela was eager to get back to her knitting too. Only one section of the cornflower-blue sweater remained, a sleeve. She knew she wouldn't be able to immerse herself in the rhythms of knitting until she'd satisfied the group's curiosity, but she began to cast on anyway.

"The main clue was the necklace that Martha wore," Bettina said. "It was a little gold charm on a chain, and Pamela recognized that the charm was a spindle."

Pamela twisted yarn around the fingers of her left hand, guided her knitting needle through the loop she'd created, and looped more yarn with her right hand, casting on stitch by stitch. She was happy when Holly spoke up, and all eyes turned in that direction.

"It was a sad story," Holly said. "Martha's story, I mean. Imagine—to be in love with a man and think he loves you back, and then your sister comes to visit, and all of a sudden he's smitten with her instead." She shook her head sadly, though her expressive features retained their charm. "Smart, serious people like that, studying ancient Greece and whatever, and almost professors. And now, of course, we know she was that person shrieking across the street last week. Who would think people like professors could get caught up in such a desperate kind of love?"

Next to her on the sofa, Gwen stirred. "*I'm* a professor." She laughed. "We *are* human."

"Oh!" Holly's eyes opened wide, and she turned to Gwen. "I didn't know," she said. "I thought you were just . . . a person."

"I should have made a more complete introduction," Bettina said from her perch across the room. And she explained about meeting Greg Dixon at Wendelstaff and how Gwen came to be a guest at Knit and Nibble that night.

"And so your love story had a happy ending!" Holly exclaimed, with a smile that brought back the dimple.

"Very!" Gwen nodded with a smile, but minus a dimple of her own. "And now"—she lifted her in-progress knitting from her lap—"I'm finishing his birthday present."

"What is it?" Holly stared at the piece of knitting—a few inches of ribbing topped by a few rows of stockinette stich, in a natural brown shade.

"The beginnings of a sleeve." Gwen manipulated the piece of knitting so it lay on her arm with the ribbing at her wrist. "I didn't finish in time, so I had to give him the sweater with no sleeves. He's been wearing it anyway."

Pamela's eyes met Bettina's across the room, and Bettina winked. So, the missing sweater sleeves had an explanation much more benign than her theory that they'd been unraveled to serve as a murder weapon!

"Now, Pamela"—Holly swiveled toward where Pamela was sitting on the little wooden chair—"how did you figure out that Martha had a motive that tied her to the murders?"

"She called me," Nell said from her end of the sofa.

"I remembered something Harold had mentioned." Pamela amplified Nell's statement. "Mary had once told him and Nell about the whirlwind romance that led to her marrying her sister's boyfriend." Then she went on, "But the real breakthrough came from an article I was copyediting for *Fiber Craft*—all about the Fates, in Greek mythology. One of them spins the thread of life with a spindle and one of them decides how long the thread will be and one of them cuts it off with shears." Pamela held both knitting needles with one hand while she made a snipping motion with two fingers of the other. "Martha was doing a research project on the Fates, and I remembered that there was a person at the bonfire dressed as a Greek goddess, and Martha wore a little spindle charm around her neck."

"Though she should have worn the shears," Bettina interjected.

Pamela continued. "The bonfire was the night the first murder took place. Martha thought the person in the Bo Peep outfit was Mary."

Despite all the talking, people had been knitting too, and not only Roland and Gwen. Nell was partway through a festive bright green stocking for the children at the women's shelter. Pamela had at least cast on for the cornflower-blue sleeve. Bettina had gotten Felicity launched on the project she'd inquired about that day at Hyler's, the boxy waist-length sweater, and then she had resumed work on the Nordic-style sweater for Wilfred. Karen was busy with the baby blanket for her friend. Holly had embarked on a sweater for Desmond for Christmas, in navy-blue merino wool.

Silence fell over the little group as industry replaced conversation and the projects on their busy needles grew, row by row. After a time, Roland paused, surveyed his progress, and nudged back his faultlessly starched shirt cuff to reveal the face of his impressive watch.

"Eight o'clock," he announced.

Gwen and Felicity looked startled as Pamela and Bettina jumped up and scurried for the kitchen—until Nell explained that Roland announcing break time was a long-standing Knit and Nibble ritual.

In the kitchen, Pamela lit the flame under the kettle as Bettina poured heavy cream into the cut-glass cream pitcher and carried it, with the matching sugar bowl, to the dining room. When she returned to the kitchen, Pamela's mixer was whirring and beaters were clattering against the side of a small bowl. She had poured the rest of the cream into the bowl, added a few spoons of sugar, and was coaxing the mixture into a sweet and fluffy cloud. The trifle sat on the kitchen table next to her, waiting for its final touch.

The whirr of the mixer and the clatter of beaters were joined by the whistling of the kettle. For a few minutes, the small kitchen bustled with activity as Bettina prepared the coffee and set more water boiling for the tea, while Pamela spooned whipped cream over the many-layered trifle and transferred the empty bowl and the beaters to the sink.

"I'll serve the coffee and tea," Bettina said. "You go ahead, with your trifle." She made a shooing motion toward the door that led to the dining room.

"Ohhh, look at this!" Holly was the first to comment as she led the way through the arch that separated Pamela's living room from her dining room.

An antique crystal chandelier, left behind by the previous occupants of the house, hung over Pamela's dining room table. Its soft light was the perfect illumination for the rose-garlanded wedding china and the apple trifle in its splendid cutglass bowl, all prettily arranged on the lace tablecloth.

Pamela stood near the trifle, silver spoon in hand, and scooped generous servings—ladyfingers, apple, and custard in alternating layers, and topped with a fluff of white—into the bowls she'd set out. Bettina stood nearby, dispensing coffee from the carafe as the tea continued to steep.

"Let's eat in here," Bettina suggested. "Eight people are a lot to crowd around the coffee table."

The dining room chairs were retrieved from the living room and the kitchen chairs borrowed from the kitchen. Soon eight people had distributed themselves around Pamela's dining room table, Pamela at the head and Bettina at the foot. The light from the chandelier softened Nell's age and lent a kind of glamour to the younger women. And once the Knit and Nibblers had tasted the trifle, pleasure caused their eyes to close and their lips to curve up as satisfied hums rose all around the table. Even Roland seemed transported, his intense expression mellowing as, spoon by spoon, he emptied his bowl.

Pamela herself was very pleased with her creation. The assertive flavor and texture of the Rhode Island Greenings had stood up to the stewing process, the ladyfingers had absorbed the apples' moisture without becoming soggy, the custard lent richness and the whipped cream a smooth sweetness. But she hastened to respond to the group's praise by pointing out that the apples had come from Bettina and Wilfred.

As people leaned back then, with bowls empty but coffee and tea still to be finished, conversation turned once again to Halloween night and the harrowing few weeks that had followed.

"But I do love this little town," Holly said, "though when Desmond and I moved here and I joined Knit and Nibble, I never suspected that I'd be rubbing shoulders with an ace detective like Pamela Paterson."

Pamela looked down at her empty bowl. Bettina had helped, and Nell too.

"I certainly hope Arborville doesn't have any more murders," Holly went on, "but if it should . . . detecting seems so adventurous. And I could help with disguises. I know a lot about hair, and wigs, and makeup . . ."

"Oh no you don't!" Nell turned to Holly, who sat next to her. "Pamela sets a very bad example."

Nell's vehemence was startling. China clunked

against china as cups reconnected with saucers. Eyes widened in surprise.

"I've never condoned lay persons meddling in police business," Nell said primly. "Never."

"But Nell—" Bettina's smile was that of a person who has a rebuttal clearly at hand.

"But Nell—" At the other end of the table, Pamela mirrored the smile.

"Never," Nell repeated. She twisted her head in Bettina's direction, then in Pamela's, and the sound that escaped her lips sounded like *shhh*.

KNIT

Trick-or-Treat Tote

If you want your tote to resemble a pumpkin—like the one I show on my website—choose orange yarn, and you will also need a bit of black felt. Small squares of felt are available at most hobby and craft stores. If you want to line the tote, you will need a piece of fabric measuring about 14" by 24". Cotton, wool, or flannel is best.

Use yarn identified on the label as "Medium" and/or #4, and use size 8 needles—though size 7 or 9 is fine if that's what you have. For the yarn, a skein of 256 yards is more than enough. The tote takes about 200 yards.

If you're not already a knitter, watching a video is a great way to master the basics of knitting. Just search the Internet for "how to knit" and you'll have your choice of tutorials that show the process clearly. This project can be made using the most basic knitting stitch, the garter stitch. For this stitch, you knit every row, not worrying about purl. But the tote looks pretty worked in the stockinette stitch, the stitch you see, for example, in a typical sweater. To create the stockinette stitch, you knit one row, then purl going back in the other direction, then knit, then purl, knit, purl, back and forth. Again, it's easier to understand purl by viewing a video, but essentially when you purl, you're creating the backside of knit. To knit, you insert the right-hand needle front to back through the loop of yarn on the left-hand needle. To purl, you insert the needle back to front.

Cast on 40 stitches, using either the simple slip-knot process or the "long tail" process. Casting on is often included in Internet "how to knit" tutorials, or you can search specifically for "casting on."

After you've cast on, knit 9 inches, then start rounding off the bottom of your tote. You do this by decreasing one stitch at the beginning and end of each row. To decrease, instead of sticking your right-hand needle through one of the stitches looped around the left-hand needle, stick it through two. Then knit the stitch as usual. Each row will thus be shorter than the previous row by two stitches. When you get to the stage where there are 18 stitches remaining on your needle, cast off. Casting off is often included in Internet "how to knit" tutorials, or you can search specifically for "casting off."

You have now finished the front (or back) of your bag. Repeat the process to make the back (or front).

For the strap, cast on 12 stitches, knit 26", and cast off. Sew the long sides together. If you don't want to knit the strap for the tote, you can use a length of canvas strapping or sew a strap from fabric.

Give the tote its pumpkin face before sewing the front and back together. For the pumpkin face, cut a mouth—grinning or frowning—and three triangles for nose and eyes out of black felt. (You can download a PDF with the pattern I invented for the face of my tote from my website.) Position the features on the tote front and pin them into place. Sew them on using black thread, a regular sewing needle, and a whip stitch or applique stitch.

Note: If you used the stockinette stitch, you will find that the edges of your knitted pieces tend to curl up. Once you've sewn the front to the back, the curling will disappear. You can pin the front to the back to stabilize things while you lay out and pin the face. Unpin the front from the back to do the sewing.

To assemble the tote, place the front and back together with the right sides facing each other. Use a few strategic pins to hold them into place and tame the curling. With a yarn needle—a large needle with a large eye and a blunt end—and more of your yarn, stitch all around except for the top. To make a neat seam, use a whip stitch and catch only the outer loops along each side. If you use all the yarn on your needle, just pass the needle through a loop of yarn to make a knot, rethread the needle, and keep going. When you've sewn all the way around, make another knot and work the needle in and out of the seam for an inch or so to hide the tail. Cut off what's left.

Lining the tote is optional, but the tote looks nicer and is sturdier with lining. And you can choose a color and/or pattern for the lining that contrasts with the knitted parts of the tote in a fun way. To line the tote, first fold your lining fabric so the right sides are together—if it has a right side—and you have a double piece that's a little wider than your tote. (I used checked gingham, which is the same on both sides.) Leaving the sewn-up tote inside out, lay it on the folded fabric, and trace around it, using a ruler to draw a pencil line half an inch outside the tote's edges. Cut along the pencil line. Stitch around the sides and bottom of the lining, ½ inch in from the cut edge, leaving the top open. You can stitch by hand or by machine.

Turn the tote right side out and sew on the strap. If you are using a knitted strap, smooth it out so the seam runs down one side. Sew one end of the strap to each side of the tote, lining up the side seam of the tote with the middle of the strap end.

If you are lining the tote, slip the lining inside the tote, leaving the lining's right sides facing each other, so when you look inside the lined tote you see the right sides. Turn back the extra ½ inch of fabric at the lining's top and pin the lining to the tote all the way around the tote's open top. Using a whip stitch, stitch it to the tote using a regular needle and sewing thread that matches the lining.

For a picture of a finished Trick-or-Treat Tote, as well as some in-progress photos and a PDF pattern for the pumpkin face, visit the Knit & Nibble Mysteries page at PeggyEhrhart.com. Click on the cover for *Knit of the Living Dead* and scroll down on the page that opens.

NIBBLE

Pumpkin-Spice Crumb Cake

Pamela and Bettina love the Co-Op's crumb cake all year round, but in the fall, the Co-Op bakery makes a special version: pumpkin-spice crumb cake. In case you don't have a grocery like the Co-Op near you, here's a recipe to make pumpkin-spice crumb cake.

You can buy pumpkin spice (often sold as "pumpkin pie spice"), or you can make your own by mixing 4 tsp. ground cinnamon, 2 tsp. ground ginger, 1 tsp. ground cloves or allspice, and ½ tsp. ground nutmeg. You will end up with quite a bit more than you need for this recipe, but you can store the extra in a small jar and use it to flavor pumpkin pie or many more batches of this crumb cake.

Ingredients for crumb cake:
  2 cups sifted flour
  1 cup sugar
  2 tsp. baking powder
  ¼ tsp. salt
  ½ cup butter (= one stick, and put it out to softening in advance)
  2 eggs, separated into medium-size bowls (yolks in one, whites in the other)
  ½ cup milk
  1 tsp. pumpkin spice, or 1½ tsp. if you want more intense flavor

Sift flour, sugar, baking powder, and salt into a large bowl. Cut in the butter with a pastry blender or two knives, or squish it in with your fingers, until the mixture resembles coarse sand. Set aside ½ cup of this crumb mixture for the topping.

Beat the egg whites until they form soft peaks and set them aside. Beat the egg yolks until they are lemon-colored and blend the milk with them.

Add the yolks and milk to the crumb mixture in the large bowl. Stir to moisten. Fold in the beaten egg whites. The batter may seem stiff and lumpy, but that's okay.

Turn the batter into a greased or buttered square pan, 9" x 9" x 2".

Blend the pumpkin spice into the ½ cup of the crumb mixture you set aside and use a small spoon to sprinkle the mixture evenly over the top of the batter. Pat down the crumb mixture with the back of the spoon.

Bake at 350 degrees for 30 to 35 minutes. Check for doneness by sticking a wooden toothpick into the middle of the cake. If the toothpick comes out clean, the cake is done.

Let the crumb cake cool before cutting and serving. To serve, leave it in the baking pan, cut it into quarters, and lift out the quarters with a wide, flat spatula or a pancake turner. This recipe makes 8 not-too-big, not-too-small servings, but it's easier to lift out quarters and then cut them into serving sizes.

Note: Crumb topping is often also called streusel.

For pictures of Pumpkin-Spice Crumb Cake, visit the Knit & Nibble Mysteries page at PeggyEhrhart.com. Click on the cover for *Knit of the Living Dead* and scroll down on the page that opens.

BONUS NIBBLE

Roland's Easy Candy-Corn Halloween Cookies

For Roland's cookies, start with a package of Pillsbury's "Place & Bake" Chocolate Fudge Brownies. You will find them in the refrigerator section of your supermarket. You will also need a package of candy corn—three or more corns for each cookie.

The "Place & Bake" Brownies are rounds of pre-pared brownie dough intended to be baked in cupcake tins. But they make great cookies. Here's what to do:

The package contains 12 of the dough rounds. Each makes two cookies. You can make 24 cookies at once if you wish, or just make as many as you like—save the rest of the dough rounds by slipping the opened package into a large ziplock bag and putting it back in the refrigerator.

It's important to leave a lot of space between the cookies so they don't run into each other. For each 12 cookies, liberally grease or butter a cookie sheet at least 10" x 14". Cut each dough round in half and push it into a ball with your fingers. The ball doesn't have to be perfect. Place the balls at large intervals on the cookie sheet and press each one down with your fingers into a circle about 2" across.

Bake the cookies at 350 degrees for 10 minutes and remove them from the oven, but don't turn the oven off. Place three candy corns on top of each cookie, pressing them down slightly into the not-quite-baked dough. You can put the points together in the middle, or facing out like a three-pointed star. Or arrange as many corns as you like in any way you like. Don't put the corns too close to the edge of the cookie or they will melt onto the cookie sheet.

Put the cookies back in the oven and bake them for five more minutes. Let the cookies cool thoroughly on the cookie sheet before transferring them to a serving plate.

Note: I tried putting candy corn on the cookies before baking them, but the candy corn melts into puddles of sugar syrup after about 10 minutes and the cookies don't bake thoroughly until 15 minutes.

For a picture of Roland's Easy Candy-Corn Halloween Cookies, as well as in-progress photos, visit the Knit & Nibble Mysteries page at PeggyEhrhart.com. Scroll down past the image of the cover for *Knit of the Living Dead.*